BEAUTY & THE BEAST

VENDETTA

BEAUTY & THE BEAST

VENDETTA

NANCY HOLDER

BASED ON THE SERIES CREATED BY RON KOSLOW
AND DEVELOPED BY SHERRI COOPER &
JENNIFER LEVIN

TITAN BOOKS

BEAUTY & THE BEAST: VENDETTA
Print edition ISBN: 9781783292196
E-book edition ISBN: 9781783292240

Published by Titan Books
A division of Titan Publishing Group Ltd
144 Southwark St, London SE1 0UP

First edition: November 2014
2 4 6 8 10 9 7 5 3 1

TITANBOOKS.COM

From the moment we met,
we knew our lives would never be the same.
He saved my life,
and she saved mine.
We are destined,
but we know it won't be easy.
Even though we have every reason to stay apart,
we'll risk it all to be together.

CHAPTER ONE

"Tess, I remembered the name of the 'intimate lingerie' shop," Cat said into her cell as she walked down the hall of her building. Her keys were in her hand and triumph wafted around her like sweet perfume. "Easy Pickin's."

"Bleah. More like sleazy pickin's," Tess said on the other end of the phone. Her voice was barely audible through the background din. Tess was still celebrating at Rosie's with the rest of the 125th precinct, where she and Cat were detectives, first grade, Special Crimes. Nobody could celebrate like the 125th, especially when a case they had cleared came back from the jury with an ironclad conviction for murder one, just as it had late that afternoon. The notorious Justus Zilpho had received a sentence of life in prison with no possibility of parole. A brutal murderer was off the streets of New York forever.

And we did it, Cat thought happily. *Tess and I.* They had been the lead detectives on the case.

"We can check it out first thing tomorrow," Cat said. "I'll stop by Il Cantuccio for the coffees and you—"

"Down, girl. Pretty sure intimate lingerie shops aren't open for business by the dawn's early light. Tonight let's

7

enjoy the afterglow from putting away Zilpho. It's like the old days, Cat. Vargas and Chandler are *back*."

"We really are." Cat smiled. "You made this conviction happen by developing that CI."

"No, *you* made it happen when you traced Zilpho's getaway car to the wrecking yard. Best partner ever." Tess sighed happily.

"We are both awesome." Cat did a quick visual scan of the hallway. No lurkers, no strangers. Good. "Captain Ward wants us to be careful," she reminded Tess. "Zilpho swore revenge."

Tess grunted. "Yeah, right. Guys like him talk big until they put on the orange jumpsuit. Then it's tears and prayers. Best thing Zilpho can do is become a model prisoner. Lay low and rack up privileges. Double servings of Jell-O become a very big deal when you're rotting your life away in jail. Oh, hey, Captain Ward is buying another round!"

"Go. Enjoy," Cat urged her.

"On it." Tess disconnected.

Cat smiled wistfully. It was only seven-thirty at night. For a minute she wondered why she'd left the celebration at Rosie's Bar so soon, why it had seemed important to rush home. Captain Ward had been so proud of his "girl team" that he might as well have bought them roses and tiaras. It seemed like just yesterday he'd been threatening to fire them both if they didn't clear more cases.

Oh, wait, it *had* been yesterday.

Well, hopefully, those dicey days were over. She was sure she and Tess would regain their bragging rights for highest clearance rate in the city.

She put her key in the lock of her front door, emotionally preparing herself for the emptiness that awaited her on the other side. Thanks to the scheming of Gabe Lowan, the assistant district attorney and former beast who had briefly been Cat's boyfriend, her *real* boyfriend, Vincent Keller, was now a fugitive again, hunted by every law enforcement agency there ever was. If she could put away Zilpho, she could figure out a way to clear Vincent's name and bring him back into the daylight once and for all. They would have a normal life together, a future, with all the wonderful things most dating couples took for granted. Such as, well, actual dates. And he would be able to accompany her to Rosie's with the precinct to savor the next sweet taste of victory.

Vincent was the one person she really wanted to celebrate with, but all she had with him were stolen moments that were few and far between.

Better one moment in a thousand with Vincent than a lifetime of moments without him, she reminded herself.

She opened the door and caught her breath in surprise at the beauty and splendor before her. This, clearly, was one of those magical times. In her living room, a dozen ivory candles gleamed from cut-crystal holders, their warm yellow light catching on a silver ice bucket containing a bottle of her favorite champagne. Beside the bucket sat two crystal champagne flutes and a small box of chocolates wrapped in gold foil and gold ribbon and topped with a gold mesh bow. Crossing to her coffee table, she examined the card slipped beneath the ribbon.

Congratulations. It was Vincent's handwriting. He knew how important this conviction was to her and must have found out about the verdict.

And he is here.

Her delighted smile widened when she saw him leaning against the doorjamb to her bedroom. He was wearing a white terrycloth bathrobe, revealing his muscular legs, forearms, and bare feet. The candlelight cast angles and hollows in his chiseled, lean face, his features honed by his life as a soldier and a passionate fighter for justice.

Now, though, his face was softened by his sexy, happy

9

smile in answer to hers. Steamy water droplets clung to his short, dark hair and his eyes blazed, not with the feral aggression of his beast side, but the passionate, human love he bore for Cat. His pleasure at seeing her thrilled her heart. It was the perfect ending to a wonderful day.

"Catherine," he said in his deep, gravelly voice, and she unslung her purse, dropped it on the sofa, and went to him. Their arms came around each other and she felt the reflexive restraint in his muscles, always careful of her. Even though she could take down gangbangers and FBI assassins, she was still fully human, and far more fragile than a beast. Vincent's beast side was stronger than the most powerful human on the face of the planet, and yet Cat never felt safer than in his embrace.

Their lips met. Rosy joy transported her to their secret place, where it was just Catherine and Vincent, and nothing could come between them. It was a world of stars and rooftops, gently falling snow, and dreams of a future where they were free to be together without fear of capture, or worse. In that world, all that mattered to her was Vincent Keller, and she knew that all that mattered to him was her, Catherine Chandler, whose life he had saved on that icy, nightmarish night a decade before.

His strong, rapid heartbeat pulsed beneath the flat of her hand as he drew her close. He could crush her.

He never would.

She shut her eyes and inhaled the clean scent of him, heard his low moan as their kiss deepened. She wondered what their lovemaking was like for Vincent, with his heightened beast senses. She was never more alive than when they were as one. Tastes were more intense. Colors were brighter. All she heard was the whisper of her name on his lips, the pull of the moon in an ocean of love, and her body singing his name in response, rushing toward him, toward their ecstasy.

Anticipating it all, her body yearned for his. She let him

know how very much she wanted him. He did the same.

"You're home earlier than I expected," he said, when they finally managed to pull far enough apart to speak, and to gaze into each other's eyes. "I wasn't quite ready."

"I'm glad you didn't have time to dress," she replied, with a teasing tug on the belt of his robe. "And as for being ready..."

"Oh, I am. I had no intention of putting on clothes. I just wanted to add this to the table."

He slipped into the bedroom, then from behind his back he held out a deep, velvety-red rose. When she took the stem his thumb brushed the back of her hand as if he couldn't stop touching her. She ran her forefinger over his warm skin. Then she kissed him again in thanks and they walked hand-in-hand to her couch.

She inhaled the heavenly fragrance. "This is so thoughtful," she said. "Thank you."

"I wanted tonight to be perfect. I know how much this conviction means to you," he said. "You and Tess worked so hard to put this guy away."

"Vincent, any time we're together, it's perfect."

His eyes flared with happiness and desire. "I'm glad you think so."

"I *know* so."

He eased her down and her weary muscles melted as she curled up, head in hand, watching as he grabbed the champagne bottle and popped the cork. He was completely unaware of his masculine beauty and the grace with which he moved. But there was much more to Vincent than physicality. He was smart, and funny, and brave. Best of all, he was a good man. His beast side had nearly dragged him down to the depths of hopelessness and brutality, but Vincent had prevailed in the battle to reclaim his humanity. His soul.

Their love.

Smiling, she opened the candy box, lifted the layer of

paper, and admired the delectable possibilities. Tonight, there were many delectable possibilities.

His eyes sparkled like champagne bubbles as he poured the first flute. His robe hung open, revealing his broad chest. She ached to plant soft kisses there.

He bent forward to hand her the glass, poured a second, and they clinked the rims together. He gazed into her eyes and she saw his fierce pride in her. Vincent admired her for being good at her job, and that made her want to do even better at it.

We are better together than we are apart, she thought. How many times had they said that to each other?

"To you," he toasted.

"To justice," she rejoined, and they sipped. This evening she and Tess had thrown back whiskey and beer, cop booze, and the sublime champagne reminded her that her life with Vincent was so different, and that so much of it was unbelievably wonderful.

He sat beside her and pulled her feet onto his lap as she popped a chocolate into his mouth. She bit into a cordial with a hazelnut center. Her shoes thunked to the floor as he began to massage her feet and she wrinkled her nose, a tad embarrassed. She had walked the mean streets of New York City today, and she felt grimy beside this immaculate man and all the luxuries he had arranged for her.

"I should take a shower," she protested gently, even as an appreciative groan escaped her. "You are *so* good at that."

"That's not all I'm good at," he said huskily.

Then he stood, scooped her in his arms, and she laughed, holding their champagne glasses in the air and balancing her rose and her box of chocolates in her lap as he carried her down the hall into the bathroom. She peeled off her clothes and he made short work of the bathrobe. Fragrant soap and steam washed away the day and by the time Vincent lay her on the bed, she felt like an entirely new person, still glowing from the thrill of victory. Today a jury of his peers had put away a very bad man. An evil man. The system had worked.

She had become a cop for days like this.

But for moments like these, she was simply a woman deeply in love. She reached for Vincent and he gently lowered himself down, gathering her up and giving himself to her. They moved together and she saw the bronze glow in his eyes, like embers, and then he willed the beast away.

When they were both sated, they ate chocolates and finished the champagne. She stroked his cheek and trailed her fingers down his arm. As tiredness caught up to the two, he clasped her fingers in his and snuggled her against his chest. His heartbeat was powerful, comforting.

There is a miracle in my bed tonight, she thought.

Somewhere in the distance a siren blared. A dog barked as if in answer.

Half asleep, Vincent mumbled, "Intimate lingerie shop?"

She laughed. "You heard that, did you? An informant implicated Easy Pickin's in a money-laundering ring—*don't* make jokes about it, Tess and I have run through them all."

"Well, I know you'll *collar* them."

"Except that one." She batted him playfully.

She told him a little bit about the case, and he listened intently even though she could tell he was weary. Then she dozed contentedly in his arms, drifting in dreams to the words of a song they had danced to together:

"You're my guiding light."

Vincent was so much more than that.

She felt the welcome weight of his muscular arm over her, the dip in the mattress from his body. He was there. It was so special when they could sleep side-by-side.

If only you could be here when I wake up, she thought. *Every morning that I wake up.*

13

But she would not ruin this night by wishing for things she couldn't have. She would be grateful for what she did have. And she was unbelievably grateful.

Smiling, she surrendered to sleep.

Hours later, she rolled onto her side to admire him in the city's light. To her surprise, the room was pitch black. She looked at the thin strip of night sky between the curtains at the window.

She frowned. She lived in Greenwich Village, a neighborhood in the city that never slept, but tonight its familiar ambient glow was replaced by an inky darkness. Something was wrong.

She eased Vincent's arm away, pulled back the covers, and sat up.

"What is it?" Vincent asked, awake in a flash. "Your heart's beating so fast." He quirked a grin. "Again?"

"Something's happened," she said slowly.

She got up, padded to the window, and eased the drapes aside. Her city block was invisible in the dark. There were no lights on the buildings, and the streetlamps and neon signs were out.

Trap. Ambush, she thought and, by then, Vincent was on his feet, too. From the glow of his cell phone, which he lifted above his head like a flashlight, she spotted a pile of clothes on the floor—his—and started to gather them up. They reeked of smoke.

"Vincent? What happened to your clothes?" she asked, trying to figure out if their condition was connected to the darkness outside her building.

The curtains fluttered and she realized that he had opened the window and was already on the fire escape to the roof. Vincent's best friend, J.T. Forbes, called Vincent's ability to move faster than the human eye could see "blurring." Vincent had definitely blurred. She dropped Vincent's clothes, dressed as fast as she could and went up to the roof, too, half-expecting him to be gone. But there he was, in his bathrobe, peering from a safe distance out at the nothingness. Not a single light shone anywhere in their field of vision.

"It's a blackout," she said. "Power outage."

For a moment she allowed herself to feel a wash of intense relief. It was doubtful that a manhunt for Vincent was the cause, and Justus Zilpho did not have access to the resources necessary to blot out the entire city. But then her cop senses took over: blackouts could lead to looting, and a lack of power meant that the average citizen was defenseless against street crime, which always increased when crooks could move about more freely.

"I have to call in," she said, and hurried back down to her apartment. As she climbed through the window, she heard the trilling of her cell phone. She checked caller ID: sure enough, it was Captain Ward. A quick glance at the time said it was 1.15 in the morning.

"Chandler," he said, "get down here. The entire borough of Manhattan has gone dark. Hold on." Listening, she moved to her nightstand to grab her badge and her gun with her free hand. "Brooklyn, too."

"On my way, sir." She ended the call and moved carefully through the darkened apartment, feeling for her purse. She drew out her police-issue flashlight and dropped in her cell phone. She had a burner phone in there, too. For Vincent. They switched them every three days, which was the protocol J.T. and Vincent had established years before Cat had arrived on the scene. For a while, they had been able to stop using them and rely on normal cell phones. But now that Vincent was on the run again, such precautions were a regular fixture in their lives.

"I heard," Vincent said. He moved to the pile of smoky

15

clothes and began to put them on. She flicked on the flashlight and shone it at him. His jeans were scorched and there were ragged burn holes in his white T-shirt.

"What *did* happen to you today?" she asked worriedly. "Were you caught in a fire? Is J.T. all right?" J.T. Forbes had protected Vincent for the ten years that he had remained in hiding from Muirfield, the secret government organization that had turned him into a beast. Now that Vincent was a fugitive again, J.T. was also at risk.

"J.T. is fine," he assured her. "And I wasn't *caught* in a fire. I ran into one. A little girl was trapped in a tenement and it would have taken the firefighters too long to get to her." He shrugged. "So I went in."

Although he was standing directly in front of her, a frisson of anxiety skittered up Cat's backbone. Fire could claim Vincent's life. When her father had turned Vincent into an apex predator, Vincent had lost his ability to heal himself. To stave off her growing panic, she reminded herself that she had seen no burn marks on his naked body, and he seemed fine. Still, she couldn't shake her instinctive reaction. If anything happened to Vincent, it would be worse than if it had happened to her.

"Was she all right?" she asked as she threw on fresh work clothes. "The little girl?"

"She was a little shaken up. Smart kid, lay on the floor below the smoke. I heard her telling the fire captain that an angel saved her." His grin was lopsided. "Good thing he didn't look up. He would have seen that angel dangling from the side of the building after the floor gave way. Without any wings."

"That was risky," she said, and he shrugged. They locked gazes and laced their hands together. She knew they were both thinking the same thing: there were things in this world worth risking everything for—their relationship, his freedom, even their own safety—and a human life was one of them. For all the suspicion and fear cast Vincent's way, and all his protests that he wasn't Batman, he was definitely a hero.

"You should leave a change of clothes here." She cupped his cheek, taking time to appreciate just how wonderful he was. "For all the other daring rescues you're sure to undertake."

He laid his hand over hers. "So far we've been able to convince everyone that you had nothing to do with my escape from custody. If you suddenly stockpiled men's clothes in your apartment, that'd look pretty suspicious."

"I could say I'm collecting things for a charity drive," she argued. "With a few on hand that aren't your size, my excuse would be more plausible."

She could tell he was thinking it over, and allowed herself a moment of satisfaction. Even though she'd become a cop instead of a lawyer, which had been her original career goal, she could still argue the finer points of any position she took. She loved that Vincent could hold his own against her, and did when it mattered to him. They were two opinionated, driven people, taking life head on, ready to fight for what was important, but learning to back off when harmony between them was more important.

A siren blared down Bleecker, which was on the south side of her building. She shifted back into work mode, zipping up her jeans, putting on her coat, and slipping on her black gloves and a charcoal-gray knitted cap. It was bitterly cold out tonight. Hopefully that would keep less-motivated would-be looters from venturing onto the streets.

"Anyway, think it over," she asked him. She rose on tiptoe to kiss him goodbye, wondering how long it would be before she saw him again. This part was always so difficult. Too difficult, and tonight it was veering on painful when she considered that he would have sacrificed his life willingly today to save that little girl.

"I have to go," she said unnecessarily. What she meant

was, *I never want to let you go.* The soft expression on his face assured her that his heart heard her unspoken words, and that he felt the same way.

"I'll patrol, see if I can keep NYPDs crime stats down," he said. "Help out a few folks."

"Thanks. But *please* be careful. It's dark, but people aren't blind. If someone spots you…"

"I'll lay low. I was Special Forces, remember? Covert ops?"

"And a fireman, and a doctor," she said. A protector. A healer. *And the man I love.*

"And a candlestick maker." He kissed her once more. Despite her captain's urgent summons, she savored that kiss. They never knew when it would be their last.

"Will you be here when I get back?" she asked, but that was a question he couldn't answer, and they both knew it. In fact, since she was a cop, there'd be no guarantee that *she* would come back, either.

"I want to be."

"That's the best answer I can hope for."

He had dimples when he smiled. Beautiful dimples. She lost herself for a couple more seconds.

Then she was out the door.

CHAPTER TWO

It was 2 a.m. and the 125th precinct was buzzing like a beehive: phones ringing off the hook, overtaxed emergency generators causing the overhead fluorescent lights to flicker. As she entered the bullpen, Cat's body responded to the call to arms, blood pumping, the last vestiges of sleepiness evaporating.

Tess was leaning over her desk on the landline with a steaming travel mug glued to her hand. She took a swig and grimaced, then hailed Cat over with the mug. Her brown eyes flashed with the thrill of the chase and Cat knew she was taking down the details of a crime report.

Tess, said, "We'll get right on it."

She hung up just as Cat reached her desk, then took another gulp from her mug and shuddered from head to toe, a total body roll of disgust. She shook her head like a wet poodle drying off and smiled her best, most mischievous smile.

"Whoa. You are not going to believe this," she said in a hushed, excited voice. She looked furtively around. "This is our case. Ours, okay? We deserve it."

Cat raised her brows. "It's clearly juicy. Let me guess. We're going undercover in Florida? At a spa resort?" She took off her gloves and hat and gave her hair a shakeout. A scattering of snowflakes had kissed her loose waves and the tip of her nose. It was January, and it was cold.

Tess smirked. "*Almost* as good. Angelo DeMarco has been kidnapped."

Cat blinked. "DeMarco? As in *those* DeMarcos? Tony DeMarco, mob boss?"

"The DeMarco DeMarcos, yes," Tess said. "Angelo is Tony's son." She got as close to squealing as a badass like Tess could get. "Captain Ward's *got* to agree that we get to keep this one. We just put Justus Zilpho away."

"Kidnapping cases are FBI jurisdiction," Cat pointed out.

Tess's eyes sparkled. "And that *was* the FBI. They're asking for an assist."

That made sense. The DeMarcos were one of New York City's most prominent families. The FBI was a federal agency, but the DeMarco Building was in 125th's jurisdiction, and the DeMarcos prided themselves on having been in New York for seven generations. Originally from Sicily, they were incredibly wealthy and powerful, and although occasionally a DeMarco would be brought in on racketeering charges, no one had ever made a case against them stick. For cops— good, honest cops—the thought of taking the DeMarcos down was the equivalent of winning the lottery.

Get to know them, help them with a legitimate issue, and you're closer to that goal, Cat thought with relish.

A family kidnapping would be a high-profile case, and even though Zilpho had paved the way back into Captain Ward's good graces, Tess and Cat still had a lot of unproductive months to make up for—the partners had spent most of their time solving beast-related crises that they couldn't tell NYPD about. Rescuing Angelo DeMarco would raise the 125th's street cred even higher.

"Beats Florida, eh?" Tess said.

"Well, we are never happy when one of the citizens we are sworn to protect goes missing," Cat said somberly. "We're both highly motivated to find this... boy?"

"Only son and heir. He's twenty," Tess said. "They've already received a ransom note."

"*Ooooh,*" Cat said appreciatively.

"See? It's gonna be a good one. Zilpho plus DeMarco equals job security. Heck, maybe even promotions. Let's go tell Ward we want this."

"In a nice, polite way," Cat added.

"Of course." Tess took another swig from her travel mug and made a face as if she had just swallowed battery acid. "I'm telling you, J.T. makes the worst coffee I have tasted in my *life*. I'm getting him one of those fancy machines with the little pre-measured cups. You can't screw that up."

"J.T. made you coffee?" Cat chuckled. "At your place or his?"

Tess scoffed. "Are you kidding? This coffee was destroyed on-site at nerd central." Tess went a little pink, but just a little. "The conditions of my man-cleanse require that no one stays at my house. Staying at my house is messy. In more ways than one."

Tess and J.T. had a complicated relationship: Tess had told J.T. to his face that he was all wrong for her. Shortly after that, she had leaped on top of him in his rolling desk chair and planted a long, passionate kiss on him. Cat hadn't been a witness to this, but J.T. had told Vincent, and Vincent had told Cat.

As for the other definition, for a neat freak like Tess, "messy" meant that one of the many framed photographs of her and Cat was a centimeter askew. J.T. had no housekeeping skills whatsoever. Give him a place to set down a bag of gummi worms and a beer and he was happy as a clam.

"Does J.T. mind that you never have him over?" Cat asked as they trooped together toward Captain Ward's office. The door hung wide open and plain-clothes and uniformed officers were racing in and out. Beyond, the windows were broad rectangles of ebony.

"The Bronx is down," a uni said as he sailed past Cat and Tess.

Rikers, Cat thought. Former FBI Special Agent Robert Reynolds, her biological father, was incarcerated there. Her stomach did a flip, but she put thoughts of him on hold. As she so often did.

"What on earth is *happening*?" Tess said. In a lower voice meant for Cat's ears, she added, "Are you kidding? J.T. *mind* that I'm staying over at his place? He's having sex on a regular basis. He's in heaven."

"A regular basis?" Cat echoed.

Tess closed her eyes and grimaced—as if to admit that she'd said too much—and looked past Cat.

"Captain," she called.

Their harried boss glanced up. When he saw them, his expression grew very somber, and Cat swallowed hard. Her cop instincts told her that he had bad news for one or both of them... and that it had nothing to do with the DeMarcos.

It can't be Vincent. Vincent is safe. He's fine.

"Chandler, Vargas," he said, by way of greeting. His manner was very grave, even stern, as if they hadn't partied together hours before, toasting Zilpho's demise. "The entire city's in chaos."

"Are they suspecting terrorism?" Cat asked. The tragedy of 9-11 was never far from any New Yorker's mind. Vincent had lost both his brothers in the Twin Towers, and their deaths had prompted him to drop out of medical school and enlist in the army. From there, his own tragedy had occurred—being experimented on by Muirfield, then hunted like an animal so that Cat's own father could put him down.

"Unknown," Ward replied. "But we have plenty to keep us busy while that's under investigation."

"Speaking of which, we have a case," Tess said. "It's a case we deserve. Right, Cat?"

Tess looked over at Cat for confirmation. But Cat was staring straight at Captain Ward. "What is it?" she asked slowly.

He returned her serious expression. "Chandler, let's take a minute." He looked expectantly at Tess.

"I'm her partner," Tess said. "You want me to butt out, Cat?"

Cat shook her head. "If it's all right with you, sir, I'd like my partner to stay."

"Very well."

Just then Pamy, one of the civilian secretaries, poked her head in, assessed the situation, and smoothly exited the room, shutting the door behind herself.

"Have a seat," he invited the two detectives.

Cat kept a lid on her nervousness. "If it's all the same to you, Captain, I'll stand."

"Me, too," Tess said.

"Chandler, it's your father, former Special Agent Reynolds." Ward paused.

"My father." That lid was threatening to blow. "Who's at Rikers."

Captain Ward said, "He's missing."

The room tilted like a ship at sea. A panic reaction, pure and simple, she told herself, but there was nothing simple about her father. Reynolds was a man she despised and mistrusted, and she had risked Vincent's life to save his. And just when she thought she was done with him, another tornado of his making tore through her life.

"As in, out of his cell," Tess said.

"As in, no longer at Rikers," Captain Ward said.

"Whoa." Tess slid a glance in Cat's direction. "He escaped?"

And then Cat was back, swallowing a flood of stomach acid so she could ask questions. But the most important question could not be voiced: *Is he coming after Vincent?*

Ward said, "As to if it was voluntary or not, we don't know yet. They had a blackout same as us. Generators didn't come on right away and the disappearance took place in that window of opportunity. Witnesses say the guards were overpowered by armed assailants in ski masks. But no shots were fired and there were no injuries."

"Rikers guards? Overpowered?" Tess echoed. "That place is like the Fort Knox of prisons."

"So it's said," Captain Ward replied.

"Any leads on the assailants?" Cat asked.

"We don't know yet. FBI's at the scene. Early reports say it looks like an inside job." He waited a beat as he studied Cat's face, and then the tornado landed on top of her:

"A job orchestrated by you."

CHAPTER THREE

We carved out a little time, Vincent reminded himself as he put on his scorched ball cap and kept his head down, quietly departing Cat's building. *We got to be together.*

But it was never enough time. And he hated how he put Cat at risk whenever he visited her apartment. When they had first met, Cat had come to the abandoned chemical factory he and J.T. had turned into a sanctuary. Her trespassing had sent J.T. into a spiral of dismay, and as J.T. feared, Cat's initial investigation into Vincent's supposed death had put Vincent back on the radar of the clandestine organization that had changed him into a beast—Muirfield. In Afghanistan, his superiors had received orders to wipe out his unit of experimental super soldiers, and he had used every bit of Special Forces training to elude the shock troops, survive, and get back to the States.

J.T. had been terrified that Cat's repeated visits to the factory would lead Muirfield right to their door. Unfortunately, he had been right, and the chemical factory was now gone, blown up to convincingly stage the death of "the Vigilante"—Vincent's nickname in the press. Now J.T.

lived in a vacated gentlemen's club and Vincent stayed on a houseboat in the 79th Street Boat Basin.

It would have been easy for someone as loyal as J.T. to resent Cat for all the danger and tumult she had brought into their lives. But thanks to her interference, they actually had lives. Before Cat, they had essentially existed in stasis, and she had been right when she had insisted that he and J.T. couldn't spend another decade in lockdown.

And anyway, I was the one who exposed us in the first place, when I went out at night to help victims.

Like I'm doing tonight, actually.

It had been inevitable that he would leave trace DNA and the occasional fingerprint when administering CPR or wheeling a wounded victim into the receiving bay of the local hospital's ER. He had always risked discovery because of his insistence on helping humanity... even though back then he had ceased thinking of himself as human. Muirfield had turned him into a monster, a beast. It had taken Catherine's love for him to see himself not as hopelessly damaged and beyond redemption, but as someone whose life had value.

Someone who was worthy of love, worth risking everything for.

I was dying inside, and she brought me back to life. J.T., too. All those years, all he was doing was treading water. Sooner or later, he would have drowned.

He surveyed the streets and buildings of her neighborhood, as impenetrable to the naked human eye as the streets of Afghanistan on those terrible, violent nights of the war and its aftermath for him and the other beasts. Lights were coming on in Greenwich Village—candles, lanterns, flashlights. Errant, handheld light sources would be harder for him to avoid. He kept the collar of his pea coat up high and his cap down low. He did not move furtively, for that would attract attention, and the street he was walking down was empty. It was the middle of the night, when most people were indoors, and civilians were wisely barricading themselves in their homes. New Yorkers would be terrified tonight. So much misery had rained down on their heads: the destruction of the Twin Towers, Hurricane Sandy. It was not lost on him that he lived in a city every bit as resilient as he was. He would do everything he could to increase NYC's odds of survival against anything that came at it—be it opportunistic criminals, a terrorist group, or a natural disaster.

He heard approaching footsteps and kept his head down. One block up, a pair of large men turned the corner and approached. Vincent could smell the metallic tang of concealed weapons and stayed loose. He was not afraid, just ready.

The men spotted him. He sensed their interest in a stranger, a potential target. He heard one murmur to the other, "Whatcha think?"

"Naw," said the other. "That guy's too strong. He works out."

Wordlessly, they passed Vincent. He waited until there was some distance between him and the two men, and then wheeled around to follow them. They were on the prowl, and he wasn't about to let them harm anyone.

Behind him, glass crashed and someone shouted, more out of anger than fear. He heard more shattering glass, and then a siren, and a man's voice shouting, "Police! Freeze!"

Vincent maintained his position, glad that there was a police presence in Catherine's neighborhood despite the fact that he would have to be more cautious as a result. With every news outlet in the city broadcasting his image as New York's most wanted, he had decreased his covert visits to Cat's apartment until he went half-crazy from missing her. He wondered if Gabe Lowan had possessed the nerve to attend the precinct party at Rosie's tonight, or if he had respectfully kept his distance. Gabe's misguided desire to "protect" Catherine from Vincent was the reason Vincent was being hunted down... again.

And to think we trusted him after his beast side died, Vincent thought in disgust. And Cat had done more than trust him...

Adrenaline rushed through Vincent's body and he forced his mind off the track it was taking before he beasted out. Caught in a romantic triangle, Cat had ultimately chosen him over Gabe. But for a while, she had shared her bed— if not her heart—with the ADA. There had actually been a time when Vincent himself had considered the other Muirfield refugee to be the better choice for Cat. But now Vincent finally had his beast side under control, tamed by his love for Catherine and his need to be a man whom she could love in return. To be someone whose existence and efforts made the world a better place, whether he remained a beast forever or could one day become fully human again.

A car horn blared and dubstep thumped on a tricked-out set of speakers in a passing Chevy Camaro lowrider. A head hung out the opened car window and Vincent kept his own head bowed but his shoulders straight. He had no interest in appearing as some cowering target for a gang of street toughs.

The horn honked again and he ignored it. The car slunk on.

On the sidewalk up ahead, the criminal duo Vincent had been trailing seemed to lose interest in sizing up prey and fell to arguing about football instead.

Vincent's path took him more deeply into Greenwich Village. Windows flickered with light. Bodies moved along the sidewalk in silhouette from the car traffic. There were a lot of vehicles on the road, especially considering the time of night and that this was Greenwich Village, not busy midtown Manhattan.

He approached an alley partially blocked by an especially fragrant Dumpster. Years of training as a soldier urged him to caution; it was the perfect hiding place for a potential mugger.

Then, through the street noise, he detected a snick from across the street in the alley opposite to this one. He sent blood to his auditory system, enhancing his hearing.

Zing!

His ears picked up the sound of a bullet rocketing straight at him. His reflexes kicked in and he dove behind the Dumpster, flattening on the ground and covering his head.

The projectile slammed into the Dumpster, rolling it on its wheels toward Vincent. He rose cautiously to his feet and crabbed backwards against the shadowed brick wall. He focused quickly down his alley in both directions, ensuring that no one was headed his way. Threatened, his beast side began to emerge; he didn't rein it in fully but he also took care to remain concealed. For all he knew, someone had taken a potshot at him just to see if they had the right man.

The right *beast*.

For years, he had been unable to prevent himself from beasting out whenever his safety had been jeopardized. But then Catherine had come into his life and he had learned to subdue it, if not entirely control it. If someone was trying to unmask him, this was a damned dangerous way to go about it.

There were no more shots. He eased around into the narrow space between the other side of the Dumpster and the wall, and squinted in the direction of the shooter. He spent a couple of seconds recreating the scene as only a beast could do. In his mind's eye he saw a single shooter in a hooded sweatshirt, jeans, and boots—looking much like Vincent himself, actually—standing in the alley across the street holding a pistol. As soon as the man had loosed the shot, he had run.

Vincent took off with a burst of speed. He could run faster

than any human alive. But once he crossed the street and leaped over trashcans and wooden pallets into the alley, he found nothing, and he couldn't track his quarry any farther. Able to see in the dark, he looked up toward the fire escape, then higher up at the rooftop. He raced through the alleys of the next three streets, hearing only his own footsteps.

He blurred west, then east, doubling back, then slowed and settled into predator mode once more. Centering himself, he allowed his beast side to collect more evidence: smells and visual clues his human side would never uncover. The man had been wiry, and none too clean. He used heroin. Vincent mentally saw the man fire off a round from a .40 caliber handgun, run, then climb into a car that was rolling along. The car was old. He couldn't tell much about the vehicle except that it had recently had an oil change.

He returned to the Dumpster and ran his fingers along the grimy exterior facing the street, seeking the bullet. It had torn through the thick metal and lodged in the other side, causing a dimple. He decided that before he went Dumpster diving to retrieve the cartridge, he'd see if he could find the shell casing. He crossed back into the shooter's alley and searched.

There was no casing, or it could simply be that Vincent missed the tiny object. That could be a telling detail. A random shooter would have left evidence behind, being either too ignorant or uncaring to bother retrieving it. A pro would have been more diligent. So the question remained: was this someone who had intended to shoot *him*?

He was just about to climb into the Dumpster to pry out the bullet when the *crack-crack-crack* of splintering wood caught his attention. He heard a shout laced with fear. Someone's apartment or business was being invaded. He cautioned himself not to blur again. As he often reminded Catherine, he wasn't some superhero. Tonight he would do what he could to protect lives and property, but unfortunately

there would be a limit. Just as there was for every other
person on the planet. That was part of being human. For
people like him—and Catherine—that was a limitation that
was difficult to accept.

CHAPTER FOUR

2.45 A.M.

The streets of New York City were as tangled as a jumble of rusty necklaces in a forgotten jewelry box. The anticipated crime wave had commenced, and citizens afraid to be in their homes had taken to their cars, trying to outdrive the darkness. The gumball lights of Cat and Tess's squad car illuminated throngs of looters hopping in and out of broken storefront windows. Gleeful men, women, and even children staggered down sidewalks and alleys carrying toaster ovens, cameras, and laptop computers. They knew that unless the police officers abandoned their vehicle, thereby worsening the gridlock, no one was going to stop them.

Tess had called in and backup was on the way in the form of a van carrying a dozen unis. But Captain Ward had warned Tess and Cat that the resources of the 125th were fully deployed. He simply had no more officers to send out. The fire department and neighboring police precincts had their hands full, too. The mayor was talking about calling out the National Guard. It all depended on how long the blackout lasted.

"It was good of Captain Ward to let us keep DeMarco," Tess said as they crawled along impatiently. "He could have put us on looter duty."

"Vincent's patrolling the Village." Cat pictured various neighbors she had befriended, some of whom were frail and elderly. They would be vulnerable, afraid. "Remember when they used to call him the Vigilante? Tonight he actually is one."

"J.T.'s probably going crazy without his electricity," Tess said. "I hope all his batteries were charged."

Cat suppressed a grin and avoided the obvious double entendre about J.T.'s batteries. Beside her, Tess huffed and muttered, "Oh, my God, how old are you?"

"I didn't say a word," Cat protested. "Hey, innocent until proven guilty." She waited a beat and then she added impishly. "Anyway, I knew you were talking about his lap. Top."

"You *are* twelve."

"I have the patience of a twelve-year-old right now," Cat said. "Let's hope Angelo DeMarco's kidnappers are as hampered by the blackout as we are."

"If they caused it, they've made plans for dealing with it," Tess countered. "Don't you think it's weird that two people have gone missing during this blackout? Both their cases coming under FBI jurisdiction? I have to think they're connected." Tess toyed with her phone. "In the old days we could ask Gabe to check it out."

"Don't even say his name," Cat grumped.

She looked out the window at the dead skyscrapers, then up at the obsidian sky, wondering where her father was. She remembered the three months of hell he had put her through when he had captured Vincent. Three months of searching. And heartbreak. And nightmares. It was ironic to her that a search for her father was underway. She would have nightmares until he was found, but her heart would never break for him.

"We'll find him," Tess said. "Hey, you know, maybe we *should* have asked for looter duty. We'd have more freedom to start searching."

Tess was right. There were other detectives who could work the DeMarco kidnapping, but no one would be more invested in finding her father... except for Vincent. Any searching she did would have to be off the books, as always. Although she had been the arresting officer who brought her own father to justice, as a rule NYPD did not allow officers to work cases involving family members—the same as a doctor would not operate on a relative. But what was done was done. They had made the request before Captain Ward had told them about Cat's father, and they couldn't exactly back out of a case to spend time doing something they weren't *supposed* to be doing. Besides, staying in the field was one way to assure Internal Affairs that she hadn't skipped town to reunite with her father.

"I can't believe IA would actually believe I had anything to do with his disappearance. Anyone with half a brain would know the last thing I would do is try to free *that man* from prison."

"Not everyone knows you hate your father's guts," Tess said reasonably. "And you know the FBI thinks you're sketchy because your 'ex-boyfriend' is New York's most wanted." She smiled wryly. "Crazy huh? Go figure."

Cat gave her horn a sharp, long honk, more out of frustration than the expectation that it would do any good. "We took Muirfield down and that secret society retreated back into hiding. Who else would want Special Agent Reynolds?"

"He knows more about beasts than anyone else," Tess pointed out. "Maybe a beast we don't know about snagged him. Maybe those masked invaders didn't rescue him from Rikers. Maybe they took him out so they could, you know, take him out."

As in kill him. Cat didn't let herself say what she was thinking: that the world would be a better place without her biological father in it. Better for her, and far better for Vincent. Every time she and Vincent thought the past was behind them and that they could build a future, her father launched some new scheme to destroy Vincent. To keep her safe, Reynolds claimed. He insisted that no matter how hard Vincent fought to keep his human side in command of his beast side, the beast would win out. He also said that beasts never got better, they only got worse, and that Vincent would one day kill Cat, of that he had no doubt.

The deaths of innocents who had crossed his path hadn't mattered in the least to Bob Reynolds. Anyone who got caught in the crosshairs was collateral damage. Those deaths had only started to bother Reynolds when they had piled up so high they couldn't be covered up or explained away, when all his wrongs had caught up with him, and by extension, his own daughter.

He had assured Cat that he had had nothing to do with her mother's murder. She wanted to believe him, but in her heart?

I'm still glad I stopped Vincent from killing him, she told herself. Not for her father's sake, but for Vincent's. *He would have lost his humanity forever.*

Tess shook her out of her reverie.

"I swear, this is the worst traffic jam in the history of New York. And that's saying something."

"It so weird to see the city so dark. It's like the zombie apocalypse," Cat said. "So what do you think happened?"

"Somebody hit the off switch with their elbow?" Tess shrugged. "I mean, one borough, maybe, but all five?"

"New York definitely doesn't need any more disasters," Cat said. "I'm sure Counter-Terrorism is all over it. FBI, too."

"Well, I hope we get the lights on soon. Look at that."

Tess gestured toward a trio of teenagers running up to a

car in the middle of the traffic. They started yelling at the driver and pounding on the windows. The driver honked. The kids laughed and moved onto the next car, and then the next.

Cat began to roll down her car window to yell at them but that would just be an exercise in futility. They wouldn't hear her in the din of blaring car horns. They were being malicious but they weren't physically harming anyone. It wasn't worth getting out of the car and chasing them down because that would worsen the gridlock. No one was paying their flashing lights and siren any mind. Two taxis, a bus, and a truck had boxed them in, and there was nowhere to go to make way for the cops.

Suddenly the sky overhead became dotted with pinpricks of light that expanded and became helicopters. They aimed their searchlights along the streets, illuminating looters, some of whom dropped their treasures and ran, while others just jeered at the choppers without missing a beat.

Then the traffic lurched forward but the bus waited, giving Cat a tiny space to pass. Exhibiting nerves of steel, she edged her way past the bus so closely that she almost scraped paint, and kept moving.

"And why would anyone frame me for my father's disappearance?" Cat said. "That's just inviting more scrutiny on the real perps."

"What kind of evidence do you think they planted in his cell to implicate you?"

Cat rolled her eyes. "Oh, I don't know. Probably something subtle like some strands of my hair and one of my business cards with a signed confession on the back."

"Plus a selfie of your father holding a thank-you card. They must not be taking it all that seriously or they would have grounded you tonight."

"Maybe this zombie apocalypse has held up the

paperwork," Cat said. "Or better yet, the zombies have devoured IA."

"Zombies would never attack IA. Zombies eat brains."

"We are *both* twelve," Cat said.

At the next intersection, a cluster of cops was directing traffic. They spotted Cat and Tess's squad car and facilitated their tortured progress through the intersection and around a corner.

"*Whoa*," Tess murmured as they came within sight of the lavish DeMarco Plaza, a towering edifice of marble, ebony, and gold. Powerful searchlights running off generators illuminated the front of the building. Embossed golden lions with their maned heads held in noble majesty flanked the DeMarco name in six-foot-high golden letters. "I haven't been by here in forever. I forgot how, well, I guess the right word is *gaudy*, the DeMarco building is."

"They do like the bling," Cat said. She spotted the uni in front of the vast complex and managed to pull over into the empty spot at the curb he had been reserving for them. She got out and Tess did too.

Flashing her badge at the NYPD foot soldier, she said, "Thanks for saving us a seat."

He gestured to the squad car. "I'll keep an eye on it for you, Detective."

Cat gave him a nod and she and Tess headed toward the dim lobby entrance. On the other side of a glass wall were four more unis and a dozen private security guards wearing earphones and carrying SIG Sauer P226s and .357 Magnums, by the looks of the gun butts poking out of various holsters. Cat and Tess were both armed but there was no need to draw their weapons as they showed their badges.

One of the private security guards, a burly bald man with very small, piggish eyes, unlocked the door and stood back to give them room as they entered. The dimly lit room was crowded with bodies and chatter.

"I'm Detective Chandler and this is Detective Vargas," Cat said. "We're from the one-twenty-fifth. We're assisting on the kidnap."

"Lizzani. Sorry to inform you that our elevators are down," he said. "Mr. DeMarco is waiting for you in the penthouse. Sixty floors up."

Cat and Tess exchanged looks. Cat said, "No problem," and the man broke into a trademark "Yeah, right" New-York grin and opened the door with a flourish. Cat pulled out a flashlight, to reveal steep concrete stairs.

"Officers," he said.

Sixty floors.

Straight up.

"Remind me again why we wanted this case," Cat said, and Tess moaned.

They began to climb.

CHAPTER FIVE

2.32 A.M.

Fully awake despite the hour, Gabriel Lowan stood inside former agent Bob Reynolds' cell at Rikers as the FBI Evidence Recovery Unit completed processing the crime scene. The two-person team had already paused once to call in the item that incriminated Catherine: a hand-drawn map of Reynolds' cell block on the back of a envelope for some junk mail addressed to her, complete with a penciled note that had already been favorably compared to her handwriting: *Have him ready.*

Gabe had been permitted to view the envelope through a sealed plastic collection bag. It was laughably amateurish because it was so clearly intended to implicate her. No one in their right mind, especially not a police detective, would have created such a document in the first place. That it was false evidence was as obvious as sixth-grader's attempt to write his own absence note to his teacher.

However, the handwriting did resemble hers. He felt a pang, remembering many scrawled notes she had left for him: *Gone for coffee, back soon. XO Cat.* And *I'll get us some takeout. Red or white wine?* All those little intimacies you built through notes, texts, quick calls. That you take sugar in your coffee. That you prefer red wine.

That her favorite way to sleep with you is spooning.

Gabe brought himself back from memory lane to focus on the situation. Law enforcement was dealing with the citywide crisis caused by the blackout. Captain Ward had informed Gabe that Agent Brian Hendricks of Internal Affairs had checked in to see if he could help with looter duty, and the *second* he had heard about Reynolds and the ridiculous envelope, he had been ready to come down to the one-two-five and interrogate her. In Hendricks's opinion, Detective First Grade Catherine Chandler had escaped justice once before, when the bullet he was certain had been discharged from her service weapon during her father's arrest had come back as a mismatch. Not from her weapon, in other words. Hendricks had been floored, and his apparent blunder had only confirmed what most cops thought about IA: that they were bumbling incompetents who got in the way of *real* cops doing actual police work.

Hendricks had confided to Gabe that he would catch Chandler one of these days. The IA agent would never know that Gabe had been the one who had taken the evidence bag containing Catherine's actual bullet and replaced it with a facsimile in order to destroy his case. Had Gabe not committed that felony, Catherine would have been charged as an accessory to her father's confessed multitude of crimes.

But there were many more atrocities Reynolds kept hidden. The secret Muirfield organization and the beasts they had created remained secrets that Reynolds, Catherine, Vincent, and Gabe shared, binding them together.

Clearly, whoever had snatched Reynolds tonight had taken advantage of Hendricks's vendetta against Catherine. Gabe felt a frisson of trepidation on his own behalf.

I was a beast, too. If the world ever finds out about

beasts, my life will turn upside down.

He could tell that the two members of the FBI ERU finishing up Reynolds' cell were surprised to see him, but they recognized him from TV and somehow that gave him permission to be there. Considering he was an assistant district attorney and not an investigator, he wound up at an awful lot of crime scenes. For some months he had literally run the 125th precinct, tasked with cleaning up the mess that the previous captain, Joe Bishop, had left behind when he'd been ousted over his obsession with avenging his brother's murder.

Obsessions were dangerous, and not just to one's career. There were no limits to the lengths Gabe would go to protect Catherine from her obsession with Vincent. If Catherine hated him to her dying day for forcing Vincent to go back on the run, it would be worth it if it kept Vincent out of her life.

"Whatever it takes," he muttered; and then, as the two techs started brushing the bars of the cell for prints, he caught the glitter of something beneath Reynolds' cot. As casually as he could, he extended his leg and swept an arc, bringing the object within his reach as he bent down and pretended to tie his shoelace. He palmed it, then glanced quickly at it, and what he saw made his heart hammer against his ribcage: it was a round pin decorated with eight small gold stars and a diamond.

This was the pin worn by members of a super-secret society of the ultra-rich and extremely powerful—magnates, tycoons, dictators—manipulating world events to a far greater extent than conspiracy theorists could ever dream of. Funding the Muirfield beast experiments had been their primary strategy for world domination, but they had fingers in hundreds of pies. They had not known each other's identities. These pins were the only way they could recognize each other.

He had taken many of those powerbrokers and kingmakers

into custody at a clandestine emergency meeting during a New York City charity fundraiser—a masked ball. Hiding behind masks, their pins had been their entrée, prominently worn on gowns and tux lapels. Catherine and Vincent had assisted, saving many of their lives when a man named Sam Landon turned one of the guests, Andrew Martin, into his own beast assassin and commanded him to rip them apart.

On that victorious night, Gabe had believed the entire organization would be brought to justice. J.T. Forbes had succeeded in decrypting the database containing their names and addresses, and that would give Gabe the first tool to build his cases.

However, the decrypted file had cannibalized itself within seconds, releasing a crippling virus. J.T.'s entire computer was wiped clean, just as Catherine's work computer had been when she'd begun her investigation into Muirfield. There was no cloud, there were no backup files, nothing, and no one had taken the time to print out a hard copy of the data during the crisis. An investigation of the few names and addresses J.T. could remember led to a mere two arrests and convictions. The secret society vanished back into the shadows.

Except… here was one of their pins. Gabe tried to follow a train of logic to a proper conclusion. Was this pin left behind on purpose to implicate the secret society? To warn off those who would know what the pin signified? Maybe it had been shown to Reynolds to assure him that he was among friends… or that he had better do as these ruthless people said, and leave with them voluntarily.

Who took Reynolds, and why?

If the so-called "Masters of the Universe" wanted to create more beasts, it would make sense for them to spring Reynolds. Or maybe they wanted to make sure that no one else had acquired beast serum, and that the beast experiments were truly over. Reynolds would be the obvious choice to consult for those end games, too.

Gabe closed his hand over the pin. Forensics would not be receiving this into evidence.

He put it in his pocket and said casually, "Finding anything interesting?"

"Prisons are tough." The female technician gestured to the residue of black powder on the cell bars. "They're dirty and there's an amazing amount of traffic. We have a jillion prints here."

Gabe glanced around the cell one more time. He said, "Be sure to let me know if you come up with anything significant."

"Like the envelope," the tech said proudly. "I collected that. It was hidden under his blanket."

I'll bet you're the one who missed the pin, Gabe thought, smiling at her. "Good for you," he said.

CHAPTER SIX

2.57 A.M.

After Tess and Cat had climbed twenty-six flights of stairs, an emergency elevator generator kicked in and Tess swore an oath that she would go on a run every single morning until the day she retired, because she never wanted to feel this winded and sore again in her life. Lack of sleep and fairly Olympic sex were not sufficient excuses for her spasming muscles.

She and Cat wobbled from the stair landing to the blessed elevator as it arrived. Inside was Lizzani, the pig-eyed man from the lobby. The doors closed and the elevator shot upward toward the penthouse.

It took Tess a minute to place him: he was a uni from the 123rd precinct. The 125th had played baseball against the 123rd—and won. This guy was an infielder.

"Hey," Tess said. "One-twenty-three, right? We kicked your butts a couple of weeks ago. Is this your side job?"

"No butt-kicking was accomplished," he countered. "The ump was blind. And yeah, I do private security for Mr. DeMarco."

It wasn't unusual for cops to have side jobs. Firefighters

did, too. A common reason for a side job was to keep their alimony and child support payments regular. The life was tough on families. It hadn't surprised Tess that Joe, her ex-boss as well as her ex-lover, had been having marriage problems when he had turned to her. What had surprised her was that she had fallen for him and snuck around with him. She'd grown up in a big family of cops and her world pre-Joe had been very black and white. There were lots of lines you didn't cross, but she had just hopped right over that one like it wasn't even there.

After his little brother Marius's death, Joe's seemingly dead marriage had revived. She wondered if it was surviving Joe's termination with the NYPD. But that wasn't for her to wonder about. She and Joe were done. She didn't even miss him any more, and it was great not to be carrying so much guilt around.

It was often said that things happen for a reason. Her relationship with Joe had definitely made it easier for her to understand why Cat had risked everything to be with Vincent. And for Tess to realize that her Mr. Right, as opposed to Mr. Right Now, was Vincent Keller's geeky best friend, J.T. Forbes.

Impossible. I have lost my friggin' mind. But the mere thought of him gave her a nice, warm tingle.

She compartmentalized J.T. and focused. She was on the job.

"So did you notice anything unusual before the blackout?" she asked Officer Lizzani. Beside her, Cat regarded the off-duty cop with a neutral expression, but Tess knew that behind Cat's nonthreatening façade lurked a bulldog of a detective eager to leap on any detail that would help them develop a lead.

"This place is a fortress and I'm sure it's no surprise to you to that people do not cross the DeMarcos *ever*. Not people like us, anyway. I can't see someone on the inside having a hand in this."

Tess took note of the man's healthy fear of his employer. That made it less likely that Lizzani had taken part in the crime.

"Can you walk us through the security system?" Cat requested.

"I'll show you as much as I can." He pulled a plastic rectangle from his shirt pocket and tapped the elevator control pad with it. "First thing is a key card and a retinal scan."

"Wow, really?" Tess said, impressed. "Do your retinas work on it?"

"You're in this elevator, right? I'm in the database," he confirmed.

"We'll need the list of names on that database," Cat said, and Tess braced herself for the inevitable stonewall. Which they got:

"Above my pay grade, and I'm betting Mr. DeMarco will require a warrant. Which the FBI, not NYPD, will ask for."

"We're trying to recover his son for him," Cat pointed out, but all three of them knew that a man like Tony DeMarco would guard the secrets of his customized security layout like a fire-breathing dragon.

"Man like him takes the long view, know what I'm saying?" Lizzani said. "He would go to the ends of the earth to get his son back... but he's gonna make sure he doesn't jump out of a plane without a parachute."

And there's our mixed metaphor of the day, Tess thought, amused.

She inspected the fisheye lens to the side of the door at the same time as Cat. Great partners thought alike. "You looked in there, right?"

He nodded. "Yes. I looked into the scanner to make the doors open. Then I looked again to make them close."

Cat said, "So it would be possible for the kidnappers to

get in and force you to look—"

"Hey, wait a sec." His brows shot up and he held his arms in front of himself. "I wasn't even on duty when this happened."

"Oh, I didn't mean you personally," Cat said smoothly, and Tess knew that until that very second, Cat *hadn't* meant him personally. But his defensive reaction was the stuff of a detective's dreams. There was more going on with Lizzani than met the eye. Could be something as minor as cheating on his time card or even on his diet, could be conspiracy to commit a major crime. Something had caused that guilty reaction, though. Now they had something to look into. It was fuel for their case. That was how detectives worked— looking for something that didn't fit, or something they could question. That was exactly how Cat had found Vincent, despite J.T.'s success at keeping him hidden for nine years.

And that was how Tess had busted Cat and Vincent's secret wide open a year later.

"This is a flawed system," Tess observed. "If all it requires is one person who's been cleared to ride the elevator, anybody could force—"

Then the doors opened, and a trio of men in black suits faced them with weapons drawn. As soon as their eyes darted toward Tess and Cat's badges, they holstered their guns and stepped out of the way. The middle one spoke into a radiophone.

"You were saying, detective?" Lizzani pointed downward and lifted his foot. A small black button was revealed. Then he gestured to the handrail that ran the perimeter of the elevator. "I step on this, I make contact with this"—he pressed the black button with the toe of his shoe and circled his thumb and forefinger on the rail—"and security is summoned."

"What if you do it by mistake?" Tess asked.

He shrugged his shoulders. "Better safe than sorry. Mr. DeMarco doesn't have a problem with mistakes like that.

Only with the kind we've got now, with his son snatched in his own home. We run drills for every possible emergency. Blackout was on the list. So was home invasion. This shouldn't have happened."

"Does the FBI have any working theories about how it went down?" Cat asked.

"You really need to talk to Mr. DeMarco about that," Lizzani said.

A man who looked like a professional wrestler approached. "He's ready," he told Lizzani. "Detectives, this way, please."

She and Cat stepped out of the elevator and Lizzani followed closely behind, almost like he was tailing them. Maybe he was. Judging from the expression on the faces of the security guards they passed, NYPD on the job wasn't all that welcome here. Wasn't the first time.

Wouldn't be the last.

CHAPTER SEVEN

3.10 A.M.

"This is like a *Godfather* movie," Tess murmured to Cat as a phalanx of even *more* security guys gave them the once-over before they were escorted into the DeMarco family penthouse. "Look over there. Doesn't that guy look like Al Pacino?"

The front door opened, revealing the ostentatious heights that alleged corruption could lift one to. The two detectives were treated to a vast panorama of white marble floors veined with gold, gilt furniture cradling mountains of black velvet upholstery, and a forest of fluted gold columns. It was blinding: gold picture frames and mirrors, gold vases containing chunky yellow flowers, and copies of classical statues—including Michelangelo's *David* adorned with a jewel-encrusted golden fig leaf.

"No way," Tess murmured, and Cat could feel her partner trembling to keep from bursting into laughter. Cat had the same dilemma. The room looked a cross between an over-decorated casino and their favorite intimate lingerie boutique, Easy Pickin's.

Among the scatter of statues and profusion of furniture,

Evidence Recovery Unit techs were out in force, their dark blue windbreakers stamped with FBI in two-foot-tall letters on the back. A young dark-skinned woman took one look at the detectives, grinned slyly, and made a point of taking a close-up of the fig leaf with her camera.

"Happy to email it to you, detectives," she said.

Tess handed her a business card. "Appreciate the help."

"Do you know where Special Agents Robertson and Gonzales are?" Cat asked her. Those were their FBI contacts.

"They're with Mr. DeMarco." The tech couldn't keep her distaste from flashing across her features. Then she hit a button. "Picture's on its way."

"Hey, Lizzani," someone called, poking his head out of an enormous kitchen shimmering with gold fixtures as Cat and Tess passed by. He had a receipt in his hand. "You owe ten from the pizza run."

Cat and Tess both eyeballed the receipt as Lizzani pulled out his wallet. The pizza delivery had occurred at 11.52 a.m. That was just a little over three hours ago. They shared a tiny but significant look. Lizzani had told them that he hadn't been here when the kidnapping had occurred, but midnight pizza suggested otherwise. The FBI contact on the phone had placed the crime at around one-thirty a.m. They'd have to do a timeline on Lizzani.

The two detectives were ushered into a room twice as spacious as the penthouse's foyer, which was fortunate because at least twice as many men in suits surrounded an ornate gold and ebony desk. Behind the desk, an older but very buff man with jet-black hair sat in a beautifully cut charcoal-gray suit and dark blue tie. He wore a Rolex and a large gold-and-onyx ring on his left pinkie. No wedding ring.

His face was that of a soulful Italian, with dark, deep-set eyes and an aquiline nose. His mouth was turned down sharply, and as Cat and Tess held up their badges, he burst into tears. At that moment, his tough-guy image was shattered, and Cat found herself confronted with a frantic parent.

"Oh, my God, Angelo," he said, and his shoulders heaved.

Cat and Tess remained impassive, their faces blank as Cat glanced into the mirror behind the distraught man. It was a two-way mirror. For all she knew, he was recording this meeting. A glance into the mirror at Tess, who moved her chin less than an inch. She had noticed it, too. They must tread very cautiously, dotting all their Is and crossing their Ts. Men like Tony DeMarco ate sloppy cops for breakfast if they didn't obtain the results they desired.

"Sir, NYPD will do everything in our power to get your son back," Tess said, while Cat caught sight of two men in the back row, wearing white dress shirts and nearly identical dark blue suits. They moved in concert toward her and Tess.

"Detectives," the older, paler one said, holding out his hand. His mouth was turned down and he had a purple birthmark in the hollow of his left cheek. His eyes were hooded and cold. "I'm Special Agent Robertson. Glad you could make it."

He had a snide tone that Cat didn't appreciate, as if he were insinuating that they had taken too long to get there. She didn't react and neither did Tess, just politely shook his hand.

"I'm Special Agent Gonzales," the second man said, in a friendlier tone. Black eyebrows accentuated chestnut eyes, and black stubble burnished a slightly rounded chin.

"I'm Detective Chandler and this is Detective Vargas," Cat said. "Would you mind bringing us up to date?"

"My son is missing. What more do you need to know?" DeMarco half-shouted, pulling a handkerchief from his pocket and wiping his eyes.

"Mr. DeMarco, please try to remain as calm as you can. We know this is a nightmare and we're sorry that it happened. But Detective Vargas and I have worked cases like this before and we've gotten results," Cat assured him.

"There has *never* been a case like this. This is about *my* son," DeMarco snapped, and suddenly the grieving parent was nowhere to be seen. The man was seething like lava, once more the most dangerous crime boss in all of New York City, if even one-tenth of the stories about him were true. Not someone you wanted to get on the bad side of. But Tess and Cat were officers of the law, not to be trifled with. If they were working on his case, that meant they couldn't work someone else's case. And the workload of a police force always exceeded manpower. So he had obligations too—to keep himself together in order to help them.

She wondered how Vincent was faring. Ten years ago, he had served his country in a war zone. Now he was serving his city—and he was just as hated and feared now as then.

"What I mean is that you will have our full attention and we will do everything we can to bring Angelo home," Cat said.

"Whatever it takes?" He raised his chin as if daring her to say otherwise.

"Of course. Within the law, of course." It was a relief to apply her skills and training to a complex case that didn't throw beasts in the mix, too. But that relief was tempered by the fact that she was dealing with a powerful man who believed that laws were meant to be shattered if they stood in his way.

He smiled slowly. "Well, aren't you a spunky lady. I like you."

Cat didn't smile back. She wasn't here to be liked. She needed him to be cooperative so she could find his son, but that was all.

Gonzales cleared his throat. "I'll debrief you. Mr. DeMarco is far too upset. At approximately one-ten p.m.

the power went out in the DeMarco building. The backup generator system did not turn on, as it was designed to do, until one of Mr. DeMarco's people physically went down into the basement to reset it."

"We'd like to talk to that person," Tess said.

"The next thing that failed was the backup for the security system."

"Wow," Tess said.

"You don't need to be broadcasting that," Mr. DeMarco snapped. "There's still a blackout, right? I don't need my business rivals thinking I can't protect what's mine. It's been fixed. All of it. We don't have any problems."

"Who's in charge of that system?" Cat asked Gonzales.

"We've already debriefed him," Robertson insisted.

Tess stayed cool. "Maybe he'll remember a few new details by restating their story to a new interviewer." Allowing other departments who were working on a case to interview key subjects was Investigation 101, no matter who you worked for. Robertson was just being a jerk.

"All you need to do is look for Angelo," Mr. DeMarco said. "You're NYPD. You know the city."

The FBI had twelve hundred agents in New York City. They knew the lay of the land as well as the police department.

"The more we know about *how* he was taken, the closer we get to who may have taken him, and where," Cat said. Surely he knew this. "I respect your need for privacy, and I'm sorry you have to permit strangers into your home."

"Strangers who can take what they learn and use it *later*," he said. He pointed a finger at them. "You can bet it'll be changed up, so don't bothering taking a lot of notes."

"If it's going to be changed up," Tess ventured, "then it won't matter if we talk to the people who put the current system together."

DeMarco blinked at her. Then he actually smiled. "You've

got moxie. Both you ladies." He looked at Robertson. "They can talk to Bailey."

"Okay."

Cat could tell by Tess's carefully neutral expression that she was finding this conversation just as odd as she was. DeMarco was dictating the terms of the investigation to an FBI agent. It spoke volumes about how powerful he was— and suggested that Robertson, at least, was content to let him take the lead.

"Okay, I see that your ERU is keeping busy. What do you have so far?" Cat asked briskly. FBI might have jurisdiction, but that didn't mean that the NYPD was somehow a lesser entity or a junior partner. If they were going to assist, they needed facts, information.

An evidence tech approached carrying a dark-blue plastic bin. "Here's the ransom note," said Special Agent Gonzales, reaching inside the bin. The tech set the box down on DeMarco's desk. Gonzales held up a clear plastic evidence bag for Tess and Cat to see. It would have been nice if they could have examined the note before it had been bagged. They had their own gloves; they wouldn't have contaminated the evidence.

"We bagged it a bit prematurely, perhaps," Gonzales added.

Cat wondered if his apology was genuine. Some FBI agents were remote and intimidating, like Robertson, but the FBI was in the business of intelligence gathering—extracting information, making connections, figuring things out. Her dad—her *real* dad, not her biological father—loved to say that you caught more flies with honey than with vinegar. Ergo, it made sense for agents to cultivate trust in the individuals they dealt with, on all levels, from criminals to colleagues from other agencies. To be a "people person," in other words... or to be able to act like one. All that "just the facts, ma'am" you saw on TV? More often, agents were friendly and encouraged chatter.

Inside the bag was a handwritten note on a piece of plain copy paper. It said, *We have your son. He will receive insulin when we receive money. Be ready.*

"Insulin," Cat said, and Special Agent Gonzales handed her another evidence bag from the bin, this one made of brown paper, like a lunch sack. Bags such as these were used for pieces of evidence that were moist, since being encased in plastic could promote molds or other bacterial growth that could compromise the item. Cat set down the bag and put on a pair of blue latex evidence gloves. Tess did the same. Then Cat reached in and carefully retrieved a small plastic box with a digital screen and a plastic tube attached to it.

"Angelo DeMarco has juvenile diabetes. It's been difficult to manage because he doesn't deal with it very well. Mrs. DeMarco has corroborated that this is most likely Angelo's insulin pump," Robertson said. "We've taken DNA samples off it. We'll have them analyzed."

"Is Angelo DeMarco's DNA in the system?" Cat asked.

Robertson shrugged. "We can use his medical records. He's been to the doctor about a thousand times." Medical records were protected information, but looking at them would be easily accomplished with a subpoena.

"Here's a good headshot of Angelo," Gonzales said, handing each of them an eight-by-ten glossy of a young man who resembled Tony DeMarco, but whose features were less sharp. Big, dark eyes, heavy eyebrows, but a softer nose and plumper lips. He wasn't smiling, and he looked as if something was weighing heavily on his mind. Haunted. "I'll email it to your phones as well."

"When was this picture taken?" Tess asked.

"About three months ago. It was for DeMarco Industries' annual report," DeMarco said. "Angelo is on the board." He gave his head a shake. "Not that he ever makes the meetings. See, that's the problem if you grow up rich."

"I wouldn't know," Tess murmured, so softly that Cat, who standing the closest to her, barely heard her. Good thing, too. They didn't want to antagonize DeMarco.

"We could help you question the security and housekeeping staff," Cat said to Robertson.

"On it," he said. "Agents are taking statements in some of the guest rooms as we speak."

"Looks like you have everything well in hand," Cat said with a trace of asperity.

"We do," he responded.

It was evident that the two men resented her and Tess's presence. It didn't matter. A young man with a medical condition was missing. Finding him was their mandate.

"Maybe it's time to speak to Bailey," Cat said.

"I'll arrange that," Robertson said. He pulled out a radiophone and began speaking into it as he walked off.

"Take them to Hallie while Bailey gets ready," Mr. DeMarco told Gonzales. "I'm not sure how much help she'll be. You know how women are." He inclined his head. "Except for beautiful lady cops, of course."

Bleargh, Cat thought.

Gonzales gestured for them to follow him out. They left the office and followed the two agents back through the foyer to a cavernous space filled with suits of armor. A large shield with a yellow-and-black coat of arms hung on the wall. DEMARCO, it read.

There was one woman in the crowd of security people. In her early fifties, she had short, feathered red hair and she was dressed in a black suit with a skirt, low black heels, and the most foreboding "don't screw with me" expression in the apartment thus far. She was on a radiophone and when she saw Cat and Tess, she walked into a room off the hall and shut the door as if for privacy. There were a few head nods in their direction as they walked the gauntlet of strangers, but for the most part they were pretty much ignored.

Then Gonzales opened a door on the right and Cat stepped through first. She found herself on a carved marble staircase that spiraled upward, and Gonzales indicated that she should go up.

Behind Cat, Tess murmured, "Oh, boy, more stairs," and Gonzales smiled.

"We were running a pool on whether or not you two would actually climb sixty flights of stairs," he said.

"Damn straight," Tess replied, and his smile broke into a big grin.

"I had my money on you, Detective Vargas. You're in shape." His gaze strayed toward her butt.

"Can we cut the chatter?" Robertson snapped.

Tess flashed him a quick evil eye out of his range of vision and Cat stayed silent as they ascended the stairs. Their footsteps rang out.

"Would the kidnappers have used this route?" she asked.

"That's something we don't know," Gonzales said. "I mean, you can hear how noisy this stairwell is. It was built that way on purpose. It's one way Mr. DeMarco kept tabs on his son. Or tried to. Somehow, Angelo still snuck in and out."

"He's twenty, right? I mean, can't he come and go as he pleases?" Tess asked, and Robertson's mouth set into a rigid line.

"Mr. DeMarco is correct to be so protective of his son. Angelo has trouble accepting that the wealth and privilege he was born into makes him a target for exactly this situation. If he was more cautious, his father would be less… watchful."

Poor little rich boy, Cat thought. She was forming a profile of Angelo DeMarco: restricted and rebellious. A volatile combination. She could remember having spats with her mom over curfews and the company she kept.

But not when I was twenty. My mom was already dead.

"The security cameras must have backup batteries," Cat said, combining two questions into one: that they *had* cameras, and that they'd been on.

"The cameras leading into Angelo's quarters were disabled," Gonzales reported. "That's not unusual. Angelo hacked them himself on a regular basis. Said he didn't want to be spied on." He gave her a weary look as if to say, *You begin to see the problem.*

The stairs ended on a landing decorated with a signed guitar in a glass case. The case stood in the direct pathway of a security camera. None of the status lights at the base of the camera was on.

"This guitar belonged to Stevie Ray Vaughn," Gonzales said offhandedly. "The kid collects."

Collects what? Cat wondered, as he opened a door in front of her. Robertson was busy typing something into a cell phone.

They walked into a messy, shabby bedroom. Cat expected to see more milling security guards, but there was only one person: a tall, seriously athletic woman maybe as old as thirty-five, with curly blond hair cascading over her shoulders and a face completely free of lines and blemishes. She was wearing a black, floor-length raw silk nightgown that exposed plenty of cleavage, with a luxurious black robe— looked to be cashmere—over it. There was no puffiness from crying around her large blue eyes. Her makeup was perfectly applied, shiny lips pursed together in a scowl. She wasn't worried. She was pissed off.

"Hey, Miguel, Jim," she said as the FBI agents walked in. Her words were slurred and she was none too steady on her feet. She looked past the men, did an eye sweep of Cat, then raised her brows at Tess as if to say, *Who the hell are you two?*

"Mrs. DeMarco," "Jim" replied, "these are the police detectives the Bureau has brought in." He turned to Cat and Tess. "This is Mrs. DeMarco." Then he walked out of the room, leaving Gonzales behind.

Hallie has to be Angelo's stepmother, Cat thought, *unless she had him when she was twelve.* She said, "I'm Detective Chandler. This is Detective Vargas. We'll do everything we can to retrieve your son."

Mrs. DeMarco made a face. "My son," she said. "Well…" She trailed off. "Thanks."

She was surrounded by open dresser drawers and jumbles of jeans, running shoes, and hoodies. An acoustic guitar had been placed in a stand in a corner. The room was decorated in early thrift shop—a cheap bureau made of painted particle board, a drawing table, and a twin bed with a peeling wrought-iron headboard. Pencil sketches of young men playing guitars and skateboarding were tacked to the walls. Books and sketchpads were scattered on top of the bare mattress. The sheets were stretched out on the floor like the chalk drawing of a body.

"I've looked through everything," Mrs. DeMarco told Gonzales. "Nothing."

Cat wondered why there was no one from evidence recovery in here. Maybe there was some concern for Angelo's privacy… or something the family didn't want outsiders to see. Drugs. Porn. They wanted to cover that up. Conceal it. Not a good plan. Anything that could provide information about where Angelo was and who had him should be available.

Just then Robertson walked back in. He was carrying a glass of what smelled like straight bourbon.

"Mrs. DeMarco, Mr. DeMarco is asking for you," Robertson said. He held out the glass. "He asked me to give this to you to help steady your nerves."

So FBI agents double as cocktail waiters? These guys were

way too familiar with the DeMarco family. It was clear to Cat that this wasn't the first time they'd dealt with each other.

Hallie DeMarco took the drink and guzzled it down without pausing. Then she handed the empty glass back to Robertson and swayed out of the room. Gonzales sighed and shook his head.

"Let's get to work." Robertson moved to the pile of clothes on the bed. He said to Gonzales, "Did she take anything?"

Gonzales colored and turned to Cat and Tess. "As you may have surmised, there's no love lost between Hallie DeMarco and Angelo. She's his second stepmother, and she's pretty new. Just two years into the marriage. He's called her a gold digger to her face."

"Is she?" Tess asked calmly.

"She's not on trial here," Robertson said icily.

Yet, Cat thought. "We're not accusing her of anything." She was irritated that she had to placate a fellow professional like this. "But if there is any reason to suspect that she had a hand in the abduction, we need to find that out."

"There's no reason," Robertson replied, but Gonzales spoke over him.

"She doesn't like Angelo. At all." he interjected.

Cat followed up. "Why not?"

"Hallie Schneider was an LVN—a licensed vocational nurse—before she married Mr. DeMarco. An... employee of DeMarco's had placed his mother in the assisted living facility Hallie was working in and she caught DeMarco's eye when he came to pay his respects."

That didn't exactly answer Cat's question. She assumed Hallie was insecure about her hold on DeMarco, and didn't like having to deal with a resentful stepson who could influence his father against her. Angelo's rebellion might be directed at her. Maybe he was worried that if his father had a child with his new wife, he would be supplanted, maybe even disinherited.

"Did she assist Angelo with his diabetic treatments?" Tess asked.

"That was his dad's hope, but Angelo wouldn't let her come near him."

"Where's his mom?"

"Undetermined," Gonzales said. "She cut off contact when Angelo was a baby and we haven't found her. Mr. DeMarco thinks she may be deceased."

Okay, that's weird, Cat thought. By her answering expression, Tess was thinking the same thing.

"Let's get back to work," Robertson said. He put on a pair of gloves and began to search methodically through the clothing on the bed. He dug his hands into pockets and turned socks inside out. Gonzales flicked on a flashlight, dropped to his knees, and peered under the bed.

He pulled out what appeared to be a sketchbook, but was actually a musical composition book. Robertson kept examining the clothing. Cat put on fresh gloves and Tess followed suit, even though it was odd to both of them that ERU wasn't performing these tasks, and soon they were slowly paging through the book. There were no lyrics, just notes on musical staffs.

"You said he collected," Cat said.

"Oh. Yeah." Gonzales walked to what appeared to be a standard clothes closet. But when he opened it, a huge room was revealed, and in it, there were dozens of guitars in glass cases like the Stevie Ray Vaughn in the stair landing. On the walls hung large black-and-white photographs of guitarists. Cat recognized Elvis Presley and Jimi Hendrix. The others were unknown to her.

"Does he play as well as collect?" Cat asked. She looked down at the music book. "Are these his songs?"

"He's terrible," Mrs. DeMarco said behind them. She came up beside Cat and tapped the book. "He liked to go to clubs and write down what he heard. So he could steal it. Sometimes the musicians invited him to sit in but trust me, they were doing it because of who he is. He was so bad he didn't even know he was bad."

Okay, and at least some parts of sentences were in present tense, Cat thought. *So maybe she doesn't have special knowledge that our vic is dead.* Speaking of missing persons in past tense could serve as an indicator of participation… and guilt.

Mrs. DeMarco ambled down a row of guitars. "You can't believe how much money is in these things. Tony's such a sucker when it comes to that kid."

"But of course you're worried sick about him," Robertson coached her.

"Huh? Oh, right. Of course I am."

And for one moment, something slipped on her face and she looked completely and utterly miserable. It was as if she forgot to be hard and instead revealed just how young and out of her depth she was. People under extreme stress did that, just dropped the act and showed their real faces. The best example of that was Vincent, whose classic stress reaction was to beast out.

Not any more. He's got it under control, Cat told herself firmly.

Cat didn't go so far as to pity Hallie DeMarco but she made a mental note to check into her history. And to see what they could discover about Angelo's mother. There was a lot going on beneath the surface of the DeMarco compound, that was for sure.

"Sir?" said a voice, and Cat, Tess, and the two agents all turned to see the dark-skinned woman from the recovery unit hovering in the doorway with a matchbook in her hand. Cat hadn't even seen her enter the bedroom.

The tech was excited. "I just found this under the vic's bed."

"You mean Angelo DeMarco. He has a name," Robertson growled. His eyes flashed with fury as he advanced on the young woman and grabbed the matchbook. "I *said* that Special Agent Gonzales and I would personally search his room."

"I'm sorry, sir. I—I didn't hear that," said the crestfallen woman.

"No matter. The damage is done now."

Damage, Cat noted. She knew Tess was listening just as hard.

Tess and Cat gathered next to Robertson. The front cover of the matchbook was gray, and the word *turntable* was printed in smeared black letters.

"That's a club," Tess said. "For people into vinyl records. You know, the classics." Cat blinked in surprise that Tess would know such a thing. "J.T. took me there." Her cheeks reddened and Cat forced away a grin. A real date. That she had not yet heard about. That was something to look forward to.

"That's the kind of place he liked to go," Mrs. DeMarco said.

Liked. Past tense again.

"Does he have any friends there, people he meets on a regular basis?" Cat asked, ignoring Robertson's baleful looks. She wasn't going to stand there and do *nothing*, for heaven's sake. She had sworn an oath to protect and serve, not to avoid offending the FBI. In fact, if anything, the FBI owed her big-time.

"No clue." Hallie DeMarco glanced over at Robertson. Clearly she was unwilling or unable to respond in his presence.

"May I?" Cat asked the tech, who looked flustered as she took the matchbook and examined it. There was a string of seven numbers written in blue ink on the inside flap. Could be a phone number without an area code. She let Tess take a picture of it with her phone, then positioned the cover for another picture. Robertson practically snatched it out of her hand.

"We'll take care of that," he said, thrusting it back at the tech. Then he turned to go back into the bedroom. Gonzales followed. After a couple of seconds, Mrs. DeMarco went inside, too.

"No kidding this is an inside job," Tess muttered.

Together the two detectives walked through Angelo DeMarco's guitar museum. Nearly all the instruments were electric, except for a very few that were displayed in the cases the farthest away from the door. Then in the very last case sat a child-size guitar, which was painted shocking pink and decorated with periwinkle-blue flowers.

"I saw guitars like this for sale when I was in Cancun with Gabe," Cat told Tess. "A street vendor had a souvenir cart filled with them, and maracas and castanets."

"Cancun. Gabe. Stop. You're making me shudder," Tess said. "I know, right? *Gabe*." Cat couldn't believe she'd ever slept with Gabe either. Repeatedly. They'd taken that trip when Gabe had pretended be dead so they could flush out Sam Landon, the man who had created new beasts to take out the "Masters of the Universe," the ultra-hush-hush organization of the rich and ruthless that had backed Muirfield.

In Cancun there had been massages and lovemaking and convincing herself that Vincent was nothing more than a memory. Just thinking about it made Cat grimace. Gabe was her bitterest enemy now, although he didn't see himself that way. He believed he was her white knight. He had made her life a living hell so that he could *protect* her.

The same as my father, she thought. *And now my father is missing*. Until that very moment, she hadn't allowed herself a single second to dwell on that, and now, just as agony had ruptured Mrs. DeMarco's mask, thoughts of him crashed through the wall she had erected so she could do her job. It infuriated her that she was being jerked around by Robertson and Gonzales instead of looking into her father's disappearance.

"And... we're back from Mexico," Tess murmured pointedly.

"Sorry." Cat opened the case and took out the pink guitar. "Why would he have this?" she asked. "Did it belong to someone famous? Shirley Temple?"

"Maybe it was Angelo's first guitar?" Tess ventured. "Wouldn't that be weird? I mean, I don't care that it's pink, but wouldn't his so-very-sexist dad?"

Cat turned the guitar over to examine the back. Something fluttered out of the sound hole and Tess bent to retrieve it. It was a blurry Polaroid of a little redheaded girl. There was something about her that caught Cat's attention, but she couldn't figure out what it was.

"Does this ring a bell?" she asked Tess, and Tess considered. She took the photograph and held it closer.

"Maybe?" Tess said. "I'm not sure." She pulled out her phone and snapped a picture of it. "I'm tempted to take it."

"Then we're breaking laws and we do that often enough," Cat said. "I suppose we should show it to the agents."

"Show what?" said a voice behind Cat, and she jerked, startled. Agent Robertson had come up behind her. He took the photograph and the guitar. "What's this?" "The photograph was inside the guitar." She pointed to the sound hole. "Maybe he hid it there. It could be a family member, or some kind of link."

"Naw. It's nothing," he replied. "I'm sure he doesn't know it's even there." He stuffed the photograph back in in the guitar and put the guitar back in the display case.

Finally, Cat lost her temper. "How can you be so sure?"

He sighed. "I just am. Just leave all this to us. We're FBI."

She said, "*We* are professionals too." As soon as she said

it, she regretted it. She didn't want him to know he was getting to her.

"Last call for clubs in the city is four a.m.," Tess said. "It's after three now. There's a mandatory curfew on businesses but they might be open. Not sure if we could get there before closing with the traffic but we might catch staff."

"You wanted to talk to Bailey Hart," Gonzales said. "I'll get someone to take you down to him."

Cat traded looks with Tess. If they talked to Bailey Hart, they would miss out on the club. But as they say, a bird in the hand was worth two in the bush. And it was doubtful that the club was open.

"Okay," Cat said.

Gonzales said into his phone, "I need someone with a retinal scan in the database."

After a couple of minutes, the red-haired female security staffer met them at a freight elevator. Her name was Claudia McEvers. She was stiff-backed and waves of apprehension rolled off her like flop sweat as she was introduced to Tess and Cat. She approached a retinal scanner and the doors opened; then she went inside with Cat, Tess, and Roberston, and used her key card to activate the elevator.

"So you work for Mr. DeMarco," Cat said. "Were you on duty when the kidnapping occurred?"

The woman hesitated. "No. I was called in shortly before you arrived. I've given a full statement to the agents." She made eye contact with Roberston, but barely.

Either they know each other or something's up, Cat mused. *She's not going to speak freely in front of him.*

They got to the sub-basement and stepped into a workspace dominated by a wrap-around computer station abutting a vast wall of monitors. Dressed in gray trousers and a chambray shirt rolled up to the elbows, Bailey Hart was an amazing piece of techno eye candy, a man who believed in lifting weights and doing sit-ups as much as Vincent did. He looked like one of the super-hunky firefighters who appeared in the annual FDNY pin-up calendar. Mr... what month was this? This was Mr. *Year*.

"Okay, so hi," he said breathlessly. He was holding a ballpoint pen and he clicked it a few times. A few more times. It was obviously a nervous habit. On the desk was an ink blotter that he had scribbled and doodled on so much there was no white space left. There were pieces of graph paper, a Styrofoam plate containing some pizza crust, more pens, and a tablet. He glanced at Robertson and completely avoided eye contact with McEvers. "Let me run you through our backup security operation."

The monitors revealed different sections of the house, and each screen was packed with people milling around in the rooms. Cat caught a glimpse of Hallie DeMarco in the kitchen, pouring herself another glass of bourbon as she chatted with a young man in an FBI windbreaker. Robertson's face hardened as he watched her.

"This is custom, in-house stuff," Hart said. "I didn't buy anything off the shelf, and no one who worked on it besides me had access to all the components. The brains are in here."

He walked them down a flight of stairs into what could only be described as a bunker designed to withstand a nuclear blast. It was guarded by two men in olive-green uniforms who were holding sub-machineguns across their chests. They stood to attention as he presented his eye to a retinal scanner and placed his hand on a print reader. Then he keyed an elaborate code into a shielded box, so that no one else could see.

A steel door at least two inches thick clicked and slowly swung open. The interior was softly lit, and as he ushered them in, the two guards turned toward them and raised their weapons.

"This is not cool," Tess said.

"It's all right. It's just a precaution," Hart said.

"It's not all right," Cat insisted. "They need to lower their weapons *now*."

"All right. Okay," Hart murmured. He said to one of the guards, "Alpha niner zulu."

Both guards lowered their weapons to their sides. Then they executed a smart half-turn and faced outward once more.

A small box about the size of a microwave sat on a black pedestal. Hart came forward and stared into another scanner, tapped in more secret code on a keypad, and the box door opened. The unit inside was a very small cube of matte charcoal-gray with no buttons or switches to mar its sleek surface. The magic was in the computer chips, to which Cat and Tess were not privy. They could only take his word that it did what he said. But give that box to J.T., and it would be like unlocking a universe.

As for what Hart said it could do: it could lock all doors, windows, safes, and computer hard drives, freeze all elevators, and activate motion-sensitive lasers in any or all of the designated "zones" throughout the house.

"No one should be able to get in or out," he finished. *Click-click, click-click.* "But someone did."

"And this comes on when the primary security system backup doesn't activate?" Tess asked.

He pulled his pen out of his pocket. *Click-click.* "It's supposed to. But it didn't. From what I can figure out, the kidnappers reprogrammed my code so that it thought the primary backup *did* go on. So that would keep my system from activating."

"So what would be a reasonable point of entry," Tess began, "to reprogram your code?"

"Well," he said. "I've initiated a debugger, and—"

"We're interviewing the entire security staff," Robertson

cut in. "We'll let you know what we find." He waved a silencing hand at Cat as she prepared to protest. "Surely you can understand Mr. DeMarco's reluctance to share the workings of his private security system with New York's finest, some of whom are not so fine. No offense intended to present company."

Because the FBI is so much more ethical, Cat thought. *Offense definitely intended to present company.*

Bailey Hart clicked his pen like crazy. He was monumentally uneasy—no; he was *frightened*. Take the situation and multiply it by DeMarco's temper, and it was clear why.

"I'm the only one with direct access to its programming. As you can see, I have a retinal scanner, a print reader, and a secret code when I program it." He swallowed hard. Of course suspicion now focused on him.

"There *are* work-arounds for scans and prints," Robertson said, as if to reassure him. Cat knew this from personal experience—Tori Windsor had successfully opened a secret vault that had belonged to her father with her retinal scan, which was of course was programmed to recognize his DNA, and Cat had read about cases where criminals had created fake readable fingerprints off glass and other smooth, hard surfaces.

They left the bunker with its two armed guards and walked back upstairs into what could only be termed Hart's lair. Cat opened her purse, grabbed a business card, and handed it to him. "Anything you can share with us that you think would be useful, we'd appreciate hearing from you."

Looking flustered, Hart glanced at Robertson and murmured, "I'll see what I can do." He sat down, his way of ending the interview.

There's another dead end, Cat thought. *He's not going to talk to us.*

Suddenly, red lights began to spin and alarms whooped at ear-splitting decibels. Cat, Tess, Robertson, and McEvers all pulled their weapons. Hart was so startled he fell backward in his chair as his pens and papers skittered to the floor. He hit the deck just as the alarms cut off.

The two guards appeared at the end of the room, weapons out. Tess and Cat raised their hands.

"Code one-two, code one-two," Hart cried. "Stand down, stand down! False alarm!"

"We're NYPD," Cat said. "Stand down."

Neither of the guards cracked an expression. As robotic as ever, they re-shouldered their weapons but didn't leave the room.

Cat bent down to help Hart back up and her business card holder and a couple of pens tumbled out of her purse, which had snapped open. Tess gathered up the scattered belongings while Cat hoisted a shaken Hart to his feet. Their weapons still out, McEvers and Robertson carefully watched. Then their radiophones rang and both of them answered in unison as a landline phone on the wrap-around desk rang as well. Hart grabbed it.

"Hello, yes, false alarm," Hart said. "Code seven-foxtrot. Seven-foxtrot. Yes, sir. I think they implemented a time delay. Rather than fool the system into not going off, they programmed it to go off later."

Someone on the other end spoke.

"I don't know." Hart thought hard. "Maybe they didn't mean to. Or they did it to cause confusion." He looked at McEvers and Robertson, then pivoted and stared at the two guards. "Maybe they were hoping someone would shoot me when it went off. No, sir, I'm not trying to be sarcastic. I'm genuinely afraid here."

"That's a lot of maybes," Tess said to Cat as she closed Cat's purse and handed it to her. Cat slung the strap over her shoulder.

"Yes, I did take them into the vault. I thought… oh, I'm so sorry, Mr. DeMarco. I thought… yes, of course," Hart said, hanging up the phone. The blood had drained from his face. "Mr. DeMarco has asked me to terminate the, ah, tour." His hands were shaking. "So, ah, if you would please…" He gestured to the elevator.

He showed us more than he was supposed to, Cat thought.

They went back up to the penthouse level. Cat was glad to see that equipment had been set up to listen in on and trace any calls DeMarco received. Since Angelo had a serious medical condition, it had to be assumed that a call would come in soon.

"Okay, so now the club?" Robertson prompted. "You want to give it a shot?"

"Do you have someone out in the field who would be closer?" Cat asked. The longer they took processing the crime scene to develop leads, the colder the trail would grow. It was common knowledge that the first twenty-four hours in a kidnapping investigation were the most crucial.

"You're probably our best choice." He pulled out his business cards and handed one to Cat and one to Tess. They reciprocated. He gave both cards a nonchalant glance and then placed them in his wallet.

"We'll stay in contact," Cat said.

"You do that." He fluttered his fingers as if to say, "Off you go," dismissing them in the most condescending way possible.

Cat bit the inside of her cheek to keep from herself from saying anything else she would regret and they crossed back into Angelo's room. Gonzales was examining another notebook and Cat would have given anything to take a peek at it. Instead she and Tess walked by themselves into the hall, which was still flooded with private security and FBI personnel. Claudia McEvers was among them. She looked left and right, then hailed them over.

Cat and Tess walked up to her, and she opened a door that led into Mr. DeMarco's office from the back way. Cat hadn't even noticed it when they'd been inside the room before. Raised brows and a headshake from Tess indicated that she hadn't seen it before, either. The place was like a funhouse.

Or a safe house. There was probably a panic room, too, in case of home invasion. Maybe more than one.

McEvers murmured, "Watch out for those two Feebs, detectives."

"Feebs" was another term for FBI. So this woman didn't like Robertson and Gonzales either.

Cat indicated to McEvers that she'd been heard and she and Tess walked into DeMarco's study. He was sitting alone with an open bottle of a scotch and a half-full glass.

"I haven't had the pleasure of working with you before," he said. "I want you to know what a lot of cops who've made my acquaintance already know: if you find Angelo, you will share in my joy. Generously."

Bribes, Cat translated.

"That's not necessary, Mr. DeMarco," she said.

He tsked. "You don't need to worry. Downtown has given their stamp of approval. I pay my taxes, sure, but a man in my position creates a lot of work for you hardworking city employees."

He waited. Cat said nothing more. There really wasn't anything to say.

"However." He held up a finger. "If you do anything to screw up this investigation, you will share in my dismay. Also generously."

"No worries," Tess said.

"Robertson and Gonzales are good guys," he went on. "They know what they're doing. I hope the same can be said of you."

"It can," Cat assured him.

But as they walked out of the office, Tess gave her a look that told her she understood what the redheaded security guard had warned them about: if the FBI agents did make any mistakes, they'd try their hardest to lay them at the door of someone else.

Guess who.

CHAPTER EIGHT

3.51 A.M.

Tess and Cat called ahead to the club and verified that it was closed. No one answered repeated calls and given the gridlock, they decided to table a visit for now. The traffic had gotten worse, and it would take them forever to return to the precinct, so with Captain Ward's blessing they assisted in minimizing the looting in the vicinity of the DeMarco Building. Interestingly enough, the looting already *was* minimal—further evidence of the powerful reach of the DeMarco crime family.

They decided to patrol a few blocks northeast of the DeMarco Plaza, away from the glitz and glam and into an older neighborhood. There were fewer businesses and more residential blocks. Their flashlights traveled over shabby buildings fronted with tidy squares of snow-covered ground. Lights flickered in windows—candles, lanterns. A sign over a padlocked gate announced that this was the DeMarco Community Garden, for local residents only.

Snowflakes drifted down. Cat hoped no one was burning charcoal indoors to stay warm. That would lead to death by carbon monoxide poisoning, and she and Tess had observed more than one of those sad scenes.

They continued northeast. The buildings became progressively shabbier and many of them looked completely abandoned. They had reached the outskirts of civilization and by tacit agreement were about to turn back when Cat heard the trill of some kind of flute. Disconnected notes hopped up and down the scale. The tuneless playing made a counterpoint to the slightly fainter but still incessant honking of car horns a few blocks away.

Beyond the garden, several rusted-out cars created something of a wall; the flicker of orange flames was visible in the spaces between the metal hulks. It was a campfire, Cat guessed. The flute "song" was coming from there.

They moved around to the right, to see an old man seated in a rotting beach chair with a blanket draped over his shoulders. He had long, scraggly gray hair that had been combed away from his face, and he was playing what appeared to be a pennywhistle. In his large ham hock hands, the metallic cylinder looked as tiny as a pencil.

When Cat and Tess stepped into the firelight, he stopped playing. Then he laughed and said, "Well, hello, angels."

"Hey," Cat said affably. "How are you doing?"

"Fine, fine." He scratched his cheek with the plastic mouthpiece of the pennywhistle. "You're *here*, right? I haven't had my medication in a while. I want to be sure I'm not dreaming."

"We're here," Cat said. "You're not dreaming."

"Did the boy come with you?" He moved sideways and craned his neck. "Haven't see him in a while. Did he die?"

Whoa, Cat thought. "The boy," she repeated carefully.

He blew a note on the pennywhistle. "Gave me this. He said when he was little he couldn't say 'tin whistle.' So he called it a tordemacto." He cracked up. "He's a good boy. Did he send me some food?" "Not tonight." Tess looked around, then climbed up to sit on the hood of one of the cars and dangled her hands between her knees. Cat leaned against the same hood and crossed her feet at the ankles.

The man sadly shook his head. "He died, then. I'm going to miss him. He brings me food."

"What's his name?" Cat asked.

He blew on the whistle. "Dead Boy, now."

"What did it used to be?"

"He give me all kinds of things. You want to see my place?"

"Love to," Tess said. She slid off the hood of the car.

The man gathered the folds of his blanket and tried to rise from the chair. He grunted and shook his head. Tess and Cat approached and each held out a hand. He gave the flute to Cat.

"Just to hold," he said. "I'll want it back."

Cat shone her flashlight on the instrument. The word *Famagosta* was printed in gold letters of the side of the whistle. Italian.

"Is the boy's name Angelo? Is that why you called us angels?"

He grunted and held out his hands so they could help him get up. Tess took one hand and Cat wrapped her fingers around the other. They both tugged and he nearly flew into the sky along with the sparks from the fire. He was feather-light, clad in oversized sweatpants and a drooping sweatshirt. The only part of his body that had any significant flesh on it was his hands.

He laughed. "Whoopsy daisy!"

Then he flexed his fingers, requesting his flute. Cat gave it to him. He held it like a scepter, turned, and walked away from the campfire. His blanket dragged in the dirt.

Cat and Tess followed as he led the way toward a dilapidated metal shed with the faded words KEYS MADE painted on the side. The man stopped and gestured at the shed with the flute. Abracadabra. He trundled along, then stepped into the shed via a door that squeaked and protested when he opened it.

The interior was pretty much as Cat expected: a profusion of canned food, a can opener, dirty paper plates and napkins, a sleeping bag. Also, incongruously: several bottles of Chianti in their woven straw cozies. She picked up a bottle and shone her flashlight on it. It was full, hadn't even been opened.

"Did Angelo bring you the wine?" she asked him.

The man sank to the floor much more gracefully than she would have anticipated and began playing the flute. He said around the plastic mouthpiece, "This is called a tordemacto."

She reached in her purse and pulled out the glossy photograph of Angelo. She held it out to him.

"Is this him?"

The man stopped playing again. He leaned forward and kissed Angelo's picture.

"He's dead."

"How do you know?" Cat asked gently.

"He didn't come. I need my medicine."

She followed his line of reasoning. "Did he always bring you medicine? Were they pills or bottles of wine?"

A single tear ran down the man's weathered cheek. Then he fished around in his sleeping bag. He showed them an old digital tape recorder and turned it on.

Music began to play. It took Cat a few seconds to place it—"Ave Maria," played on an electric guitar, not too well, but with a lot of emotion. Reverential, haunting. He set down the tape recorder and began to tootle along on his flute, his notes entirely out of syncopation and discordant... but no less heartfelt.

"Is that him?" Cat asked. "Is that Angelo playing the guitar?"

"She's an angel," the man said. "She's dead."

Variations on a theme.

The man picked up one of the Chianti bottles and shook it, then yanked the cork out with his teeth and began to throw it back.

"Sir, it's going to be very cold tonight," Tess said. "Let us take you somewhere warm."

He gave his head a quick shake. "I have to wait here."

Cat tried to take the bottle from him but he held it indignantly against his chest.

Cat said, "People are looking for Angelo. They're very worried about him. We'll get you some hot soup and warm clothes."

Tess pulled out her phone. "Should I call the DeMarcos?"

"Given the blackout, I don't think we have a choice except to take him there, if they're agreeable," Cat replied. "And it sounds like he'll be able to provide information if he just gets a little encouragement. Can you walk, sir? Hey, what's your name?"

"I can walk. He calls me 'Buddy.'"

"Yes, hello," Tess said into her phone. She lowered her voice and walked a distance away. Cat walked slowly beside the man as he shuffled along.

"How did you two meet?" she asked.

"He came by." *Shuffle shuffle shuffle.* "Playing his guitar."

Tess rejoined them. "They're bringing a golf cart."

It didn't take long for the cart to arrive. A man Cat didn't recognize was driving it, and it was a two-seater. It took some convincing to get the man to sit in the cart, and he only agreed to it if the driver would go slowly enough for Cat and Tess to walk beside him. He began to play his flute and Cat felt unaccountably protective of him. She hoped no one would confiscate his tordemacto, if it was indeed Angelo's.

Soon they were back on the busy, noisy thoroughfare.

The dedicated uni was still faithfully guarding their squad car. His breath wreathed around him like a ghostly presence, and Cat waved at him. He waved back.

The cart stopped at the lobby entrance and Cat helped the old man out.

"Come with me, sir," the cart driver said.

The driver didn't invite Tess and Cat back in. Cat expected the old man to insist that they accompany him. But he shuffled away without looking back at Tess or her. To his escort, he said, "I need medicine."

"We'll take care of you, sir," the driver said. Then they went together into the lobby and, from there, into an elevator.

Gonzales leaned out of the elevator, gave Tess and Cat a wave, and mouthed "Thank you." But he made no move to invite the detectives inside as well.

"Well, humph," Tess said, "and why am I not surprised?"

"I second your humph. Let's call in."

Tess and Cat walked over to the uni just as two more officers approached him. They were also being released from the DeMarco building. The streets were just as busy, the car horns just as deafening. A sharp wind tore through Cat and she shivered.

Cat said, "You guys up for patrolling together? We'll come too."

Everyone nodded and Cat and Tess voted that they go past the DeMarco Plaza in the other direction. As the group began to move, Cat got through to Captain Ward.

Cat hung back and asked, "Are there any new developments on Agent Reynolds?"

"All I know is that there's a case number and an APB," Ward said. "If there are any leads I'll let you know. What's the status of the DeMarco case?"

She told him everything, from the booze for Mrs. DeMarco to the guitar collection, the visit to the sub-basement and finding the old vagrant. She was frank about their reception and Robertson and Gonzales's behavior.

He sighed and muttered, "I really hate the FBI."

"You're not alone, sir."

She heard a scream; the others did, too. She told her captain she had to go.

They ran en masse in the direction of the scream, car headlights dissecting their forms into bands of light and dark. Flashlights bobbing, they followed a second scream down the steps of a rank public toilet, to find two men cornering a terrified woman inside a pitch-black ladies' room.

"Stop! Police!" Cat yelled. She drew her weapon; the others did, too, and they pointed their beams directly into the faces of the two scumbags. The woman ran toward Cat and threw her arms around her. Cat held her, and it was probably the best thing that could have happened, because she was so exhausted and furious with the DeMarcos and her father and now these two slime buckets that, looking back later, she had to admit that she'd been on the verge of pistol-whipping them. All she wanted to do was hurt them. She didn't want justice, or to protect a defenseless victim, or to stop them. She just wanted to deal pain.

As the unis cuffed them, her savage impulses ebbed but didn't disappear. The primitive part of her saw herself doing horrible things to them, sadistic acts she couldn't unsee. And she thought, *If this is what happens when I'm pushed, how can I expect Vincent to do any better?*

CHAPTER NINE

4.12 A.M.

*D*ing.

Wreathed in darkness, J.T. stared at the laptop screen in disbelief. His stomach dropped to the floor. This could not be real.

It was his worst nightmare. And Vincent's, too. Cat... *God*, did she know? With the blackout and all the chaos... but it was on the Internet. She *would* know.

Had she reached Vincent?

He tried to breathe but his chest was too tight. He could barely think. It had to be some sort of sick joke. But no one J.T knew would do something like this. It would be like telling your best friend you had a terminal illness... to be funny.

This is like a terminal illness, exactly like it. It will be the death of us.

He leaned forward, examining each pixel as if by sheer force of will he could make the image disappear or change or be something else.

"No," he said aloud. "No, no, no. Wrong."

He took a screenshot. At that exact moment, the front door began to open. The glare of a flashlight blinded him.

He pushed away from his desk, grabbed his baseball bat, ran at the door, and swung.

The intruder must have ducked. J.T.'s bat smashed into the wall.

"I guess I should have knocked," Vincent said, turning his flashlight on himself so that J.T. could see his face. J.T. also saw that he had taken out a vintage sconce, but better a shower of old, powdered plaster than Vincent's skull and brain matter.

"You should have *called*," J.T. said, and then he shook his head. "But you couldn't get through, am I right?"

"Right," Vincent concurred. "All I got was a message from our cell phone company that there is no service available at this time."

"There's signal gridlock same as out on the streets," J.T. said. He swallowed nervously, appraising Vincent's mood. He didn't *look* like he was turning into a rage-monster. So he must not know.

And I have to be the one to tell him? J.T. thought, not loving that idea at all. *Really?*

"So, ah, to what do I owe the honor?" J.T. said.

"Someone took a shot at me. I don't think it was me personally. But I got worried about you and I decided to come over."

J.T. studied him. He had known Vincent for most of his life, and he had delivered horrible news to his best friend many times—that their latest attempt to create an antidote had failed, or that Vincent's DNA was mutating and he was becoming more beastlike. Now J.T. fidgeted and weighed the pros and cons of not telling him. But if Vincent didn't know, Cat might not know, and someone was going to have to be informed real fast, if they were going to do anything about it.

"Want a beer?" he asked Vincent. "How about a bottle of scotch?"

"What's wrong?" Vincent asked warily.

J.T.'s smile stumbled before it was even out of the gate. "Huh, see, you aren't supposed to answer a question with a question."

Vincent was not amused. "There's something seriously wrong. Your pulse is skyrocketing and you're sweating."

"Please don't smell my sweat. That's just..." At Vincent's withering look, he caved in.

"Okay." He crooked his finger in a "follow-me" gesture and walked Vincent over to his computer. Wordlessly, he pointed at the All Points Bulletin announcing that Former Special Agent Robert Reynolds had escaped from Rikers. There was a description of the event, Reynolds' mug shot, his case number, and the name of the Special Agent in Charge, one Gayle Thurman.

Vince was eerily quiet. J.T. started completely freaking out.

"It just showed up. Just now," J.T. said. However, according to the FBI data sheet, Reynolds had escaped hours ago. "I was looking for information on the blackout, you know, what the police are doing." He looked a little abashed. "To see about Tess, and wow, luck of the keystroke..."

"*Reynolds*." Vincent said the name like a curse. And Reynolds was a curse. He dogged them and he dragged them down and he wouldn't stop until Vincent was dead. "She didn't tell me." Vincent's voice was dangerously close to a growl.

"How could she? Maybe she doesn't know."

Were Vincent's eyes beginning to glow? The tranq gun, where was it? J.T. had stopped keeping track of it because it no longer seemed necessary. Vincent was in command of his beast side. Or so J.T. had thought... until now.

He was definitely changing—veins bulging, jaw extending, those *teeth*...

"Vincent, they've gone after him. See? They're looking for him. Not everyone in the FBI is corrupt. There are good people, professionals, and if they're hunting him…"

"*How did he get out?*" Vincent raged. He turned his back on J.T. and flung his flashlight across the room. It hurtled end over end, a strobing projectile, and from the thunderous crash and the smell of more plaster dust, J.T. guess that it had smashed *through* the wall. The room was dark except for the faint light emanating from his laptop screen. He wasn't even certain that Vincent was still there… then his bones vibrated as Vincent let out another deep growl.

"Hey, big guy, stop. Think. Vincent, you can't beast out. You need your human side for this."

Suddenly, J.T. couldn't breathe. His feet were dangling off the floor. Panic surged through him like an electric shock. Vincent was losing control in a way that J.T. hadn't seen in over a year—when Catherine had come into his life.

His arms windmilled and then he grabbed wildly at the hand around his throat. His best friend's hand. He couldn't speak to Vincent, couldn't reason with him. The beast side was dominant, and J.T. was starting to pass out from lack of oxygen.

Then suddenly he was dropped to the floor and Vincent fell beside him with an anguished cry. J.T. contracted, making himself as small as possible, and tried to roll out of Vincent's reach.

"J.T., man, I'm sorry." Vincent sounded entirely human. But J.T. was too terrified to respond. "Oh, God, I can't believe I did that."

I don't want to believe you did that.

Vincent got up and went to J.T.'s computer. He sat at the chair and peered disbelievingly at the screen, just as J.T. had done.

"How did it happen?" Vincent muttered.

"Maybe he wasn't rescued," J.T. offered. "Maybe he was abducted."

"And killed," Vincent said. "God, if he was killed..." His voice trailed off.

"You can't be the one to kill him, Vincent." J.T. got to his feet; he still kept his distance. His throat hurt. Vincent could have collapsed his windpipe, but he hadn't. He had stopped himself. He'd been in shock, and yes, he'd beasted out. But a year ago, in a tantrum, he had destroyed J.T.'s car. Tonight he'd only screwed up a wall. So he was doing better.

"Vincent." J.T.'s voice rose. "Are you hearing me? You cannot go near Reynolds."

"Don't you get it?" Vincent pushed away from the computer bank. "He will stop at nothing until I am in the ground. *Nothing.*"

He stomped across the room, disappearing into the darkness. The front door slammed open.

Slammed closed.

"Vincent!" J.T. shouted. "No! Do not do *anything!*"

Rising unsteadily, he shambled through the blackness, his shin connecting with the coffee table. He got to the front door and opened it. Swirling red lights bounced off the walls of the buildings on the other side of the street. For one horrible moment he thought Vincent had been arrested. Then he saw that a police cruiser was parked in the center of the street and police officers were lining up a barrier of sawhorses topped with the red lights. They were closing off his street.

He saw no sign of Vincent. Wiping his forehead with a shaking hand, he faced into the room, using the light to get the lay of the land. He shut the door for safety's sake and counted off steps back to the computer. He emailed Tess and Cat, then tried to text and call them on his phone. He still couldn't get through.

85

Then he refreshed the page with Reynolds' APB to see if there had been any responses. So far, no one had seen or made contact with him. J.T.'s fury as he stared at the man's face was equal to his fear. He touched his swollen neck and then he shuffled to the bar and fumbled around until he found a liquor bottle. Full, too, by the heft of it.

He opened it and drank it down.

CHAPTER TEN

Back in his loft after a thoughtful drive from Rikers, Gabe lit a large candle, pulled the stolen pin from his pocket and tilted the golden disk right and left in the light of the flame. The matte gold finish had been rubbed off along a section of the edge. He held it closer to his eyes and caught his breath.

Copper-colored circuits on a black plastic plate. As the implication hit home, Gabe's mind began to race.

A computer chip.

Ever since they had learned of the pins, Gabe had wondered about their origin. He had been in possession of three pins and he had asked J.T. to examine them thoroughly before he had relinquished possession of them. If the other pins had contained chips, J.T. had been unable to detect them. So maybe this pin was unique. Maybe it belonged to the head of the society. If Gabe could crack it, maybe he could find out who the leader was and bust the rest of the group.

Surely someone wanted him to know that information. Him, or someone connected to Reynolds. But why leave it in his cell like that? What if the FBI ERU had simply admitted it into evidence, thus locking it away from examination by someone knowledgeable?

I've appropriated evidence before, he thought. *Unless it was dropped for someone else to acquire. But I got to it first.*

A sudden feeling of unease washed over him and raised the hair on the back of his neck. What if there was a tracker on it? Maybe any second, armed troops would invade his home, possibly even kill him. Except... he had been in possession of the pin for some time. He checked his watch. It was nearly five a.m. He'd had it for two hours. And no one had come.

He carried the candle and the pin to his dining room table. Case files lay in organized profusion. A jeweler's magnifying glass was clamped to the edge of the table and he set the pin on the examination plate while he pulled up a chair. He sat down and adjusted the magnification to its highest value.

Gabe rooted through a box of items he had retrieved after J.T. had ruined his lab, back when he'd still been a beast, and selected a scalpel. An image of Tyler blossomed in his mind. She had been the beautiful scientist who had figured out that they could stabilize Gabe's beast DNA, but only by extracting Vincent's entire lymphatic system. It would have killed Vincent, but Gabe had been so desperate that he had agreed that Vincent's life was a price he was willing to pay. He was about to fully beast out for the rest of his life.

That just proves what beast DNA can do to a person, he thought. *Fully human, I would never have condoned killing Vincent to save my own skin. I wouldn't have harmed him for any reason except to protect Catherine. And now I have no choice.*

Someone had killed Tyler and Gabe didn't know who. He wished she were here now. She might have been able to hack this chip. He was an attorney, not a scientist, and the best hacker he knew was unavailable to him. J.T. Forbes wasn't speaking to him. Gabe wondered if one day he and

J.T. would have a meeting of the minds. Of all the people who knew Vincent, J.T. had to know that one day eventually, Vincent's beast side would burst free and he would once more become the killing machine he had been designed to be. It was inevitable.

Seated at the table, he gently scraped at the finish. More channels of shiny copper and were revealed. He almost accidentally cut into one of the threads with the ultra-sharp blade and stopped, alarmed. He needed help with this. But who could he go to?

A name appeared in his mind.

His lips parted in shock.

"No way," he said aloud.

Still, he pushed back his chair, found a small padded mailer to put the pin in for safekeeping, and grabbed his coat. About then he realized that it wasn't yet five in the morning. He laughed mirthlessly and put back his coat. His interview would have to wait. He tapped his fingers on the mailer, wondering if even now, someone was on the way to retrieve it.

Then he opened up his computer to see if there had been any updates about Reynolds' disappearance. There was an APB out, but so far, no hits. However he was traveling, whoever he was with, Cat's father had not been seen.

He queried IA about their investigation into Cat's alleged complicity in her father's escape. No one replied to his email. Apparently no one else was working by pre-dawn's early light.

He got up and paced. As he looked out over the cityscape, lights began to wink on. Outside his loft, cheers rose. Crossing to his flat-screen TV, he experimentally pressed the power key. It turned on.

Power had been restored. The Big Apple was back in business. The part of Gabe that was still a protector rejoiced that fewer crimes would be committed now that the perpetrators would be deprived of the cover of darkness. He fidgeted with the curtain pull as he observed increasingly greater sections of the city coming back to life. It was almost as if he could feel the electricity surging through the soles of his shoes and up into his brain.

Things are going to change, he promised himself. *I'm going to change them.*

He was going to penetrate the layers of secrecy surrounding those in the upper echelons of world power who knew about beasts. He was going to know who they were. How they had conducted their research. What they had found.

And then something... shifted... in Gabriel Lowan's psyche. He could almost see the shiny thought bubble over his head.

Once he had this information, he was going to do something with it. Something he would never have dreamed of doing.

Yes. It is. Down deep, you've been thinking about doing this for quite some time, he told himself. *You just didn't want to admit it to yourself.*

He had said he would do *anything* to protect her. But that? *That?*

"Oh my God," he said aloud, because he was so stunned. It ran counter to everything he claimed to believe. But he wasn't going to argue with himself or attempt to justify what he was going to do. Somehow the decision had already been made below the surface of his consciousness. How long ago, he had no idea. All that was left was to act. With any luck, he had been given the means to accomplish his new plan.

His path was clear.

His conscience, on the other hand...

His conscience didn't live here any more.

Gabe waited for morning, and the bright sunshine was a welcome sight. The restored lights of the city winked back out one by one. Then he headed back to Rikers.

By the time he arrived, the inmates in gen pop had also eaten breakfast. Some were milling in the yard; others had jobs or were attending classes. Outsiders complained that prisoners had too many privileges. But when you were trying to control a population of over eleven thousand incarcerated individuals, you filled their hours with activities and goals beyond returning to the lives that had landed them at Rikers in the first place.

And one of those individuals had been pulled off laundry duty and escorted back to his cell, because the ADA wanted to have a private word with him. Away from prison phones, and security cameras, which made sense because the District Attorney's office occasionally met with prisoners to discuss plea deals, solicit cooperation, nail down confessions.

Gabe decided that the reason for his visit could theoretically be termed "soliciting cooperation." But as soon as the prisoner saw who it was he had been fetched to meet with, his face went purple with rage and despair.

He was Sam Landon, the archeologist-turned-beast-maker who had kidnapped J.T. Forbes and forced him to make a beast serum. Landon had even tried to use that serum to turn Gabe back into a beast, but Catherine had intervened.

"What are you doing here?" Landon demanded. "Have you come to gloat?"

"Hello, Sam," Gabe said amiably. "How are they treating you in here?"

"What do you want?" Landon said.

Gabe stayed loose and relaxed. Sam was facing a thirty-year sentence. For Gabe, that was a fortunate thing. Sam could be persuaded to take risks he might not have otherwise even contemplated. That gave Gabe leverage.

"I asked you what you wanted," Sam repeated. "If you won't tell me, I'll call for the guard to throw you out."

As if a prison guard would lay hands on an ADA, Gabe thought, amused. Poor Sam. When he had still possessed control over his life, he had lashed out because he had felt powerless. Now he truly *was* powerless, but he had yet to grasp that.

This won't happen to me. Ever. Gabe was flush with excitement over his new plan—the decision he had made last night that would alter his life forever.

"I've come here because I want to continue the work you began, Sam," Gabe told him. "I was only able to convict two people, but so many of the guilty remain at large. I know that's not your idea of justice and it's not mine, either. And I promised you justice."

"I *told* you that they're above the law," Sam flung at him. There were deep rings under his eyes. He wasn't sleeping. He was suffering.

"But they aren't above the law," Gabe replied. "We obtained two convictions. And those two would have exchanged information for plea deals if they had known *anything*. I want to get convictions for every single member of that society. So give me something to work with."

"I don't have anything," Landon insisted. "You people took my database."

And we lost it, Gabe thought. *They wiped it clean.* But Sam didn't need to know that.

"You should have let my beast kill them all when it had a chance. They would all be dead now!" Sam cried. "It's over."

"It's not over," Gabe said.

"You're useless. Incompetent." Tears welled in Sam's eyes. "You ruined everything. All my years of planning, waiting. They killed my son. They killed thousands of people and ruined their lives. They ruined *your* life."

"No. I'm still standing," Gabe said.

"Go away," Sam muttered.

"Landon, look at me. Look."

Gabe turned back the lapel of his suit jacket, to reveal the pin attached to the underside. He made sure Sam zeroed in on it.

"A pin, so what," Sam said, but he was clearly on alert. "That night you had what, three of those?"

"Yes. But this is a fourth. Notice anything unusual about it?"

Gabe unfastened it and held it toward Sam's cell bars, turning it left and right so that Landon would catch sight of the circuitry. Success; Sam's mouth dropped open in an expression of astonishment. The man's hand shot out but Gabe pulled the pin back. The prisoner rose from his cot, transfixed.

"Where did you get that? What is that?"

"Data, I'm willing to bet," Gabe said. "Looks like a chip."

"Let me see that." Sam eagerly stretched both his hands through the bar.

Gabe shook his head. "Oh, I'm not letting go of this for a second." He paused dramatically. "What if this contains *more* information than your flash drive? Names and addresses of all the members of the society, sure, but what if it's the key to completely gutting the organization?"

"You don't know how to access the information." Sam couldn't tear his gaze away.

"You're a smart man." Gabe put the pin in his pocket. "But smart doesn't mean all-knowing. Smart means admitting when you need ask for help. And whom to ask."

When Sam looked at him in confusion, Gabe explained, "When you began your revenge plot, you were an archeologist, not a hacker. So who helped you connect the dots? The society's secret server was hidden away, and all of the files were encrypted. How did an archeologist figure out what to do with them?"

Gabe patted his pocket. "How would you know what to do with *this*?"

Sam's eyes gleamed as he realized that he, too, had leverage. He folded his arms and pursed his lips, the very model of small-minded petulance, although his excitement was impossible to conceal.

"What do *I* get?" he asked. "If I put you in touch with someone who can help you?"

I'm in, Gabe thought excitedly. *I'm going to make this happen.*

"What do you want?" Gabe asked, deliberately keeping his own tone of voice far more casual. As if all he wanted was to identify more criminals and lock them up.

Oh, no, I want something far more incredible.

"What I want is *out*. I heard someone *else* left Rikers last night," Sam said slyly. "I want a 'get out of jail free' card too."

"You don't know *how* he left," Gabe retorted, but his interest was piqued. What had Sam heard about Bob Reynolds' escape? "You want to leave here alive, am I right?"

"Don't bluster. I know very well that Reynolds was alive when he escaped," Sam sneered.

Gabe kept a poker face. "Really."

Sam smiled. "But *you* didn't."

"You're bluffing."

Sam's smile grew and his eyes took a faraway gleam, as if imagining all the things he would do once he was a free man again. Gabe would support his pathetic little fantasy. He might promise Sam his freedom, but in truth, Sam wouldn't set foot out of here until he needed a walker to do it.

"I want something in writing," Sam said. "Tell the DA I want a reduced sentence and credit for time served. And I want out of gen pop. These people are animals. Worse than beasts."

Gabe almost sighed at Sam's naiveté. Vincent had also

demanded something in writing—his pardon—but Gabe had succeeded in ripping it up anyway.

"Give me a name and I'll see what I can do," Gabe said. He arched a brow as if to say, *Your move*. As if they were playing chess. Or poker.

The game that was life.

"Agree first," Sam said.

"I'm not taking this to anyone until I know what I've got," Gabe insisted. "And until then..." He lifted his shoulders. "I've really got nothing to lose if this doesn't work out."

"I *do* know your past, you know. You were a beast. A first-gen," Sam said fiercely. "I'll tell everyone. I'll blow it wide open."

Gabe said, "And when they come for *you* in the middle of the night? What then?"

Sam paced. He stopped and wrapped his hands around the bars. "I hate this, I hate being caged," he whined.

Been there. Done that, Gabe thought. *Never going to let it happen again.*

"No promises," Gabe said. "If I can't get you out any sooner, maybe I can get you a nicer, bigger cage. In a minimum security facility."

Sam gestured for Gabe to come closer. His eyes were shining in an almost predatory way, and Gabe grew wary. Sam had operated on hatred and rage for six years. His revenge had not been complete and, in his despair, he had attempted to jump off a skyscraper. That kind of energy didn't dissipate. It simmered and steamed, and waited for another change to boil over.

Gabe stayed light on his feet as he approached. For one terrifying moment he thought Sam was going to bite off his ear as he urged Gabe's head against the bars.

Then Sam grabbed Gabe's shoulder, pressed his lips against his ear and whispered very softly, "Cavanaugh Ellison."

"Helped you," Gabe murmured.

Sam said nothing more. He released Gabe and Gabe would have stumbled if he hadn't grabbed onto one of the prison bars. Sam snickered.

"Helped you," Gabe said again.

Shaking his head, Sam crossed his arms. "Never met him. Don't know him."

"Then—"

His smile was slow and lazy, and perhaps a little mad after all.

"That's his pin."

CHAPTER ELEVEN

B lessed dawn.

Cat leaned her weary forehead against the door of her apartment and took deep breaths to keep herself from bolting back into the streets to search the city, New York state, the *world* for Bob Reynolds. She cared nothing for him, felt no bond with him, although there would always be a connection: he had done terrible things to Vincent and would continue to do them until either he killed Vincent or was stopped.

Or if people finally saw Vincent the way I see him— strong, compassionate, fighting against a terrible curse and winning—then my father couldn't hurt him.

When. I almost lost him, I lost part of myself. I didn't know who I was. And then I realized that I am the woman who is in love with Vincent Keller, and whom he is hopelessly in love with. And there is nothing on this earth that my father can do to change that.

Her hand shook. Love was one thing. Survival was another.

Tonight, she, Tess, and their band of unis—Officers Tanaka, LaRochelle, and Kent—had taken on more gangbangers and street toughs than Cat could count. Her knuckles were bloody and Tess was going to have a shiner. LaRochelle and Tanaka had been totally psyched, loving every second of "World Wrestling New York," but Kent, who sheepishly confided in Cat that her dream was to retire with nothing but a paper cut, had mostly hung back and offered helpful advice such as *"duck!"*

Cat had tried to call Vincent dozens of times with no luck—so many, in fact, that her phone battery had died. As soon as she got in the house and plugged her cell in to recharge, she'd tell him about her father.

She turned the knob and pushed open the door with her last vestige of strength. Vincent was standing so close that the opening door missed his nose by a fraction of an inch. He was wearing a black turtleneck sweater and jeans. He'd gone to his place and changed before returning to her apartment.

"Catherine, what's this about your father?" he said by way of greeting.

She stepped back, startled, then composed herself and shut the door.

"How did you hear about that?" she asked. She put down her keys and started taking off her hat, gloves, and coat. Buying a little time.

She knew, Vincent thought. He could hear her heart racing. She was nervous. He had to stay calm, keep the beast side down, but if ever he had a trigger, it was anything to do with Bob Reynolds. Reynolds had turned him into a beast, recaptured him and made him even more dangerous, wiped his memory, and programmed him to kill other beasts. Then Reynolds had planted the heart of one of them, Curt Windsor, in Vincent's refrigerator to ensure a murder conviction against him. Vincent hated Reynolds as much as he loved Catherine.

Catherine, who, even now, was trying to figure out what to tell him; he could practically see the wheels turning in her mind.

She knew, and she didn't tell me.

"Don't spin it," he warned her. "Just talk to me."

"Okay, so did you *do* anything? That's all I want to know," she said, searching his face. He saw the worry there. The fear.

"Do?" he repeated.

"Just… did you track him?"

"How?" he demanded. "How can I track him when I don't know anything about this?" *Because you didn't tell me?*

Her heart was beating fast. "How did you find out?"

"There's an APB," he said. "J.T. saw it on his computer. Which I only discovered because I stopped by to check on him." He felt a rush of shame. He had hurt J.T. His best friend. Over *Reynolds*. His hatred of that man was compromising his self-control. Bringing out the beast in him, literally.

"Yes, okay, yes," she said. "He is missing."

"And you were going to tell me when?" That was exactly the wrong tone to take with her but he couldn't help it. He was afraid for her, and that fear sharpened his tone.

She lifted her chin. "When I had a chance to tell you face-to-face because I couldn't get through on my phone."

"You couldn't find a charger? Or use Tess's phone?"

"I have to be careful, Vincent. Whoever took him, or helped him escape, left evidence that implicated me. And my boss told me that IA's all over it."

From her reaction he knew that his eyes had begun to glow. His fingernails stretched in their nail beds; he gave his head a shake and stared past her at the wall. He was spinning out of control. He knew she was a powerful woman who was more than able to hold her own in fair fight. But this wasn't fair. None of it was.

I'm going to kill Reynolds, he thought. And in that moment he knew that if her father had been in the room, he would have gone after him.

After promising Catherine repeatedly that he would never take a human life again when there was another choice, he was afraid that he would have broken that promise, and thrown his head back in triumph when Reynolds lay dead at his feet.

"You should have told me as soon as you heard," he insisted. "I've lost so much time—"

"Time for what?" she demanded. "You don't know where he went. And you can't get into his cell to gather clues. Don't even think you're going to use some stupid false identification to fake your way into Rikers again. You're as blind as I am."

Right now I am, he thought. But he would not sit idle. He'd figure out a way and he would run Reynolds to ground like the dog he was.

"How are they tying you to this?" he asked.

"It's obvious that someone's trying to frame me," she said. "There was an envelope with a map on it and words that are supposedly in my handwriting. It says *Have him ready.*"

He blinked. "You've got to be kidding me. Who'd believe that?"

"The same people who believed that you would keep Curt Windsor's heart in your refrigerator," she replied. She clasped one of his hands with both of hers. Her fingers were like icicles. "I think this was orchestrated to draw you out, Vincent. Don't take the bait. Let other people look for him."

"What other people? The FBI?" He could feel his hand trembling between her palms. "The same organization that has my blood on its hands?"

"People *are* after him already. He was found guilty on multiple counts of premeditated murder. He betrayed his own agency, reinforced people's belief that the entire department of justice is corrupt—"

"Because it *is!*" he shouted. "I can't believe you're talking like this! The FBI probably broke him out themselves! They just waited for the right moment and swooped in just like they always do. Took the law into their own hands and paid him back for years of loyal disservice."

"No—"

"*Yes.* He got me indicted for murder while he was behind bars, Catherine. Why couldn't he organize a breakout?" He shook himself free of her. "Why was there a blackout tonight? Oh, I'm going after him, believe me."

He looked at her face, saw that same sickening despair and disbelief as when he had attacked Reynolds the night Cat had arrested him, and Cat had warned Vincent off. He hadn't listened, and she had shot him, Vincent. Here, now, she was rocketing back to that horrible moment that had cost them so much. He had come so far...

Have I? Didn't I just admit to myself that if he were here, I'd kill him?

No, he wouldn't. He wouldn't kill Reynolds. He was in better command of himself than that. *I just said that because I was angry.*

But was he telling himself the truth? *And didn't I choke J.T. tonight?*

"Catherine," he began, and she choked back a sob.

"I need you to not do this," she said. "*We* need you to not do this. Listen to me, *please*. You've come so far. *We* have. And you know... you know that as awful as it is to stand by and let someone else handle this, you *have* to."

He rubbed his forehead, to find it smooth and human. He couldn't go so far as to feel remorse for his fury, but he could refuse to give into his hatred, for Catherine's sake. There was a world of difference—a world of hurt—between feeling something and acting on it. He had been raised to be a man of action, someone who took care of things. He had been a firefighter. His medical specialty—ER medicine—required an immediate response. He hadn't simply joined the army—he had put in the extra blood, sweat, and tears to join the elite ranks of Special Forces. Always eager to take the next bold step, he had volunteered for Muirfield.

To him, doing something to affect any situation he found himself in was as natural as breathing. To sit by passively? That felt exactly the same as holding his breath.

But for Catherine, he would do it.

"Catherine," he said, and walked toward her. At first she stiffened, but as his arms came around her, she laid her head on his chest.

She said, "I've been so afraid that we would wind up back in the past. You know what I did to avoid it."

You tried to convince yourself that you loved Gabe, he thought. *And I tried to be there for Tori Windsor. Poor Tori. She didn't deserve the terrible things that happened to her.*

"What can I do?" Vincent asked. "To make all this easier?"

She relaxed against him and gathered up the fabric of his sweater. Her warmth was like a caress against the chill that had supplanted the heat of his anger.

Then she reached for her purse, pulled out a glossy color photo, and showed it to him. It showed a young man with curly black hair and large, sad eyes. He looked like a figure in an Italian fresco.

"This is Angelo DeMarco. Yes, *the* DeMarcos. He was abducted last night."

"That's weird," Vincent said. "Two abductions? Was it planned?"

"Yes. Extracting him from his father's penthouse was probably trickier than getting my father out of Rikers." Her expression told him that she wasn't kidding.

"Tess and I haven't found the link yet between the two

cases but there's got to be one. The kidnappers left a ransom note. And his insulin pump. When they get their money, he'll get his insulin." Vincent swore under his breath. "Bastards," he muttered. His protective instincts kicked in. Part of his mind was already classifying Angelo DeMarco not as a police case, but as a patient.

And someone he had to help.

"So how fast will it get bad?" Cat asked.

Way too fast.

"It depends on the severity of his condition—how much insulin he takes, how often, if he's brittle. 'Brittle' basically means that his disease is difficult to control. Having a pump is one indicator that he is highly dependent. A brittle diagnosis is quite rare, but stressful environments can increase the severity of the disease."

"His environment is stressful," Catherine said. "His father has a terrible temper and he has a stepmother he doesn't like. Their penthouse is guarded like a prison."

Vincent nodded. "Then you might want to assume the worst. So. He'll develop DKA. Diabetic ketoacidosis. His body won't receive enough glucose and it'll begin attacking itself for energy. He'll get flushed. He'll vomit. There will be severe dehydration. He'll have trouble breathing and his brain will swell. He'll lapse into a coma. And then..." He blew the air out of his cheeks. "...he'll die."

She slumped, dejected.

He regarded her. "I thought the FBI handled kidnappings."

"We're assisting. And frankly—and I'm sure this will convince you that there *aren't* any good FBI agents—we don't like the agents we're assisting. At all. The DeMarcos are treating them like extended family members. Or employees. We think they're dirty."

Typical, Vincent thought.

Catherine's expression went flinty. "They really didn't

want us there. For sure they didn't personally request an assist. We did find one thing: this poor old homeless man Angelo went to visit. Angelo brought him food and wine, and some kind of medicine. I guess they played music together."

"Is there a connection? Was he someone Angelo knew?"

"We don't know. The old man obviously cares about him very much."

He heard the concern in her voice for this missing young man. He seemed like a good person, even if his family did despicable things.

"Did the FBI agents follow up with you? Fill you in?"

"Not so far. I doubt they will. We got dumped on them. They made it clear they're not going to share information with us."

"In other words, this is a waste of your time." *Time that you and I should spend searching for Reynolds.*

She smoothed her hair away from her face, a nervous habit of hers. "The whole time I was out there, I kept wondering what my father was doing. If he had known someone was going to break him out. If they hurt him when they took him." Her hard expression told him that she wasn't worried about Reynolds for Reynolds' own sake, and he realized their crisis had passed. For now.

"If they killed him," he finished. "Exactly," she said, and he led her to the couch and poured her a glass of water. Then he set the kettle on for tea. He didn't know if Catherine would last long enough for tea, but he'd get it started just the same.

"Hours have passed since the ransom note," she said, and he realized she had switched gears. Her mind was racing, and she was too exhausted to control it.

"Considering that the case is a kidnapping of a potentially brittle diabetic, I'd be handing out assignments to anything that moved if I were in charge," he said.

"Me too," she said. She made a strange sound, not quite a sob, and when he glanced up from the stove he saw that she had covered her eyes with her hand. She was in torment.

I hate him. I swear I'm going to...

Stop it, he told himself.

"Maybe they're just giving you some time to rest up before they put you to work."

She leaned her head back on the couch. "Maybe someone wants to know about beasts." She raised her head and looked at him. Her face was drawn and pale. When Reynolds had confessed to murder, he had not volunteered that the dead men had all been beasts—and that a brainwashed Vincent had actually killed them on Reynolds' orders

"As long as we're in this together, we'll win," Vincent said, and the look on her face was his reward. He was tapping into emotions deeper than hatred and rage.

He was drilling down deep, into the firm bedrock of love.

"But in the meantime, tell me what *I* can do. How I can help."

"Okay. An off-duty cop working security says it had to be an inside job." She smiled grimly. "He's on our suspect list, actually. And the security cameras focused on Angelo's room weren't working, the security backup didn't work, and the *extra* backup system didn't work. We were told that Angelo likes to disable the cameras on his room, which must mean he has some computer skills. But the techie in charge of the last line of defense says that the only way to reprogram that system is through directly programming it, and he's the only one who can do it. It's password-protected, for starters. Fingerprint and retinal scan."

"All of which can be beaten."

"Yes. But if you're twenty and more interested in collecting guitars, do you really know how to compromise sophisticated computer programs and fool bio-scanners?"

She tapped her finger against her lips. "Or maybe you want everyone to *think* of you that way…"

"If you're a kid who feels like he's got no way out, you take desperate measures. You learn things, or you find people who know how to do what you need done. And twenty's not all that young. It's not like he's ten."

"Exactly." She nodded thoughtfully. "I'm going to ask Captain Ward to talk to Tony DeMarco directly, explain that we can be a real help in the investigation. But we need a longer leash, you know?" *I know about leashes*, he thought, as he got out two mugs for their tea and two herbal relaxation tea bags her sister Heather had left behind.

"I'll go places you can't. Track. You can feed me information from financials, check phone records, whatever you want me to know. We'll find Angelo together."

"That would be *great*," she said. Then she caught herself and added, "But you have to be very careful. Promise me." She leaned her head back on the sofa and closed her eyes. "You have to promise me."

He held up his hand. "Scout's honor. Okay? Truce?"

Catherine's answer was a deep sigh, the closest thing to a little snore he had ever heard her make. She also made the clucking noise that he'd teased her about before. He left the steeping cups of tea beside the stove and gathered her up in his arms. She was feather light… and fast asleep.

He carried her into her bedroom and lay her down gently. He took off her shoes and loosened her clothing. Her knuckles were bloody and he inspected them tenderly. She'd been in an altercation. More than one, by the whisper of a bruise on her jawline. He ghost-kissed every injury he found, and then he made himself leave. He had stayed too long—it was daylight out—but he had wanted to talk to her about Reynolds. Talk? He had confronted her. Accused her of hiding the truth from him.

I'm so bullheaded, he thought, and his brain obligingly dredged up proof of that—the image of J.T. dangling from his outstretched arm. One of these days, J.T. was not going to forgive him when he lost control. He understood now that it was important to remain forgivable. Cat and J.T. deserved that.

And so much more.

He went to the roof, keeping to the corners, and blurred away.

CHAPTER TWELVE

Gabe left Rikers, went to his office and called Cavanaugh Ellison. He was told that Mr. Ellison wasn't in and his secretary didn't know when he'd be back—or wouldn't say—and Gabe decided to drive out to his home, see what he could glean.

He made the drive from Rikers Island to the north shore of Long Island, also known as the Gold Coast, where Gilded Age New York financiers and industrialists such as the Vanderbilts and the Astors had once owned huge mansions. Many of their palaces to greed and excess had burned down or been demolished. Others had become colleges or museums. But some of them were still private homes.

The Ellisons lived in one of them, and it was a huge, stately Tudor. It was so enormous that it could fit two copies of the mansion Gabe had grown up in, and possibly more, since Gabe couldn't see the sprawling estate in its entirety. Sturdy, leafy trees and formidable stone walls hid much of it from his view. But he could trace the silhouette of turrets and gables, and at least half a dozen brick chimneys. A large weather vane twisted in a building wind. The place was truly magnificent, and he studied it as he pulled over to the side of the road, his engine left idling for warmth. He had stopped to buy himself a croissant and a coffee, and he ate his little breakfast now. After a sleepless night and very little to eat before he'd gone to Rikers, he figured he'd better get some energy before he took on Cavanaugh Ellison.

Gabe had also taken some time to research Ellison. Ellison held several patents for innovations in communications systems, and numerous competitors had sued him for unfair business practices. He was a Page Six society type; his wife had died eight years ago, and his usual companion was his daughter, Celeste. She was twenty-eight, and she was beautiful, with skin the color of mahogany and eyes as shiny and dark as jet.

After quickly absorbing as much information about Ellison as he could, Gabe felt fairly certain that Ellison was indeed the leader of the secret society. There was a preponderance of news articles and photo calls placing him with the two members of the society Gabe had managed to put away. In the photos, they stood deferentially, while Cavanaugh Ellison appeared tall, his shoulders back and chin held high. Ellison deferred to no other person, not even in photos with kings and queens, dictators, movie stars and world-class athletes. It appeared less and less likely that it had been an accident that his pin had been left in Reynolds' cell.

Mention was made in several articles that Ellison was supposed to have attended the ill-fated charity gala. Ellison's private jet had suffered an equipment failure, and he'd been delayed in Miami because bad weather had rolled in. Gabe wondered if he had intentionally absented himself from the top-level emergency gathering for some reason.

Gabe finished his croissant and wiped his fingers on a paper napkin. He remembered breakfasts in bed with Cat. Mexican hot chocolate and her joyous smile. Her tears when she had arrested her father, and Reynolds had told her that Vincent must be put down. How she had melted against him, bereft. He had hesitated to hold her, aware of her vulnerability, and of how much he had loved her even then.

She didn't seem to remember that comfort. Could no longer acknowledge how right they were for each other. *Still were.*

She had utterly discounted the sacrifices he had made. He was incredibly rich. He didn't have to work. No longer a beast and with Muirfield out of business, he had had very little incentive to stay in New York City. But he had remained in the ADA's office specifically to make amends to Cat and Vincent. At first they had treated him like a pariah, but he had stayed. He had risked his life more than once to help them. None of it had played out the way he had hoped.

Plan B is looking better all the time.

Stepping into dappled sunshine, he went around to the trunk of his car, popped it open, and pulled out his .9mm Beretta. He loaded it, then slipped on his shoulder holster, inserted his gun, and put on his suit jacket. As his final touch, he fastened the pin to his lapel, making sure it was positioned up high, so that when—not if—security cameras inspected his face, they would see it.

Then there was nothing for it but to get back in his car and drive up to the guard station of the estate, an imposing edifice that looked to be heavily reinforced steel and glass beneath a brick façade. Cameras mounted on both it and the other side of a steel gate swiveled as Gabe stopped and rolled down his window. A square-jawed, broad-shouldered man with a rock-hard gaze stepped from the guardhouse. He was wearing a black business suit very much like Gabe's.

Gabe showed his work credentials. "I'm ADA Gabriel Lowan. I don't have an appointment, but—"

"One moment, sir," the man said. He pulled out a smartphone and took a picture of Gabe. He pressed a button and then he lifted the phone to his ear.

"The police are back," he said.

Back?

"Yes," the man said, and then he lowered the phone. "Go on in, sir. There's a circular drive at the front of the house. Just park there and someone will escort you to her."

Her?

"Thank you," Gabe said. The large gate slowly slid back, allowing him a view of sweeping lawns and mature oak trees, hedgerows that appeared to comprise a maze, and a large pond overhung with willow trees. White swans were swimming in the pond, and a small octagonal building sat at the water's edge. Ellison really was the lord of the manor.

Glorious beds of rose bushes and all sorts of flowers created living rainbows as Gabe drove along a gravel path, then reached the circular drive. The front of the house sported a massive wooden door carved with unicorns and lions and the initials CC entwined with thistles and Tudor roses.

A black-haired man stood at the top of a trio of stone stairs. On either side of him, white marble statues of enormous lions growled in perpetual silence. The bulge in the man's jacket suggested that he was armed. Gabe figured he would be asked to give up his Beretta or leave it in the car, but there was no harm in trying to protect himself.

"Mr. Lowan," the man said, as Gabe got out. "I'm Bruce Fox. What can I assist you with?" Then, before Gabe could answer, Fox asked. "Are you here because you have a new lead?"

Is he referring to Reynolds? Gabe wondered.

"Is someone from the family here?" Gabe asked carefully.

Gabe's hand began to stray to the pin but he put it in his pocket instead. His palms were sweaty; his face tingled with anxiety. Something was going on and Gabe wasn't sure what it was. The man beside him seemed affable enough, but Gabe knew professional politeness when he saw it. He braced himself for the situation to change once they got inside the house, behind closed doors.

There was a woman in a gray-and-white maid's uniform hovering just inside the door. Her eyes were swollen from crying.

Fox said, "*Policia*," and she nodded. She asked him in Spanish if the *señor* would like coffee. The man said yes to the coffee and asked her to serve it outside, on the patio. Gabe spoke some Spanish—a lot of people in New York law enforcement did—but he didn't let on that he understood.

"*Have* there been any new developments?" Fox asked him. "Is that why you came out here?"

"I should probably speak with a family member first."

"Of course."

Fox led him through room after room of fine art and what appeared to be authentic furniture from different historical periods. It reminded Gabe of The Cloisters, a museum in northern Manhattan, which had been assembled from sections of medieval monasteries and convents. There was stonework everywhere, and the walls were covered with tapestries and oil paintings of knights and aristocratic ladies in gowns and elaborate headdresses. Hanging vases of flowers decorated the bannisters of a sweeping staircase, and there jungles of potted palms. But the house felt strangely lifeless, and a sense of foreboding crept over Gabe.

Then Fox opened a door that led onto a patio covered with wisteria vines. On a low stone table flanked by two chairs upholstered in green canvas sat a green enamel coffee pot decorated with a white Tudor rose, two matching cups and saucers, sugar and creamer.

Fox raised the pot, Gabe said, "Thank you," and the man poured Gabe a cup.

"Cream? Sugar?"

Gabe shook his head, still trying to get his bearings. He accepted the cup and then Fox left him. Bemused, Gabe drank his coffee. It was smooth and rich, perfectly brewed.

"Hello?" said a woman, and Gabe turned to see Cavanaugh Ellison's jaw-droppingly gorgeous daughter Celeste striding toward him. She was wearing black leggings, a black tunic, and heeled ankle-boots. Her hair was piled on top of her head and amethysts set in platinum glittered in her ears. A matching platinum-and-amethyst choker set off the velvety brown hue of her complexion.

She approached, and he saw how anxious she was. Her forehead was wrinkled and her plucked, shaped eyebrows nearly met above her nose.

"Mr. Lowan?" she said. "I'm Celeste Ellison. Tell me who you are, exactly, and what is going on."

Gabe took another sip of coffee while he considered his next move. Celeste didn't seem to notice the pin on his lapel. Or if she did, it was of no import to her.

"Would you like some coffee?" he asked her.

Her frown deepened. "No. I'd like to know where my father is."

He tried not to let his hand jerk. Cavanaugh Ellison was *missing?*

"I think you should sit down," he said gently, stalling for time. That was why Ellison hadn't been in his office, and his assistant had been so vague about where he was. Fox had been asking for developments about Ellison's disappearance, not Reynolds'.

She sat none too steadily. Her hands were shaking. Gabe set down his coffee and leaned forward, doing his best to appear nonthreatening so that she would trust him and open up.

He told her he was from the District Attorney's office and she sat up straight, hope brimming and threatening to spill over. She reminded him of someone who was afraid of heights preparing to sky dive.

"Have you found him?" she asked.

"Not yet. When did you talk to him last?" he asked her.

She wilted. Edgy anger replaced the hope. He could practically taste her disappointment.

"Like I told the other detectives, he went pretty crazy during the blackout. He left and then he called me around three in the morning, and said to stay in the house until he contacted me."

The other detectives? He'd have to log into the NYPD database and see if he could locate any information about the situation.

"And since that call, he hasn't contacted you?"

"I already told you people all of this!" she cried. Then she drew a breath. "I'm sorry. I haven't slept all night and I haven't had any sleep, really, since the break-in. Neither has he."

The break-in. Gabe was taking mental notes as fast as he could.

"Did he give any specific indication as to why he was particularly upset during the blackout?"

She shook her head. "I—I'm just so worried. When Bruce told me the police were here I thought you were going to give me news. Good or…" She trailed off. "But you haven't heard anything." She picked up a sugar cube, toying with it, setting it down on the saucer of her empty cup. "You said there were developments. *Please* tell me what they are."

Gabe let his hands dangle between his knees, assuming a posture of familiarity.

"Have you had any new reports from the authorities on the break-in? I only ask," he added quickly, as she began to flare with renewed irritation, "because I'm trying to run through the possibilities of where your father might be right now."

"He was so upset. He hasn't been the same since," Celeste said. As she talked, she poured herself a cup of coffee, then added a liberal dollop of cream and several sugars, including the one she had set on her saucer. Catherine loved cream and sugar in her coffee, too.

"What was taken?"

"Secrets," she said, surprising him. "A laptop with encrypted files."

"And the nature of these files?" She shook her head. "I don't know."

It didn't take beast sense to know she was lying. He looked at her calmly, without blinking, inviting her honesty. It was a trick of his, and it no longer surprised him how often it worked.

"My father's involved in a very high-stakes field," she said. "His clients are billionaires, entire countries. Dozens, hundreds of competitors would like to hack into his systems, clone our products." She gestured to their surroundings. "There are security cameras everywhere. And yet someone was able to invade our home and take sensitive material. My father's been frantic. He hasn't had a moment's peace since that night."

"When did this happen?" Gabe asked her.

"The night he was stranded in Miami. We were supposed to attend a charity event. A masked ball. My father phoned me several times. He tried to charter another jet but the weather was terrible that night and no one wanted to risk it."

She took a shaky sip of coffee. "Thank God we didn't go. A friend of ours was murdered. Andrew Martin. You must have heard about that."

"I did, yes." Gabe cocked his head. "I was there. I helped clear the room when that madman Sam Landon began his killing spree. I developed the case for the DA's office, and I obtained his conviction." He didn't mention that he had also convicted two of the pin-wearers for conducting lethal medical trials on juveniles, one of whom had been Sam's son.

She gaped at him. "You *did*?"

When he nodded she leaned forward and put her arms around him. "Thank you," she said. She smelled delicious.

Then she shuddered and silent tears rolled down her cheeks, and after a moment's hesitation, Gabe put his arms around her and held her. Then as suddenly as she had begun to cry, she stopped. Pulling away, she picked up a white cloth napkin embroidered in green from beside the coffee service and dabbed her eyes.

"Enough of this." She cleared her throat and looked hard at him. "If you didn't come with news about Dad's disappearance, why did you come?"

"Last night, a former FBI agent who was convicted of a string of murders escaped from Rikers. When his cell was searched, this was found." He pointed to the lapel pin. "We believe it belongs to your father."

"Oh." She bent forward, examining it. "Of course. I thought it looked familiar. But it was in someone's *cell?*"

It was obvious to Gabe that she didn't know what it represented—the ID card into the top stratum of world domination. Nor that she had fully absorbed everything he had just told her. He was fine with that. The fewer questions she asked, the better.

To his intense relief, she handed it back to him. A shadow crossed her face and her hand darted forward as if to pluck it back out of his hand. He made a fist—an authoritative, possessive gesture—and she lowered her arm to her side.

"We've admitted it into Evidence," he said. "Of course we'll get it back to your father once we've closed our case. Do you think someone might have taken it from your house during the break-in? Maybe to implicate your father in what happened last night?"

"I don't know. I suppose so." She chewed her bottom lip. "This FBI agent who escaped…"

"*Former* FBI agent." Gabe decided to go for it. "His name is Bob Reynolds, and we found his fingers in all kinds of pies. Unfortunately, sometimes people in influential positions misuse their power and wind up hurting a lot of people. Reynolds was one of those people."

"But why would he have my father's pin? How would he get it? And how would that implicate my father in his dealings?" Then she pressed her fingertips against the bridge of her nose. "Dropped when he escaped. Right."

He couldn't decide if she was shell-shocked, playing dumb, or truly naïve about the way the big bad world worked. As he observed her, he noted telltale signs of chronic stress—circles under her eyes not fully concealed by makeup, a gauntness that spoke of not eating rather than dieting and, perhaps most revealing, she needed a manicure. Gabe had grown up surrounded by extreme wealth—perhaps not at this level, but close—and the women in his adoptive mother's circle always made sure their nails were perfect. Some of them even had on-call manicurists who came out to their palatial homes to repair chips and change nail colors to go with various outfits.

"Its presence doesn't implicate your father in Reynolds' crimes," he said. *Necessarily.* "The more pertinent issue is whether your father had anything to do with his disappearance." He was repeating himself deliberately to let the information sink in. Sometimes he had to tell a subject the same thing half a dozen times before they absorbed it.

"You must think I'm the stupidest person you've ever met. In all honesty, I'm losing it, Mr...."

"Gabe." He took another chance. "I want to be honest with you in return. I'm not here officially. I was responsible for the conviction of the man who escaped last night, and I've made it my personal mission to find him and bring him to justice."

"But what about the police?" she asked, and he shook his head. He wasn't about to tell her that it was an FBI matter. That would only raise more questions about why *he* was there, since he wasn't in the FBI.

"They're taking too long. They're ignoring half the things I tell them," he said, laying on a level of frustration that mirrored her own. "There's so much bureaucracy…"

She pursed her shiny lips. "That's been our experience with them too. My entire life. We only deal with government agencies when we just can't avoid it."

As Gabe would have expected from a man in Cavanaugh Ellison's position. He was grateful to have a way into her good graces. Having grown up a beast, Gabe had refined his ability to manipulate people simply by echoing back their own thoughts and opinions.

"Okay," he said, "Here's the whole truth: I'm off the grid. Way off. I'm looking for the escapee on my own. It's personal for me, and I'm like you; I can't trust a bunch of bureaucrats who have nothing invested in the situation to put in the kind of time and attention that I'm willing to spend." He cocked his head and delivered his ace in the hole, "And now I'm wondering if this man's escape is linked to your father's disappearance."

He assumed she would react in shock, maybe even fall apart again. Instead she finished her cup of coffee, blotted her mouth, and stood. "Then can you help me look for my father? Maybe if you find him, you'll find the man you're after."

And just like that, I know she's not going to the police today, he thought triumphantly.

"I will. I'll stay in contact with you, let you know what I find. If you'll give me a direct phone number, I'll call you as soon as have something."

She raised her chin. "No. What I meant is, I've decided to take matters into my own hands, too. I'm going to look for my father. We can go together."

There were pros and cons to her suggestion, but more cons—lack of maneuverability and privacy, not to mention that his end game extended beyond locating Reynolds and her father. What he had planned, she could never know.

"It would be better if you did as your father asked, and stayed here. Where you're safe," he emphasized. *But safe from what?*

"I can take care of myself," she insisted.

"I can move faster on my own," he said gently. "And time is of the essence."

"Oh. I see. Well, then." She got up out of her chair and began to walk away without a word. Gabe watched for a moment, bewildered. Had he offended her? Was she leaving?

"Miss Ellison?" he called after her.

She kept going. He rose and took a few cautious steps in her direction, then began to pick up speed as he saw that she was, indeed, taking her leave of him.

He was about halfway to her when she whirled on him and flung herself at him without a moment's warning. He tumbled hard onto his back; his breath was knocked out of him and then before he knew what was happening, she wrenched his elbow backwards in an excruciating arm lock and pressed the heel of her boot against his Adam's apple. He gasped for breath. Her hair broke free and tumbled around her shoulders as she applied pressure, and fresh, hard pain shot up into his shoulder while his vision clouded, then flattened into a gray field punctuated with yellow sunbursts. Then she raised her heel and she was backlit by sunlight, an avenging goddess tossing her hair.

"I *said* I can take care of myself," she said. "And it looks like you can't."

Despite his predicament, Gabe laughed. He held out his hand and she helped him up. Her hand was strong around his.

"How many black belts do you have?" he asked.

"Four. And I'm a sixth-degree in taekwondo," she said. She made a fist with her right hand, pressed it against her open left hand, and bowed. "Although we are taught to remain humble about our achievements."

He imitated her gesture and bowed back. "I honor you."

She straightened and began to walk again and this time he kept up with her. He had no idea where she was taking him and he was glad he was still armed. He spotted security cameras pointed at strategic spots and wondered who was monitoring them.

They came to a large building attached to the main house that Gabe assumed was a garage. She keyed in a code and the door thrummed open. She stepped over the threshold and Gabe followed after.

They were standing in a weapons armory. Submachine guns hung from racks and semiautomatics and other sorts of handguns lined metal shelves. Boxes of ammunition were arranged in rows the way some people lined up their spices.

"Welcome to the Batcave," she said.

Her demeanor had changed. She was not the shrinking violet she had originally portrayed herself to be. He wondered if she had a society pin of her own, and if she had been at the meeting that night. It would have been a simple matter to take it off and conceal it once it was clear that the authorities were trying to round up the organization's members.

"Well," he said, "it looks like you're up to the task. Do you have any idea where your father might have gone that you haven't shared with the police? If you had reason to withhold information—" she drew herself up, offended "—I understand, and I need to know it. Now."

She looked at him blankly. Then she studied the arsenal of weapons and crossed her arms. Whatever bravado she had mustered to take him down and lead him here, it was evaporating.

"You said he called you," Gabe said. "Did you inform the police of that that last night?"

She hesitated, and then she shook her head. "He told me not to."

"That's okay," he soothed. "Did you try calling him back?"

"Yes. It was blocked."

Not for law enforcement, he thought. He said, "If you know your father's password we can try to trace the GPS coordinates of where he used it." It was a long shot, but maybe Ellison had a system in place to allow his daughter to contact him when other people couldn't.

She hesitated. He just waited. Then she nodded and said, "Okay. I do know it. All right."

Once Gabe had the coordinates, he punched them into the map function on his own phone. A map came up with a pin for a location in upstate New York, near the Canadian border. He showed it to her and she nodded eagerly.

"We have a lake house there."

"Okay." He nodded. "Now we have somewhere to look."

"Then let's pack."

She picked up an Uzi and handed it to him. She hefted a Glock G28—available to law enforcement only—and set it down. She selected a G26 instead. The G26 was smaller, more lightweight. It was telling that she didn't have a packed "go" bag containing weapons, clothing, money, and other necessities. She didn't embark on commando raids like this as a matter of course. But her single-mindedness also told him that she knew how to use these weapons, and had before, in some capacity.

She reached beneath the shelf and picked up a leather bag. She put the Glock into a holster and grabbed a box of the correct caliber of ammunition. She took the Uzi from him as well and packed it.

When she was finished, Gabe hoisted the strap over his shoulder. Soon they were heading toward the front door. Bruce Fox met them there. He looked from Celeste to the bag to Gabe and subtly blocked the exit. Gabe noticed and went on guard.

Inside job? he wondered. *Can Fox be trusted?*

"Miss Ellison, may I ask where you're going?"

"Just downtown to look at some photographs," Gabe answered for her. "We may have a lead regarding her father's absence."

"We were told we couldn't file a missing person's report for twenty-four hours," Fox said.

"That was before I became involved," Gabe replied. "Now if you'll let us pass."

Fox looked at Celeste. "May I ask what's in the bag?"

"Is this an interrogation?" Gabe asked.

Boom, his hackles were raised. He said, "As you may surmise, Mr. Lowan, I'm charged with ensuring Miss Ellison's safety when her father's not present."

"Duly noted," Gabe said. He flashed his own version of the polite, professional smile and made it clear that he and Celeste were leaving together. Fox scowled at him, then sighed and made way.

"Please check in, Miss Ellison," Fox said to her. "And if you hear from your father, please let us know."

"Please do the same," she said crisply.

Then they were out the door.

"We'll take my car," Gabe said. When she looked over at him, he added, "Less easy to track."

"Okay," she said. "Let's do it."

CHAPTER THIRTEEN

Noon

Cat forced herself to doze until she just couldn't lie still any longer. She groaned, turned over, and covered her head with her pillow, but it was no good. Her brain was engaged, puzzling the few clues she and Tess had gathered about Angelo DeMarco's disappearance, then shifting to pondering her father's. Her heart thudded as if it were revving up to normal speed through her exhaustion and she licked her lips. Then she slid a hand over to Vincent's side of the bed. An experimental touch of the mattress came back empty; Vincent was gone.

But he had programmed her coffee pot to begin dripping at eleven-fifty-five—*how had he known?*—and as she finished her shower, put her hair in a ponytail, and padded out to the kitchen, her first cup of the day was steamy and tasty.

Like him.

There was a text on her phone: *Nothing yet.* The number was one she didn't recognize. A new burner phone for Vincent. She counted back three days. Yes. It was time for her to switch, too. It was like their first months together, stealth and phone numbers that lasted three days, stolen moments… and falling in love.

Despite everything—the seriousness of Vincent's predicament, Angelo DeMarco's dire situation—it felt good to collaborate on a case with Vincent the way they had in early days of their relationship. It felt right. They had done a lot of good to protect victims, exonerate the falsely accused, and deliver the guilty to the DA. Although Vincent was in terrible danger, he had been back then, too, and they had still managed to help a lot of people. In some ways it was easier now, because they could include Tess and J.T. in their work. They had procedures in place to protect themselves. And they had a clearer view of who their enemies were.

Like Gabe.

But Cat refused to give Gabe any more space in her mind as she quickly dressed in a blousy white shirt, dressy jeans, and her flat boots, and met Tess at the precinct. Tess was glowing—at least, she was until she took a sip from her travel mug—and Cat grinned at her.

"Why didn't you just dump it out and go to Il Cantuccio?" Cat asked her.

Tess rolled her eyes. "For the dumbest reason I can think of: J.T. made it for me." She held up a hand. "Don't tease me. I'm so mortified."

"Tess, I wouldn't tease you about that. It's sweet."

"He looks so happy when he makes it. It would be like kicking a puppy."

Cat thought a moment. "Does he drink it too?"

"Yes. He doesn't seem to think there's anything wrong with it. He thinks a French press is something you would buy at Easy Pickin's."

"You should tell him. He's smart, Tess. He'll figure it out. And it'll be like the Valentine's Day flowers—more embarrassing than if it comes straight from you."

Captain Ward was in, and they made known their

objections to their treatment at the hands of Agents Ass and Hat—their private names for them, of course. Captain Ward surprised them by telling them that Gonzales had personally called him that morning to praise them for locating the vagrant and "saving his life." If that was a move calculated to take the wind out of the sails of "the girl team," it didn't, but it did reinforce Cat and Tess's observation that Gonzales was at least trying to act like less of an ass than Robertson. Or else he was just shiftier.

They tried researching the alleged phone number on the Turntable matchbook, sampling a wide variety of area codes, with no luck. Then Cat suggested they try changing the last numeral at the end of the string and bam, success:

"Maple Studios," a woman's voice said.

"Hello, may I ask what kind of studio you are?" Cat said, as Tess began typing into her desktop computer. A website popped up. Maple Recording Studios, located on Long Island.

As Cat tapped the screen with her finger, the woman said impatiently, "A recording studio." As if that should be obvious and Cat was an idiot for not knowing. Pure New York all the way. "Like for musicians? Is there something I can help you with?"

"I'm working with a guitarist named Angelo DeMarco," Cat said. "He told me to book another session with you and to set it up for the same time as before, but I, well, I can't find my notes and I don't remember what he told me. Can you help me out?"

"No," the woman said.

"Please?" Cat pushed. "He said he'd, like, fire me."

"Wait. Are you talking about Angel?"

Cat looked at Tess, who silently applauded. Cat reached in her purse and grabbed Angelo's eight-by-ten glossy photograph. She described him to the woman.

"Yeah. Sounds like Angel."

"Oh my God, *please* help me out," Cat pleaded. "It's Tuesdays at three, right?"

"Look, we promise our clients privacy."

Cat sniffled. "He said one more mistake and I'm history." She sounded indignant. "Are you kidding? What is he, sixteen?"

"He's rich." Cat sighed. "And I really need this job."

"I thought so." The woman sounded smug... and resentful. "I figured he must have a daddy paying the bills. Because he's not making any money with *that* voice, know what I mean?"

"I *do*," Cat whispered. "So... wait, it was Thursday, right?"

"Yes. It was always Thursdays. But he hasn't been in nearly a month."

"Oh." Cat feigned confusion. "He told me he was just there."

"Nope."

Cat was just about to thank the woman for her time when the woman said, "Have you tried Soundaround? He went a couple times, told me they overcharged. Maybe he went back, gave them another shot."

"That doesn't sound familiar," Cat said. "Can you think of anywhere else I might try?"

"Are you sure you're cut out for this line of work, honey? My niece just graduated from beauty school. She's set for life. People will always need their hair done."

"Next time I come in with Angel I'll have to check out your hairstyle," Cat said.

"DeMarco," the woman mused. "That sounds familiar."

"It's a very common name," Cat said. "There's DeMarcos all over New York."

"Well, I wish I could help you out, but just look in the phone listings and maybe you'll find the right studio. You know, you can specialize in beauty treatments. Do waxing, or nails…"

"Okay, thank you so much." Cat hung up.

"Got it and got it," Tess said. "Good work."

Cat had to go to court to testify on an unrelated case—testifying was a frequent duty for law enforcement officers—and when she returned after lunch, Tess had acquired a warrant to begin a financial forensics investigation into Angelo DeMarco. At the suggestion of Captain Ward, the warrant had been carefully worded and kept very narrow to avoid a toss-back from a judge, none of whom wanted to go toe-to-toe with Tony DeMarco.

Still, through the years, Cat and Tess had refined their ability to find one breadcrumb, then two, until they launched themselves on a trajectory to answers. They would never have lost their bragging rights as having the most cleared cases in the city if it weren't for the fact that most of their recent work had been off the books.

One of the first crumbs they examined was a series of payments Angelo had made to Claudia McEvers, which stunned them both. That was the redheaded security staffer at the penthouse, the one who had provided a retinal scan *and* warned them to steer clear of Robertson and Gonzales.

As detectives do, they tossed theories back and forth about why Angelo would have dealings with McEvers. Their ideas ranged from the reasonable—maybe she did side work for him off the books, went on errands for him or made payments he didn't want his father to know about—to the ridiculous: she was his mother, her appearance altered by plastic surgery, and he wanted to help support her without drawing attention to his actions by doling out too much cash.

"Or how about this: Claudia is *blackmailing* Angelo," Tess ventured.

"But the amounts are never the same." Cat opened

up more windows on the screen. "She's got a decent bank balance. Savings, retirement plan."

"She buys his beer," Tess said. "Or his cocaine. Or pays for his recording time. About Maple's policy about protecting clients. If you were a famous rock star, you wouldn't want your groupies to know your schedule."

"Or a kidnapper. Maybe the kidnapper followed him there, and targeted him," Cat said.

"Exactly," Tess replied.

Because they could now look into McEvers bank account to follow Angelo DeMarco's payments, they were able to justify prying into her work history. By mid-afternoon, they had established that she had once worked for Curt Windsor, and the breadcrumbs became nuggets of gold. Curt Windsor was Tori Windsor's father, and the man Vincent had been recently indicted for murdering. And yes, Vincent *had* murdered him, after Windsor had beasted out. Cat had watched Vincent break Windsor's chest open with his fist and yank out his still-beating heart.

Curt Windsor had been a beast, but not like Vincent. He had been a corrupt, evil bully who transformed into an even worse beast, and he would probably killed his daughter, Tori, if Vincent hadn't "kidnapped" her. It turned out that when beasts were in each other's presence, they had a multiplying effect on their bestial natures—they were more aggressive and feral, mindlessly violent. Once that had been made known, Cat had better understood Vincent's barbaric execution of Windsor.

How much does Claudia McEvers know about the Windsors? Cat pondered. *And why is she working for the DeMarcos now? What was she warning us about, and why is Angelo giving her money?*

"I don't see anything that ties her to Angelo," Cat said. "Let's go back into his financials."

Tess angled her neck left and right and made grumpy noises.

"Are you okay?" Cat asked her, and Tess scrunched up her face.

"I have a crick in my neck. I'm not used to sharing a bed all night."

"'All night?'" Cat peered up at her. "*All night?*"

"Don't get excited," Tess muttered. "He was hyper when I got there and I figured he was, y'know, scared because of the blackout. Then I told him about the hacked security system at the DeMarcos and that *really* set him off. He wanted to theorize about it for*ever and* he had to go teach a class at the crack of dawn. So it hardly qualifies as a real all-nighter."

Cat considered. "Did you take a shower?"

Tess nodded. Cat dimpled and looked back at the screen.

"A shower defines it as an all-nighter."

"It so doesn't." Then she grinned. "But does bringing me the world's most wretched coffee in bed?"

"*Yes.* Coffee in bed means there is no getting around it. You had an all-nighter."

Tess covered her eyes. "It's so embarrassing. I don't understand this at all. He's such a *nerd*. Oh, my God, Cat, he eats Cheetos and gummi worms!"

"Smart is hot. And J.T. is brilliant. Plus he's forthright. He wasn't afraid to come right out and ask you how you felt about him."

"I'm still not exactly sure how I do feel," Tess murmured. "I mean, when I think about it, I'm all 'wait, *what?*'"

"With you and J.T., it's not about what you *think* about him. It's how you *feel* about him," Cat said.

Tess considered that. Then she said, "Plus, when I think about *him*, I mean, just *him*, not questioning the relationship or what it means or where we're going…" She nodded in Cat's direction and the smile was back, accessorized with sparkling eyes. "You're right. Smart is hot. And he's super-smart."

"I get that." Cat was loving Tess's happy confusion. "Enjoy it, Tess. You've been through a lot. Knowing I was hiding something, the disappointment over Joe, plus, at base level, it can be hard for cops to find people who aren't cops who accept what we do. J.T. totally accepts it."

"He does, huh," Tess said thoughtfully. Then she stirred herself. "Okay, well, enough about my love life. Let's get back to doing what we do. So J.T. said that if he could talk to Bailey Hart he might be able to reverse-engineer the system to figure out how the kidnappers hacked into it."

"I'm sure Robertson and Gonzales would just jump at that offer," Cat said sarcastically. "And I'd be concerned that we'd be putting J.T. on the radar of people who shouldn't know that he hacks into the Homeland Security surveillance system for us."

"I thought the same thing. So I got him to give me a list of questions to ask," Tess said proudly.

"That's great. And very hot." She grinned and looked through her notes. "Here's the number to reach Hart."

Tess punched it in. Waited. Waited some more. Said, "Hello, Mr. Hart. This is Detective Vargas. We have a few more questions to ask you. Please call me back."

She hung up and they looked at each other. Cat tapped her fingers against her bottom lip. "Okay, say you're in charge of the last line of security for a crime lord's home and his son's been kidnapped because your system failed. Do you not answer your phone?"

"Maybe not if your boss has told you not to. Maybe if he has told you that you need to do nothing but work on your system." Tess frowned. "Except, what's that saying? 'The barn door's shut after the horse has bolted?' I mean, the kid's been taken."

Cat considered. "I'm sure DeMarco's fearing for his own safety. And his wife's. He's probably got a thousand enemies. He must be afraid that if word gets out, he'll be vulnerable."

"Speaking of the wife, Sleazy Pickin's," Tess said. "We didn't go. We're missing out on bargains on crotchless underwear."

Cat mock-shuddered. "And the good news is? That case will still be there once we clear this one." The caseload of NYPD detectives was staggering.

"If something has happened to Hart, we might never know it," Cat mused. "Unless we specifically develop him as a case."

"I hate to say it, but he's not our subject at the moment."

"Then we need to clear the case we're on," Cat said decisively. "What's the next item on Angelo's expenses?" She scrolled down.

"Well, speaking of Maple Studios," Tess said, pointing to the next line on the screen, "he paid for time about a month ago, just like your career counselor said. With a check he wrote himself." She sat back. "So it's doubtful those payments he made to Claudia McEvers were for studio time."

Cat used a pencil to tap the next item. "He paid for flowers to be delivered to Woodlawn Cemetery in the Bronx. We haven't established his mother's status. Alive, dead, missing?"

They tried to find out the delivery instructions for the flowers but both the florist and the cemetery refused to give out details. They put in for a warrant and while they were waiting to see if they were going to get it, they discovered that they couldn't locate a death certificate for Angelo's mother, who, they discovered by reading old Page Six entries, was, or had been, named Angelica. They also could not find a dissolution of marriage, which put Tony DeMarco's marriage to Hallie in question.

"What if the mom's alive? Maybe she snatched him," Cat

suggested. "He's almost twenty-one. A legal adult. Could be there's an inheritance."

"Or a statute of limitations on some capital offense she committed," Tess mused. "Maybe she went into hiding." She blew air out of her cheeks. "You know, Cat, it looks like Tony DeMarco can redact anything he feels like. Public records should be available to us for inspection. You could make an argument for obstruction of justice."

"Could and won't, just yet," Cat said.

"Chandler," said Captain Ward, walking up to Cat's desk. "Internal Affairs is waiting for you. They have a couple of questions."

Tess went bug-eyed and Cat's heart stuttered.

My father's escape, Cat thought. *Here we go.*

"They just said they had to go over a few things," he said.

"And you asked them for clarification, right?" Tess said.

Ward eyed her coldly. "I'm sure Detective Chandler will do fine. He's in Interview Room A."

He, Cat thought. *Please don't let it be Agent Hendricks.*

"And so is our union rep, right? In Interview Room A?" Tess said as Cat fought for composure. "And you'll be there too? Sitting right beside your officer? ADA Lowan was there when he ran the precinct."

"It might not be your best move to remind me that Detective Chandler has been under scrutiny before," Captain Ward advised Tess.

"But you're her captain," Tess said angrily. "This is our house. You're supposed to back her up. *All* of us."

He flushed but said nothing. Cat wondered if he had been warned not to interfere, and that chilled her to the bone.

"Justus Zilpho," Tess shot back. "Ours. We are your stars."

"And it takes a village to convict a murderer," Ward retorted. He gazed down expectantly at Cat. "I wouldn't keep him waiting."

He moved away and Tess said under her breath, "I can't believe he's not going in there with you. Where's your backup?"

Cat rose and smoothed her white shirt. She put on the black jacket she had slung over her chair. She added some lip-gloss and wished fervently that she weren't swimming in exhaustion. She reminded herself that she had lied to IA before to protect herself and Vincent and she had withstood the pressure of a subsequent cross-examination. She was a detective, so she was used to developing the narrative of a case and following it through the myriad false leads and distractions that inevitably arose. She would be able to anticipate where Hendricks was trying to go and if it was the wrong place, she could block him.

Or try to.

"If it's Hendricks, I'll just bite down on the cyanide capsule," she told Tess.

Tess smiled. "That's the spirit."

Cat could tell by the way the other detectives and unis were shuffling away from her in the bullpen that they knew what was going on. Maryann, one of the civilian secretaries, flashed her a good-luck smile and Cat made a note to buy her some candy on Administrative Assistants Day. She pushed open the door to Interview A—

—and there he was. FBI Agent Hendricks, with his video camera and his case file and his smug, smug smile.

"Good afternoon, Detective Chandler."

"Good afternoon, Agent Hendricks." She looked around. "No union rep."

"She said she was tied up in traffic. We can wait. I understand, however, that you and your partner are involved in a high-profile kidnapping case. Time being of the essence, perhaps your captain might feel the need to hand it off to another team?"

I hate you, Cat thought. She was cornered. The reasonable

thing to do would be to wait for her union rep and let the case go. It was a bad case anyway.

Except that Curt Windsor was at least peripherally involved, and her boyfriend was wanted for his murder, and if she stayed on the case, she could monitor the information arising from the DeMarco investigation and feed it back to Vincent.

"I reserve the right to stop this interview if I feel that I need to consult with my rep," she said.

Hendricks looked like a very full cat with canary feathers sticking out of his mouth. Alarm bells went off and she nearly announced that she wanted to stop right now. But she also wanted to know what he had on her. Correction: What he *thought* he had on her.

He pressed a switch, and the digital recorder blinked red to let her know that it was recording her. They went through the preliminaries and then he began his witch-hunt.

"You went to Rosie's Bar early last night to celebrate a conviction," he said.

"Yes." *Oh, for God's sake, he's not going to write me up for drinking and then coming in to work the blackout, is he?*

"And then you met a confederate outside Rikers to prep for your father's escape."

Her mouth dropped open. "*What?*"

With an air of satisfaction, he flipped open the case folder on the desk and slid a photograph toward her. It was a picture of her talking to a C.I. from at least six months ago, but it *was* in front of Rikers. The picture was grainy black and white, grabbed off security footage, and her C.I.'s face was away from the camera. She was glad of that, because he had risked a lot to come to her with information about gang activity.

The date and time stamp on it indicated that it was recorded at 11 p.m. last night. She had been in bed with Vincent at 11 p.m., but of course she couldn't say that.

"I wasn't there last night. This has been doctored." He started to take it back and she kept her hand on it. She felt as if she were tumbling end over end in blackest space. IA would have checked and double-checked their sources. "Who gave you this?"

"We received it directly from Rikers surveillance."

"Who?" she repeated. "I want to see the report."

"I'm not authorized—"

"We're done." She rose.

"Then you're off DeMarco. And suspended. I believe you know the routine."

Damn it, she thought, and sat back down. "There is no way I was at Rikers last night. You know my father is former FBI, and that he was in charge of a *lot* of spooky stuff. I have absolutely no motive for helping him escape from prison."

"We're not certain if he escaped or was abducted."

"But you're certain, based on a picture of me with one of my C.I.s, that I participated."

"A C.I., or one of the masked, armed men who broke open his cell and hustled him out?" he asked. "Perhaps if you give us his name and contact information, we can verify your story."

"He is still in danger. And we gave him a bus ticket out of town. Six months ago." *And I wouldn't give him up anyway. Not to you.*

"This raises serious questions," Hendricks said, and Cat narrowed her eyes.

"This raises no questions. As I said, this has been tampered with. Second of all, even if I *had* been recorded at Rikers last night, there is no way to link me to my father's disappearance."

That last assertion was a fishing expedition, to see if he had more false evidence to smear her with. But he didn't respond. He sat quietly. She glanced at the blinking red button. She was still being recorded.

"I drove straight home from Rosie's," she said. "You can check the GPS on my car. I also got a phone call from my captain—"

"—much later," he finished for her. "Hours, in fact."

She fought to stay civil. "If this is all you have, I'll get back to my case. You wouldn't want a concerned citizen to learn that the investigation of his son's kidnapping was held up for frivolous reasons, would you?"

"Oh, this is anything but frivolous." He reached forward and turned off the recorder. "I just wanted to give you a chance to come clean before it was too late."

"Don't threaten me," Cat snapped. And she was snapping. She was pumped full of coffee, anger, and anxiety. She made a point of keeping the photo though she expected him to ask for it back. But he remained silent as she walked straight-backed out of the interview room.

Tess was waiting for her with a cup of coffee made just the way Cat liked it. She held it out to her and looked with concern at the way Cat's hand trembled when she took the cup. Cat handed Tess the picture.

"I can't provide an alibi," she said simply, and slumped into her desk chair.

"This is ridiculous. Let me take this to J.T. Maybe he can figure out how to refute it."

Cat nodded. "Tess, he was so *smug*. Like he had more on me."

"Next time, union rep," Tess said.

"That's just it." Cat looked around to make sure no one could hear them. "He kept threatening to take me off the DeMarco case. And that wouldn't have bothered me at all until we discovered a link to the Windsors. So... does *Hendricks* know that? Is someone feeding IA information about *Vincent?*"

Tess caught the side of her lower lip and wrinkled

her nose. "Okay, see, back when I knew you were hiding something and I wanted to stop being your partner? I miss those simpler days." She laughed ruefully. "We'll get J.T. on this and meanwhile, our warrant hasn't come through and I thought we could drive out to the cemetery and wander around. Maybe there's a row of headstones or, y'know, a bunch of DeMarcos stacked up in a tomb."

"Maybe it's the anniversary of the death of a famous guitarist," Cat said, grateful for the distraction of a puzzle to solve. Her insides were quivering.

"*Elvis*. He played the guitar. Didn't he?"

"He's buried in Memphis," Cat told her.

"Or... *is* he?" Tess whipped out her trilling phone. "Hey, yeah, how's my favorite deputized computer hacker? Yes, it's that time again." She lowered her voice and said huskily, "*Rikers*."

Cat could hear J.T. sputtering as Tess held out her phone. She felt ten times better. She told Tess the approximate date she had met her C.I. and Tess relayed that to J.T.

"I'll scan it in for you," Tess said into the phone. "Just use the fancy software. That's what it was created for. I deputized you."

She disconnected. "J.T. fears a raid from Homeland Security."

"At this point, I don't blame him."

Tess put the photo in the scanner's bed and hit send. "Off it goes to hot smart guy."

"I hope he figures something out." Cat turned to her computer and scrolled down to the bottom of the page she was on, to the section that listed signers on the bank account: *Angelo Antonio DeMarco*. As would be expected. But there was a second signer, and Cat stared at the name for a couple of seconds before she found her voice.

"Hey, Tess." She pointed.

The second signer on the account was *Tori Lynne Windsor*.

"Wait, *what?*" Tess said. She leaned forward until her eyelashes were practically brushing the screen. "*Tori?*" She looked up at Cat. "He knew Tori?"

Cat didn't respond. She was scared. This was too connected. Fake footage, DeMarcos, Windsors, Vincent. Her fingers lifted off the keyboard as if by their own accord as she drew in a slow breath and held it.

"Okay, listen," Tess said. "You stay on this. I'll try to get the florist or the cemetery to tell me who he sent flowers to, and if I can't find out I'll drive there myself." Cat didn't respond, and Tess put a hand on her shoulder. "Cat, we'll figure this out."

Wordlessly, Cat opened up a grave-finding search engine and clicked to Woodlawn. She typed in Tori's name and death date. *No match found*, the computer reported. She opted out of specifying a burial place and tried again.

No match found.

"Tess," she rasped. "What's happening?"

"We'll find out," Tess said again. She raised Cat from out of her chair and gave her a hug. Cat couldn't feel Tess's arms around her. She was numb from head to toe. "C'mon." Tess gave her a gentle shake. "You're stronger than this. *We're* stronger. And we are smart, too. We're Vargas and Chandler! We'll get to the bottom of it."

And then Cat was back. She jerked and sucked in a deep breath as if someone had just shocked her heart. Exhaling, she nodded at Tess. "I'm okay."

"I've never seen you freeze like that," Tess said. "Ever."

"I think it was because I could. I wasn't standing in an alley with an armed suspect, or facing down IA. I've carried around such fear for him for so long. And I hate that you've been sucked into this."

"I sucked myself in," Tess replied, and she made a face.

"That sounds very wrong. But you know what I mean. I wouldn't let it go. I pushed until I found out everything. And I am going to push on this, too. And so are you. It's what we do, and we are good at it. And we need to do it. Fast."

"Yes."

"So let me work on the cemetery. You continue with our forensic accounting. J.T. will work on the Rikers footage. Vincent needs a job."

Cat hesitated. Then she said, "Take him with you to the cemetery. If Angelo sent flowers to Tori... he'll be able to help."

Tess blanched. "Seriously." When Cat nodded, she made her bad-coffee face and said, "Okay. You want to set that up? I'm going to call the florist again, maybe save myself a trip. I don't know why we're not getting that warrant. Unless our judge is someone else's judge."

They traded dour looks. Then Cat pulled out the bottom drawer of her desk, where she kept her purse, slipped out her burner phone and stepped out of the bullpen. In a stairwell, she called Vincent's new number and he answered on the first ring.

She told him everything, and in the telling, every part of her that had been frightened was angry instead. She tried to stay on an even keel so they could move forward, and she couldn't tell how he was taking all the news because he was so quiet.

"So I need you to meet Tess at the cemetery," she said.

"To look for Tori's grave." His voice cracked.

To scent her dead body. That was what she wasn't saying. He could do that. He had known that her mother wasn't buried in the grave Cat had brought calla lilies to every anniversary of her death. And he had been able to confirm that she was buried in a lonely grave behind an old abandoned farmhouse. But this was a vast field of four hundred acres of graves. Hundreds of thousands of internments.

What was she thinking? What would that be like for him? And how could he find Tori?

By sticking to the newer graves. By beasting.

"Wait," she said.

"Forget it."

"It's all right."

"No. We'll find it some other way. We're developing information."

"I'll do it. Tell Tess to meet me."

He hung up.

Cat went back to tell Tess the plan. Tess had a funny look on her face.

"Hey, remember that picture?" she said. "The one in the guitar. I just put it into our imagining system and aged it up."

She moved away from the monitor so Cat could have a look. The face of the young woman who stared back at her was unmistakably Tori Windsor.

"Go. Quickly," Cat said.

"Gone," Tess replied.

CHAPTER FOURTEEN

OUTSIDE THE DA's OFFICE, NYC

As soon as Gabe and Celeste left Long Island, Gabe drove his car to a parking garage and exchanged his car for the plainest, most boring sedan on the planet. He hadn't rented it; he'd phoned ahead and asked to borrow it "for a couple days" from Shannon, one of the secretaries in the DA's office. Gabe could tell that Shannon thought it was a little odd but he knew she had a crush on him and would be happy to help. She had cleared out all her belongings and made plans to carpool.

Celeste looked impressed that he'd taken this action and loaded her weapons in the trunk. Gabe was feeling a bit caught up in this manhunt, which was not at all what he had expected when he'd driven to the Ellison compound. He managed to switch a few things around at the office, and as everyone was still flush from the victory of the Zilpho conviction, the DA was happy to give Gabe some personal time.

Celeste had tried her father's phone at least a dozen times. All calls continued to be blocked. Her thirteenth call was to Bruce Fox, informing him that she was going to be gone overnight. When he began protesting, she hung up on him.

Then she turned to Gabe and said, "Even if we come up empty, we'll be gone so long it may as well be overnight."

He detected a hint of interest in him and wondered what kind of woman would be able to contemplate spending the night with a companion on a search for her missing father and his potential connection to an escaped convict. Then he figured he was being a little hard on her; under stress, people's minds wandered through all kinds of strange fields. He remembered one time when he was locked in the safe room of his adoptive parents' house, clawing at the walls and roaring, he had wondered if they made Spider-man footie pajamas.

He knew he shouldn't react to her perhaps-unconscious invitation; he was certain she was unaware that he'd read her. He was trying to figure out how to approach her. After getting decked by her and seeing the weapons arsenal at her disposal, he knew there was more to her than met the eye.

"Do you know why your father might be at the lake house?" he asked her.

"There are so many reasons, Mr. Lowan. As you might imagine, he has lots of enemies." She waited a beat and then she said, "Powerful people usually do."

He felt her eyes on him. He inclined his head. "That's true."

"How did you know that pin belonged to my father?"

He cocked his head as they began to maneuver out of the city. It was snowing, lending the day a gloomy air as they passed boarded-up windows, reminders of the blackout. It suddenly hit him how tired he was.

"How did you know I was right?"

She looked out the window as if at the blustering white. She tapped her fingers against the face of the phone and sighed.

"I haven't trusted Bruce Fox for quite some time. I'm not sure what he's up to, but he's been acting sketchy for a while. I don't know if he had anything to do with my father's disappearance, but he didn't like you." She smiled faintly. "That was an endorsement, in my book."

The fact that she didn't answer his question was an answer. He was certain that she had recognized the pin.

She said, "Gabe, yes. As soon as I saw it, I knew it was his. He showed it to me once and he told me that he belonged to a group like the Freemasons. He said they all had pins but that his was special. There's a band of gold around the edge. That's because he's the president."

Gabe's lips parted in surprise. A band of gold? He hadn't even noticed. Was that how Sam Landon had known it was Cavanaugh Ellison's pin, and not because of the circuitry?

He wanted to take it out and look at it but he was afraid that if he did, she might push harder for him to give it back. He didn't know what she would do if he refused. They were in a car loaded with weapons and she was lethal. He was certain she could take him out with a single blow.

"Why did you pretend not to recognize it?"

"I'm an Ellison. We thrive on lies and secrecy." She crossed her arms. "And I think you do too." *Well*, he thought. *She's perceptive*. And the thought skittered across his mind that she was probably good in bed. And that maybe he'd be in a position to find out.

"How much longer until we get there?" he asked her.

"Five hours."

He took a deep breath. *What the hell. Nothing ventured and all that.*

"Do you know about a group called Muirfield?"

WOODLAWN CEMETERY

There were a lot of boarded-up storefronts on the drive into the Bronx and an almost equal number of trucks from glass replacement businesses parked in front of them. A few stores were offering "Blackout Savings!" and Vincent was glad they still had things to sell. The dollar value of the merchandise stolen during the blackout was shocking.

Then Vincent was walking among centuries-old headstones and tombs topped with weeping angels, holding a printout of internments that had taken place within the last year. His stomach clenched and he balled his fists. The smell of death was not new to him. He had been a soldier and a doctor. And he had scented out death for Catherine before. He had known that her mother was not buried in the grave Catherine had visited on the anniversary of her death every year. Now she knew it too.

And now I'm looking for the grave of someone who gave up her life for me.

"There are too many graves," Tess said as she loped up beside him. "This is hopeless."

They walked slowly together. He said, "How's she holding up?"

Tess slid a glance at him. "She's scared. For you."

"Maybe it's time I went to look for Reynolds."

"Didn't she ask you not to? Then don't. Help us find Angelo."

Before he could speak, she turned and faced him.

"I'm serious, Vincent. Cat is scared that she's going to wind up coming to a place like this to stand at *your* grave."

"Then I should do everything I can to make sure that doesn't happen. Which means finding Reynolds."

Tess stuffed her hands in the pockets of her coat and huffed. He backed down. He had already agreed to make Angelo DeMarco his priority. It was just that he felt so terrible looking for Tori. She had lived in fear because of men preoccupied with hunting—and creating—beasts.

"This place is going to close soon," he said. "Maybe you

could take another row." He was uncomfortable doing what he had to do around her.

"Right." She moved away.

Then fresh anger surged through him, and he was worried he was going to beast. Nervously he scanned for visitors to the cemetery; he should not be seen. But he was becoming so *angry*...

Then his phone rang. It could only be J.T. or Catherine. He stilled the beast, and answered the phone. To slake off energy, he kept walking past the graves. Faster. Faster still.

"Hey." It was Catherine. "Vincent, I discovered something. Angelo's birthday is in two weeks. He'll be twenty-one. He's going to inherit a lot of money from a trust fund. Millions of dollars. He's going to be incredibly wealthy."

He kept moving, using up the adrenaline. He stayed quiet. He knew there was more. He could tell by the strain in her voice.

"The money coming to him is from Tori's mother's estate."

Suddenly he stopped. He was standing in front of a grave decorated with a large bouquet of yellow roses. Tori's favorite flower.

The white marble headstone was very plain, the inscription simple:

Tori Lynne Windsor
Beloved Daughter

He hadn't known that she'd been buried here. He hadn't even known if there was a funeral service, if people had come to pay their respects. Or if she had lain, alone, in the cold ground, with no one to mourn her.

Who had arranged for all of it?

He had grieved for days, weeks, and was still grieving.

And he had felt so cast out that he hadn't even thought to see if someone had made arrangements for her.

To the last, I put her third, he chided himself.

"Someone sent her yellow roses," Vincent said. *I didn't send her any flowers at all*.

"You found her? I'm sorry, Vincent. This must be difficult." Cat discreetly cleared her throat. "Did you hear what I said about the inheritance?"

"Yes." He sensed that she was asking him for information. He had none. "Tori never talked about her mother. She never went to see friends. She didn't seem to have anyone else in her life."

That had been the topic of his last real conversation with Tori. She had been lonely, and he had already admitted to himself that they weren't good for each other. They brought out the beast in each other. Tori relished the sense of power her beast side gave her, which he could understand. Her father had been a domineering bully who had gone so far as to surgically implant a tracker in her arm. She had trouble controlling her beast side because she didn't really want to control it. Vincent did. He identified with his human side.

The part of him that Catherine brought out in him.

He had been on the verge of breaking up with her, and she had risked her life for him and his friends. Risked it, and lost it.

"So there are yellow roses?"

He examined the bouquet. "Yes, and a card. It says, 'For Torimacto.'"

"That's him. That's close to what he called a pennywhistle. We learned that from our homeless man last night."

Vincent wasn't quite following. But he trusted Catherine and if she had just confirmed that these flowers were from Angelo, then he was satisfied.

"Can you take a picture for me? And can you take the card?"

"Sure."

"I have to go," she said. "I'll call you soon. And... Vincent? Thank you."

"Of course."

She disconnected. He did as she asked, plucking the card from among the roses, putting it to his nose then slipping it into his pocket. Diabetics secreted an odor that even normal humans could detect. The smell altered depending upon whether they had taken their insulin or not. There was no diabetes scent on the card. Ergo, Angelo had not touched it.

The flowers were wilting, the edges of the petals turning to brown. All things must pass, but Tori had been so young. As she lay dying, she had admitted that her love for Vincent was doomed. He was destined for Catherine, not her. She was glad that she had sacrificed herself so that he could live, and be happy, and be with Catherine.

And now here you are, he thought. His guilt was overwhelming. Tori was one more example of the danger anyone who got close to him was in. She had paid the ultimate price for knowing Vincent Keller. But worse, she had paid that price with a broken heart. She had died knowing he didn't love her.

"I'm sorry," he whispered. And in that moment, he made a vow that he would find this Angelo. To save his own life, yes, but more importantly, to save the young man's.

Even then, it was as if Vincent's beast-self ripped free, like a shadow over Tori's resting place, and protested. It wanted to go after Reynolds.

Not now, he thought.

He leaned forward and pressed a hand on Tori's name. Tess had joined him, and she said, "I'm sorry, Vincent."

"She just didn't have enough time to get used to her new life. Her world." He lowered his arm. "We should move on. What's next for your investigation?"

"Well, you heard about the inheritance, right? We need to look more deeply into the McEvers-Windsor-DeMarco connection. So we need to take a look at Claudia McEvers' apartment. We have an address."

"I can do that."

"That'd be great. Then Cat and I can go Turntable. It's a club."

"J.T. loves that place. He told me he took you there on a date."

"Yeah." She sounded shy, and it made him smile a little. Tess and J.T. were perfect for each other. It was obvious to everyone, including him.

"Okay, so I'll give you her address," Tess said. She hesitated. "As usual, we have a lot of stuff going on that we can't disclose, but we want to find this kid. And we need to do as much of our investigation by the book as we can."

"I'll be careful, Tess," he promised.

"We have to make Angelo our priority, but once we find him, we'll throw everything we have into finding Reynolds." She looked at him expectantly. She needed him to promise that he'd stick to their agenda.

"We're good," he said.

Except... none of this was good.

CHAPTER FIFTEEN

ON THE WAY TO THE LAKE HOUSE

The snow had begun to fall in earnest, and the road conditions as the drifts piled up urged Gabe to drive slowly. Celeste was about to answer his question about Muirfield, and his heart was pounding in anticipation. She knew something. She hadn't asked him what "Muirfield" was or told him that she didn't know. She was thinking it over.

"My father had some documents about Muirfield," Celeste said, "that I happened to read. I know it was a classified government experiment that resulted in the deaths of an entire unit of Special Forces soldiers from friendly fire. The government hushed it up and there have been all kinds of wild rumors ever since."

Stunned, he realized that her account could be one interpretation of what had happened. Substitute "friendly fire" for "on orders from their superiors" and you had *exactly* what had happened.

"Were any of those rumors described in the document you happened to read?"

"I'm not ashamed that I pried," she said defiantly. "He keeps so much from me. I should be more in the know.

Ignorance leaves me utterly defenseless in situations like this. And it puts him at risk."

"Well, sometimes people have an overprotective streak," he said. "We want to look out for the people we love. It's an instinct."

"It's demeaning."

She sounds like Catherine, he thought. It was, in his mind, a flattering comparison.

He changed the subject. "So what kind of experiment was it?"

"Soldiers were given a drug that was supposed to heighten their reaction times. The Special Forces troops were returning from a firefight and the other soldiers weren't expecting them. They opened fire and gunned them down."

Was it possible that Muirfield had lied to the secret society about the fate of Vincent's platoon? Did Cavanaugh Ellison actually believe that story? Or did Celeste's father plant misleading information for her to find to keep her out of this most dangerous loop?

Or was this a *different* failed experiment?

His mind boggled. He tried to figure out a logical path through the forest of lies. What if Cavanaugh had been deliberately kept in ignorance all these years? Was it possible that his delay in Miami was engineered so that he couldn't attend the gala?

"Why did you ask me if I know about Muirfield?" she asked.

"Reynolds, the man who escaped from Rikers, has admitted that some aspects of the experiments—" Gabe decided to leave open the possibility of other experiments "—were not sanctioned by the Pentagon and that a number of government officials conducted them anyway. He was one of those people. He killed at least three men to keep the secret from getting out."

Hitching a breath, she smoothed her hair away from her

face. "Do you think that's what's going on? Reynolds broke out of Rikers to kill my father to keep him silent?"

"Why warn him by leaving the pin behind?" Gabe asked.

Her eyes widened. "By accident? Or to flush Dad out? To make him run? So he could go after him?"

"Reynolds couldn't know that he would do that. It would make more sense to break out without telegraphing his plans. We can ask your father when we see him."

Gabe wondered if Ellison himself had orchestrated this entire escapade, possibly out of revenge for Gabe's busts at the gala. Leave the pin knowing that sooner or later the DA's office would examine the evidence... and that Gabe would figure out how to trace him?

What if I didn't? Would he have a plan B? Would he risk his daughter in a scheme like that? What if she's in on it? What if she's steering me right into a trap?

He had quietly placed his Beretta under his seat. He was glad of that now. He couldn't connect the dots and that made him anxious. His entire life had been a strange journey made in deepest secrecy and punctuated by instances when all was revealed. He was the king of spin, a skill that had helped him survive and made him an excellent ADA, not because he spun the truth during criminal cases but because he could anticipate how the attorneys for the accused would attempt to spin their defenses.

"I just wish he would answer his phone."

"Me, too," Gabe said. As far as they could ascertain, Ellison hadn't moved since they had called, going on over six hours ago. Gabe was concerned. It could mean he was hunkered down, safe and sound.

Or that he was dead.

After a few minutes, she said, "It seems off that we haven't reached Preston yet. Can your driving directions be wrong?" Before he could protest she picked up his phone, which had been resting in one of the car's cup holders, and stared at the little map in the window. "Your bars are low. It's probably the snow."

She put it back, and when they stopped to get something to eat and stretch their legs, Gabe checked the Internet for dings on Reynolds' APB and possible leads in Ellison's disappearance. He couldn't connect; the signal was too weak.

Gabe put his phone in his pocket as Celeste sighed and hung up her phone again. As they sat facing each other in the booth of a diner that had once been a railroad car, the flicker from a pear-shaped glass candleholder caught the gems in her earrings and necklace and sent scintillating sparks over the walls. They ordered hamburgers and beers and a basket of fries, and as the other diners watched the news, they moved from talking about their mission to inconsequential topics such as the snow and the stories unfolding on TV.

A man from Con Edison, the energy company, named David Whiteside was being interviewed about the blackout. Gabe couldn't hear what he was saying, but he took note of the name. He wanted to find out who had engineered the blackout, and why. Whoever extracted Reynolds had known it was going to happen. Had someone made it happen specifically for them? He tried to look up Whiteside using his cell but he still had too few bars.

Then he and Celeste opened up a little bit about themselves and their childhoods. Cavanaugh Ellison had made no secret of the fact that he had wanted a son. Old-fashioned in the extreme, he had tried to force Celeste to take ballet and horseback riding lessons. She had rebelled and become a martial artist.

"I actually thought about doing cage fighting," she said, and they both laughed.

"My adoptive parents were equally indulgent," he said. It wasn't true, but he wished it were. *I spent half my childhood beasting out, and the other half hiding who I was from the rest of the world.*

"*Indulgent*," she protested. "But I just said—"

"That you have four black belts." He raised a brow. "He might have preferred that you take dance lessons, but he didn't prevent you from doing what you wanted."

"Only because he *couldn't*," she said with a flash of fire in her eyes, and then she laughed a little. "I've never thought of it that way. But you're right."

She leaned across the table and brushed her lips with his. Neither one of them closed their eyes and she kissed him again. As she tilted her head, he felt himself stir.

Be careful, Gabriel, he ordered himself. But Celeste was so beautiful and, truth be told, the prospect of a little danger and mystery was exciting. He wasn't married, or even spoken for. Did it make sense to carry a torch for a woman who actively hated him?

He returned Celeste's kiss. Her lips were smooth and promising, like fine wine. Her fingers slid across the table and entwined with his.

"This feels good," Celeste breathed. "I'm attracted to strength, Gabe. But so few people are really strong." She gave his hand a waggle. "It's not just muscles. It's attitude."

"You were playing quite the shrinking violet back at your house."

Catlike, she moved her shoulders. The long hours in the car had also taken a toll on him and he stretched a little.

"I do that so they'll underestimate me. I've lived a sort of double existence for as long as I can remember. Surely you know what that's like."

That threw him. Did she know about beasts? He almost sat back as if to put up a protective barrier, but he stopped himself in time.

"Meaning…?" he asked silkily.

"Handsome, by-the-book ADA by day, vigilante by night."

Vigilante. Surely she had plucked that word out of thin air. She wasn't trying to send him a message about Vincent or Gabe's place in his world.

Was she?

"You look… uneasy," she ventured.

He thought fast. "Apparently I'm only handsome when I'm an ADA."

"Oh, now you're fishing for compliments. You already know you're extremely handsome, Gabe." She struck a pose. "Do you see yourself as the arm candy of a rich young socialite?"

"No. The companion, perhaps. I think I should mention that I have means. I grew up in a wealthy family and my parents have both passed on. I'm certainly not in your league financially, but I'm quite comfortable."

She dropped the pose. "That's wonderful to know."

He thought of all the pictures that had accompanied the articles about her father. In none of them had Celeste been pictured with anybody her own age. She must be lonely.

He was, too.

They got back on the road and it was dark by the time they reached Preston, a little village near the Canadian border that signaled the end of diners, gas stations, fish bait, and paved roads. Celeste made him go slowly so she could get out of the car and look for landmarks. Snow flurries obscured her vision and even more time elapsed as they worked their way to the lake house.

And then the lake house rose into view like an island.

Gabe was used to magnificence, but the lake house was a work of art. Illuminated by powerful exterior lights, it was built of timber and half of it hung suspended in mid-air over a frozen expanse of a vast lake. All the surrounding trees and vegetation were coated in sparking white snow, also illuminated. Gabe looked up to see if he had missed rising smoke from the immense stone chimney, but there was none.

Celeste typed in a code on a keypad beside a gate, which then pulled back. There was no guard gate here, and no on-site security staff. Celeste told him that the property was protected by state-of-the-art security that included several lasers activated both by motion and heat. She assured him that she had disarmed them.

"The garage is around back," she said.

Gabe drove in a semicircle to a concrete outbuilding decorated with stamped pine designs. Celeste typed in a code and one of several garage doors rose, allowing them to enter. Gabe guided in their borrowed car among a trio of exquisite classic cars: a Bugatti, a Rolls, and a beautiful old Morgan.

All this time Celeste had been dialing her father's number. Her left hand was a knot against her thigh, bloodless. As the sedan cooled down, the engine ticked.

She took a breath and whispered, "I'm scared."

"Maybe you should wait here."

"No. Pop the trunk. I'm not going in unarmed."

He did as she asked, grabbing his Beretta but wondering why he was bothering when she had enough weaponry to outfit the army of a small country. She handed him an Uzi submachine gun as before, put on a belt holster, and slid her Glock into it.

"For luck," she said, and kissed him.

She took point, guiding him not to the ostentatious main entrance of carved wood and stained glass, but toward a door that blended in seamlessly with the timber exterior. She ran her hand across a space beside the door and a rectangle slid up, revealing a keypad, and she punched in a code. He memorized the sequence of numbers.

The door opened and she crept into a mudroom containing duck boots, fishing tackles, and a pair of waders on a hook. On the wall was a photograph of Celeste wearing a toothless grin as she held up a tiny fish on the end of a line.

"Daddy?" she called. She hit a panel and lights came on.

She moved from the mudroom into a broad hall papered in hunter green, then down the hall into a sweeping living room, its walls were decorated with abstract canvases and its cathedral ceiling stretched at least thirty feet in the air. An octagonal skylight capped the planes of the ceiling.

And beside Gabe on the wall was *not* a modern art painting but a cloud of blood and brain matter stuck to the wall. In an instant Gabe went for the floor, dragging her down with him. As she fought him, she threw him off balance. He pitched forward, falling onto his chest.

His face pressed against what was left of Cavanaugh Ellison's head.

He covered her mouth to keep her from screaming and rolled on top of her to shield her. She jerked and fought and he knew he had maybe three seconds before she did serious damage to him. He whispered into her ear, "They may still be here."

She fought him like a madwoman, flinging him off, but he grabbed hold of her and jerked her off her feet. She fell hard; her momentum knocked him down and he threw his arms across her chest. She threw back her head and screamed the most inhuman shriek he had ever heard spring from the mouth of someone who was not a beast. She kicked and flailed and Gabe had no idea how he hung onto her, but he did.

Horrible as it would have been for her to touch her father, Gabe had an ulterior motive: he didn't want her to disturb the crime scene. His lawyer's mind was already trying to parse whether he should call this in and if so, how he could explain why they had come up to the lake house.

Celeste thrashed against him like a Fury from a Greek myth. She clocked him with a knife hand jab under the jawline, forcing him to let go of her. The back of his head hit the edge of a coffee table and the world blazed gray and yellow. When next he could move under his own steam, Celeste was cradling what was left of her father. Gabe had seen many awful things in his day, but this was one of the worst. Her black sweater was covered with gore and her cheeks and forehead were coated with her father's blood.

Then above them the skylight exploded. A red laser centered on Celeste's chest but as she leaped out of the way, her father's corpse was torn apart by bullets. Gabe aimed his Uzi upward, spraying the glass octagon with bullets. Celeste was screaming and sweeping up, down, everywhere with her submachine gun. She was as likely to hit Gabe as any invader.

"Let's go, let's go, let's go!" he bellowed. Something boomed and shook the walls and then he couldn't hear. Glass and wood plummeted, chunks of timber and steel slamming into the floor like bombs. Gabe reached for her but the room was filling up with smoke. His eyes began to water and his nose and throat burned, closed up. Tear gas.

He put his hand over his mouth as he coughed. He stumbled, reaching for Celeste, seeing nothing in the murk. He wouldn't leave her here.

Then someone had a hand around his forearm and they were dragging him somewhere. He couldn't see. The *pop-pop-pop* of gunfire penetrated his muffled hearing and he decided his best course of action was to allow himself to be pulled along. He hoped Celeste was doing the pulling.

He was yanked outside into the frigid, clear air. Then, as he tried to get his bearings, someone pushed him hard and he sailed out into nothingness. He couldn't make a sound, could only cough and retch, and then he hit the snow face first. Everything hurt. The air was knocked out of him and he couldn't move.

Celeste, he thought, and then *Catherine*.

And then he passed out.

CHAPTER SIXTEEN

Turntable.

Cat met Tess at her apartment, to find Tess wrapped in a bathrobe, her hair up, and nearly every item of clothing she owned strewn on her bed. Misty perfume hung in the air.

"Tess, this isn't a date," she said.

Tess gave her a look. "I can't hide my feelings for you any longer, Catherine Chandler. Every stakeout, every canvass… they've been like dates to me." She dimpled. "J.T. said he'll meet us there and introduce us around. We won't just be the cops. We'll be the friends of a regular."

Cat liked that plan. "As my dad always said, 'You catch more flies with honey.'"

"Speaking of your family, does Heather know any of this stuff? About Reynolds being your birth father?" Tess asked her as she picked up a turquoise top then put it down and examined a white blouse.

Cat picked up a red satin blouse with black inserts. "You should wear this. You look good in red. And no. When she moved to Florida, I knew it would make my life easier, if emptier. But that was back when the only secret I had to hide was that Vincent was a beast. I can't imagine juggling all my other secrets, too, if she was still living with me."

"Then maybe they shouldn't be secrets," Tess said. "Next time you get together, maybe you should tell her." After a beat, she added, "I told J.T. about his coffee." Cat raised her brows. "And?" Tess lifted up one of the piles of clothes and extracted a burgundy gift bag. Inside the bag was a box, and inside the box was a French press.

"He'll be thrilled." Cat was sincere.

"I know, right?" Tess said. "A present from a hot babe." She put the press back in the box, the box in the bag.

"I think this is the first time either one of us has brought a present to an investigation." Cat nodded approvingly as Tess modeled the red blouse. "It's perfect."

J.T. checked the time on his phone. Tess and Cat were supposed to meet him at 9 p.m. and it was nearly 9.03. Rationally, he understood that three minutes was a trivial amount of time to wait, but ever since Vincent had lost his temper and beasted during the blackout, he had felt a little needier about connecting with the people who mattered to him. And those people were Tess.

9.04.

"They are... *wow*," J.T. said.

Tess and Cat sailed into the busy club together. He could tell that his eyes were actually bulging. Tess looked so beautiful that his knees gave way. Red was her color. But black was nice too. Also white. And blue. And... no colors. Flesh color. Turntable was lit with dozens of candles on a score of tables. The warm glow made Tess look radiant. She was so *hot*.

Tess gave him a wave and he really wanted to walk over to meet them but he had momentarily forgotten how to walk.

Or breathe. A warm rush of happiness pushed a little grin across his features as he waved back.

He stumbled, then manfully wove his way among the tables and reached Tess's side. She smiled at him and he thought about kissing her but she was on duty. So near and yet so far.

"Hey," Tess said. She kind of ducked her head and smiled her bashful smile, which was the one that signaled she was feeling awkward about their relationship in the presence of someone she knew. The smile no longer offended him. He had categorized all her smiles—after all, he had eight units of psych under his belt from grad school—and then he had quantified their implementation on a spreadsheet. During any typical week, Tess smiled *at* him 11.72 times more than she smiled *about* him, either awkwardly or positively. The odds were in his favor. And besides, *she* had called *him* to suggest he join them. That meant she knew his schedule, that he had no classes to teach tomorrow and so he would stay up until all hours working on Cat's bogus footage, seeking a way to crack the case, and doing whatever he could think of be a useful member of the team.

"Hey, J.T.," Cat said.

Cat looked amazing too, but he didn't want to violate the bro-code by staring at her. She was Vincent's to stare at. His current awkwardness around her was based on a completely different set of factors—he didn't know if Vincent had told her that he had pretty much attacked his best friend. Vincent was trying so hard to prove to Cat that he had his beast side under complete control. Except… he didn't.

"Okay, the person you want to talk to is Surfer Joe," J.T. said. "He's a co-owner and he can show you the security footage. He's got forty-five more minutes of DJing to go and then he'll come to you."

Surfer Joe was J.T.'s favorite disc jockey at Turntable.

He played the classics like the Beach Boys and the Ventures. Strangely, J.T. liked surf music. He'd never been on a surfboard in his life, but he could easily see Tess in a bikini.

"Oh, hey," Tess said brightly as a waiter in a Hawaiian shirt approached. "We want alcohol for my man here."

The waiter nodded. "The usual, Dr. Forbes?"

J.T. nodded.

"A light beer it is." The waiter smiled pleasantly at Tess and Cat. "Surfer Joe wanted to let you know there's a kid who's been trying to audition as a DJ so he's going to give him the rest of this set. He'll be over in about five minutes."

"Good," Tess said. "Thank you." She looked at J.T. "Oh my God. Light beer? What am I doing with you? What about a Sex on the Beach?"

"Light beer is fine," J.T. told the waiter, who nodded and left. Then he said, "Cat, I'm making progress on your bogus footage. I found out that Rikers archives all their security footage in a database and I've gotten in through the Homeland Security system. I've isolated a batch of files from the dates you gave me and I'm going through them one by one."

"Thanks, J.T.," Cat said. "That sounds like a lot of work."

"No," he said, although it was. "I'm hoping it will lead us to whoever broke Reynolds out."

"You're so smart," Tess said. She beamed at him. "Smartest ever."

Cat's phone rang, and by the way she lit up, J.T. knew it was their favorite beastie boy. She listened for a few seconds, and then she said into the phone, "In a way, the fact that there's nothing is more telling than if there had been something. Okay, thanks."

She hung up. "V just finished going through Claudia's apartment," she informed Tess and J.T. "He said it was like a hotel room. Very sterile. Her stuff was there, but *she* wasn't.

In other words, no personal items like notes or receipts, and no laptop. Also he couldn't really scent her. He thinks she used some kind of olfactory dampeners, like Landon did."

"So what does that mean?" J.T. asked.

"Remember how I scared Vincent back when I first met you guys and he just left?" Cat asked him, and of course he nodded. How could he ever forget? "He packed up anything that could be linked directly to him. I think Claudia packed up her past. And anything that could link her to our investigation."

"We need to talk to her," Tess said, and Cat nodded.

"I just wonder if she'll talk to us. We haven't heard from Bailey Hart, either. Robertson and Gonzales have a lock on them, I'm sure."

Tess blew the air out of her cheeks. "Well, as a case, this sucks, but as a close call…"

"Hi, beach bums," said Surfer Joe. Tall and thin, with bleach-blond hair, bronzed skin, a Hawaiian shirt and jeans, the DJ sat down at the table. "Dr. Forbes," he said, with a nod. "I told the kid to spin you some Jan and Dean. 'Surf City.'"

"That's great," J.T. said. Then he huffed as Tess gave him The Look. Meaning that he was supposed to go amuse himself elsewhere, because they couldn't let him sit in on an official police investigation. She mouthed *sorry* and he forgave her at once because, after all, she had thought they would have a good solid forty-five minutes to hang out before her interview. And hopefully, they'd have some time after the detectives were finished with Surfer Joe.

J.T. moved off to another table while Cat, Tess, and Surfer Joe sat in a huddle. A different waiter walked up to him, lanky muscles, lots of blond hair, towering over him, and said, "Hey, cool cat, I'm Cowabunga Chris. Can I get you something? Curly fries? Nachos? We're trying something new tonight: popcorn sundaes. Two popcorn balls infused with maraschino cherry juice, dusted with toasted coconut and then drowned in vanilla ice cream and chocolate syrup."

"Oh, dear God, no," J.T. said. The mere description made him want to toss his gummi worms.

"Too bad, hodad," Cowabunga Chris said with mock sorrow.

"I have a light beer coming," J.T. said.

The waiter blinked. "Seriously?"

"Yes." J.T. cleared his throat. "That is what I ordered, because that is what I want to drink."

"It's cool, man. I'll just go check on that."

His beer came and he petulantly sipped it. Someone at the next table over ordered the popcorn-ball sundae and J.T. wondered why that was considered to be cooler than a light beer.

He was on his second beer when Tess and Cat came back. The thrill of their victory was tempered with some consternation, which they explained to him: security footage had revealed Claudia McEvers and Angelo DeMarco here, together, arguing. Clues were always good, hence the thrill of victory. But their consternation was due to the fact that they had decided they had to tell the two FBI agents whom they didn't trust about the footage. They had to stay on the books. It would be an easy thing for Robertson or Gonzales to check with Turntable and discover that NYPD had already been by, but had not bothered to let them know what they had found.

"What were they arguing about?" J.T. asked.

"We don't know," Tess said. "There was no audio, and no one we've interviewed so far witnessed the fight. So we need to canvass the club."

"Can I help?" he asked, but Tess shook her head.

"We have to do this one a hundred percent kosher."

Then they talked to the other patrons and the waiters, showing them Angelo's photograph. The club was filling up, and soon he lost sight of them in the crowd. He watched the guy who had ordered the popcorn sundae make a face and push it away. With some petty satisfaction, J.T. ordered another beer. He listened to surf music and got out his smartphone, performing a net search for Tori Windsor's funeral. Her death had been kept out of the papers, so it was no surprise to him that he could find no information about a service or internment. He did searches on Angelo DeMarco and the rest of the DeMarco family, but only came up with superficial stories about their charity work and business dealings. All of it was very dry and gave no insight into what they were like as people... kind of like Claudia McEvers' apartment.

"Zilch," Tess announced about an hour later as she and Cat sat down at J.T.'s table. "I decree that we are now off-duty." She waved a hand for service.

Then Cowabunga Chris appeared with a tray containing two Mexican beers decorated with lime wedges, two shots of tequila, and a salt shaker.

"Compliments of Surfer Joe."

"Nice," Tess said, clinking bottles with Cat. "Hang ten." Then she placed the bottle to J.T.'s lips, tipped it back, and he swallowed down some beer. She held up the lime wedge and the shot. He opened his mouth and it all went down the hatch. She beamed at him.

"Good, right?"

"Yes."

"And think how good your coffee will be with the French press." She yawned. "I'm dead. I need to get some sleep."

"So, you can come back to my place," he ventured. He was still shy about inviting her.

She yawned again. "I'm really tired... and it's awfully far away."

He was disappointed, but he tried not to show it.

Then she grinned her mischievous Tess grin at him. She patted the French press. "My place is closer. So what do you say we break in this bad boy in my kitchen?"

J.T. felt as if his head had just exploded. He had never been to Tess's apartment *ever*. He didn't even know the address.

"That'd be great."

Tess put her arms around his neck. "Cowabunga," she whispered.

Cat went home to an empty apartment, no return messages, and made herself go to bed. Investigations were equal parts maximum overdrive and hurry-up-and-wait, and she owed it Angelo DeMarco to rest up when she could so that she'd be on the money when it was time.

Vincent didn't show, didn't call. They had left things in such a weird place, he standing before Tori's grave and she having sent him there. Vincent often shut down when he was dealing with strong emotions—or *not* dealing with them—and when he did, there was no space for her. He was aware of it and he was trying to change. Years of living in hiding, protecting a terrible secret, had shaped him just as her mother's murder had shaped her. Tess and J.T. were their trusted confidantes, but these horrible things had not happened to them.

Cat knew exactly what it felt like to watch someone who loved you die right before your eyes. She stared at the ceiling, trying not to see all the blood gushing from her mom's wounds, or Tori's bloodless pallor after Sam Landon's henchman had drained her dry. She remembered something one of her instructors at the police academy had told her: "*If you become a cop, you will see terrible things, unbelievable things, and you will not have the luxury of looking away. You will have to examine, study, and memorize gory, awful details. They will be your clues, your cases. You owe it to the public, the people you will swear to serve at your graduation, to know that you can stare straight into hell. If you can't, then you should not be a cop. You should walk away now, no harm, no foul."*

She and Tess both had stayed.

"And we're still here," she murmured. "We'll find you, Angelo."

Blackness.

No, moonlight on snow.

As Gabe raised his head, something slid off his face—a blanket—and he pulled himself up to his elbows and looked out over the frozen lake. Painfully he rolled over onto one side and inspected the silhouette of the Ellison lake house. It appeared to be intact, although he knew that the skylight, at least, had been destroyed.

There was a rock beside his elbow. And something white beneath it. Disoriented, he moved the rock and picked up the white thing, which was a piece of paper. He tried to read it but it was too dark. He scooted in the snow, realizing that he was half-frozen, until the moonlight hit the words on the page, written in black marker.

I AM SAFE. TURNED LASERS ON. DON'T GO IN THE HOUSE. LEFT YOUR CAR IN GARAGE. GET OUT OF THERE ASAP I WILL CONTACT
21992

He felt in his pockets to find his wallet, phone and car keys. His blood was beginning to pump faster; he grabbed onto a pine tree and pulled himself up. The world swam and the lake slid onto its side. He took a moment to assess his surroundings, listening for telltale movement, and heard only the rush of the wind.

The beautiful Bugatti—or what was left of it—was a charred hulk facing away from the garage, as if it had started to drive off and then caught on fire.

"No, Celeste," he whispered.

Staying to the shadows, he staggered to the garage and studied the closed doors for a moment before making the connection that 21992 was the key code. The one he thought he had memorized. He punched it in and the same garage door they had used rose up.

He smiled.

She had taken the Rolls. The Morgan was still in the garage. She must have had the presence of mind to drive the Bugatti out and douse it with gasoline or some other accelerant. They must not have looked too hard for bodies.

Unless she had had some contingency for that. He smiled grimly at the thought.

And there was Shannon's sedan, unharmed. He clicked it open and slid in, utterly baffled. What had happened? He cautiously backed out, then turned the car around, braced at every juncture for an attack.

He didn't know how he found his way to the paved road, and from there to Preston, but he did. He wanted to take a break but the little village was shut down for the night and he was still afraid of an ambush.

He started the drive to New York City—six hours—checking his phone for messages. Finally one came in, from Celeste.

I have the pin.

He swore, then reminded himself that he was lucky to be alive. The pin had been a freebie… or, as he had suspected, some kind of lure. He still didn't know Celeste's part in all of this—if she had been an innocent bystander, somehow complicit—

To people crashing into her house and shooting at her?
But… he didn't think that they had hit her.

Gabe kept driving, though he felt eyes on him, guns pointed at him. The fear was replaced by anger. The anger by a promise.

Whoever did this is going to pay.

CHAPTER SEVENTEEN

Cat and Tess met at the precinct the next morning and Tess made a show of guzzling the contents of her travel mug and smacking her lips.

"The French press is *it*," she proclaimed. "But I have even better news. We got up super-early because we couldn't stop thinking about your Rikers smear job and we went to J.T.'s place. He was able to look at the raw footage from the range of dates you gave him. It turns out that you see a whole bunch of information when the recording initializes. Whoever slapped that fake date and time stamp on that footage forget to erase a line of code visible during initialization that includes the *actual* date and time. Which was about six months ago. Which is when you said it was taken. It is irrefutable proof that it is *not* from the night before last *and* that someone is trying to frame you."

"Whoa, J.T.!" Cat high-fived Tess.

"So while he was doing that, *I* decided to look at Robertson and Gonzales. They've had numerous complaints lodged against them. IA cases that were inconclusive. But the evidence suggests that we are dealing with two very dirty, mobbed-up FBI agents."

Cat considered. "Did you find anything that could link them to Reynolds? Or even Muirfield?"

"Not yet. But I got their addresses, and Robertson's house is a little closer than Gonzales'. Maybe we should take a little drive, see if there's anything to see."

"Sounds like a plan."

Just then, Cat's landline intercom buzzed. It was the main switchboard. She pressed the connect button. "Yes?"

"There's a Claudia McEvers on line one, detective."

Cat and Tess just looked at each other. Then Cat said, "I'll take it." She gestured for Tess to listen in on her own landline. "This is Detective Chandler."

"What the *hell* did you tell those two?" Claudia hissed.

Cat decided to be as forthright as possible and see what shook out. "We said that we saw security footage of you at Turntable with Angelo, and it looked like you were fighting."

The woman swore. Colorfully. Tess, who was listening in, pretended to plug her ears.

"Okay, I have to meet with you," the woman said. "I have information you should know."

I hope it includes an explanation of what Angelo was giving you money for.

"Can you tell it to me over the phone?" Cat pulled back her chair to sit at her desk so she could type.

"No. Only face-to-face. And only if you swear not to tell Robertson and Gonzales that you are coming to see me. After we talk, you can decide what to do."

That sounded promising. And a little ominous.

"All right. Where?"

"There's a diner near the Javits Center," McEvers said. "It's called Mars. By the water. When can you meet me?"

Cat typed in "Mars Diner" and found the address. She checked her schedule and Tess gave her a shrug indicating that she had no hard appointments. "Forty-five minutes,"

Cat said, and Tess nodded. That allowed for delays and traffic. There was a lot of construction going on in the area.

Claudia grunted disapproval. "Sooner would be better but I'll make it work. Don't bring anybody but your partner. I see you with the Feebs, any other PD, or DeMarco's people, I'm leaving."

"Are you in danger?" She caught Tess's eye and Tess raised her brows.

There was no reply from McEvers. Cat figured that meant yes.

"Do you want protection? If you can give us some indication of—"

"See you in forty-five minutes." McEvers hung up.

"Wow," Cat said.

"Awesome," Tess shot back.

They got their purses and coats, and soon Cat was negotiating the traffic.

"I swear these are the exact same vehicles we were inching along with during the blackout," Cat said. She pointed at a boarded-up storefront window. "I hope those guys were properly insured."

"I'm dying to get the skinny on the blackout," Tess murmured. "I wonder what's up with Claudia."

"She didn't need to check her schedule to meet up with us. If she doesn't have the day off, maybe she's been fired. Or on the run."

"I noticed that too," Tess said. "Look."

She pointed to a white storefront with a neon sign of a bumpy planet surface with the word Mars shooting in 3D letters from the planet's surface. MARS was also painted in futuristic 3D letters around the front window.

They could double-park in the street but traffic was heavy. Much of the parking in the area had been cordoned off because of the construction, but they found a police-legal place to stash the squad car and got out. They walked into the diner, which had a sci-fi theme, the walls painted bright red with a mobile of planets hanging from the ceiling and oilcloth on the tables stamped with 1950s rocket ships. A cute Japanese couple was sitting at one of the tables and a woman was seated by herself with a large pile of paper at her elbow. There was a row of stools at the counter and behind it stood a girl dressed in a silver space-commander top complete with blue epaulets texting on her phone.

There was no Claudia McEvers, in other words. Cat checked the time on her phone. They were fifteen minutes early.

It began to snow, coming down pretty heavy.

They took the table farthest from the door so they could have privacy. They sat undisturbed for five minutes. The texting girl came over and they ordered a couple of sodas. That held them for another ten minutes. Then Tess added an order of "Rings of Saturn," and the order came up five minutes later—a startling stack of onion rings. Tess looked worriedly at Cat.

"I'm ordering onion rings. Nerd food. Oh, my God. Be honest. Am I turning into a nerd?"

Cat cocked her head. "A cross-species DNA mutation may have commenced."

Tess dipped an onion ring into the ketchup. "This is nerd food, Cat. It's fat and salt. Add sugar, and those are the food groups."

Cat smiled and pulled out her phone. McEvers was now ten minutes late. Cat got up to check the bathroom and wandered down the hall toward the kitchen. A door led outside and she pushed it open. Sheltered from the snow by an awning, a young red-haired man in a white apron was sitting on the concrete steps smoking a cigarette. He looked very startled, put out the cigarette, and flashed her a very uncertain smile.

Hmm, she thought. What was that all about? Just a simple case of smoker's guilt? Maybe he was trying to quit.

She shut the door and went back to the table. Before Tess had a chance to suggest it, she dialed McEvers' number. It rang at least twenty times, but there was no voicemail. They called the precinct to see if they had any messages and checked the voicemail on their desk phones. No McEvers.

"Yeah, I'm getting concerned, too," Tess said, reading Cat's mind, as good partners did.

Cat stared at the onion rings. About half of them were gone. "You've eaten a few of these, right? Maybe you're pregnant."

She ducked as Tess made a fist.

Then Tess slid out of the booth. "I'll look around."

Tess went out the front door. Cat waited. The cute Japanese couple paid and left. The woman with all the pages of paper was nursing a cup of coffee.

Tess came back, shaking snowflakes off her coat and taking off her knit hat. She reported that she had nothing to report. It occurred to them that it was actually lunchtime and they ordered two cheeseburgers, which seemed to annoy the texting girl, who took it out on the other diner by pretending not to see her requests for more coffee.

"Okay, so no-show. Won't be the first time," Tess said, "but I've got a bad feeling."

"So do we call G and R?" Cat asked. Tess scowled. "We can say that we heard from her. That's all."

"Okay." Tess nodded.

Cat called Gonzales. He picked up.

"Hi, this is Detective Chandler. We were wondering if there was any follow-up on that security footage from the Turntable."

"Oh, sorry, we forgot to get back to you on that," Gonzales said. "We interviewed McEvers. She said she was there as his bodyguard that night and he had a couple of drinks. That was the cause of the argument. Mr. DeMarco terminated her and she left."

Cat's brows shot up. "When was this?"

"About three hours ago. Something go down on your end?"

"Yeah, she called us and she wasn't happy, but she wouldn't say why. She said she wanted to meet us but we haven't heard from her since." She winced at the almost-lie-by-omission, and Tess nodded encouragingly. "Do you have another number for her? We'd like to see if we can get anything more out of her."

"So would we, but we can't find her," Gonzales said. "What number did she give you?"

Cat's bad feeling got worse. She read him the number. He said, "That's what we've got." He thought a moment. "Now we have probable cause to go in without her permission."

We already went in without her permission, she thought.

Cat said, "Okay, well—"

"Hold on."

He went away for so long that she thought about hanging up. Tess looked at her questioningly, Cat shrugged, and they both waited.

"We just got another ransom note. It says *Angelo's not feeling so good. It's one point five million now.*"

"How did it arrive?" Cat asked, and Tess sat forward. Cat held the phone out so Tess could hear.

"It was sent to Angelo's email account."

"The IP address—"

"Scrambled. It ricocheted all over the world. To Mars and back."

Mars. She and Tess stared across the phone at each other at his use of the word. Coincidence? Some kind of code? A test?

"Hello?" It was Tony DeMarco. "Did he tell you what just happened here?" "Yes, Mr. DeMarco," Cat said. "You know we're doing everything we can, sir—"

"No, I *don't* know that!" he shouted. "I find out my security detail's been letting my diabetic son get drunk in bars and sneaking around God-knows-where and no one has a clue where he is!" He trailed off in a flurry of expletives.

Cat spoke slowly and calmly. "Do you have additional contact information for Claudia McEvers?" Cat asked. "We'd like to question her."

"I told the guys to get it from my HR department. Whatever we've got, the guys have got."

"The guys" had to be Robertson and Gonzales. "Where did she sneak him to?" Cat asked. "Are you referring to Turntable?"

"At least a dozen 'clubs.' So he could audition for *gigs*. They're dives. They're filled with losers. 'Musicians'? More like drug addicts on welfare."

"Could you provide a list of those clubs? We'd like to check them out," Cat told him. "Sometimes those kinds of places are fronts for organized crime."

Tess shot a look heavenward, a commentary on the irony of Cat's statement when she was probably speaking to New York City's king of organized crime.

"It could be that someone recognized him and devised a kidnapping scheme. Maybe Claudia McEvers was involved. She could have been meeting with her co-conspirators while he thought he was auditioning."

"Hold on," he said.

Cat waited again. Tess ate another onion ring.

Then DeMarco said, "I just got informed that Lizzani didn't show up for his shift today. My people called his house and I'm sending someone over there."

"Sir, we can handle that for you," Cat said. "Law enforcement—"

"No! You haven't done squat!" he yelled, and disconnected.

Cat texted Gonzales instead of calling, in case he was in

the middle of placating DeMarco. Gonzales texted back an address in Queens. Then he phoned.

"Get the address?" he asked her. "That's for Lizzani. We're going to McEvers. Do you think you can beat DeMarco's people to Lizzani?"

"We'll do our best," Cat replied. She added, "We tried to reach Bailey Hart yesterday."

"Also missing," Gonzales said. "I feel a conspiracy in the air."

She took that in. "Have the kidnappers left instructions for a drop? How can they increase the amount if they haven't left payment instructions for the first demand?"

"Because they're criminals?" Gonzales said.

"Maybe they did make a demand but DeMarco never got it. What if they think he ignored them or screwed up the drop?" Cat tested her theory. "Wouldn't they have said something about that?"

Gonzales was quiet for a moment. He said, "What if two messages from them weren't received? The first demand and then the reprimand for missing the drop? Say their communications protocol has a glitch in it, and maybe they know that and maybe they don't."

"They scrambled their IP address so you couldn't trace them," Cat said. "Maybe they accidentally sent their messages pinging around, too. Can that happen?" She'd have to ask J.T.

"It looks like the answer's yes, but this is way out of my league," Gonzales said. "We've got people we can put on this."

So do we.

"We'll get on the road to check out Lizzani," Cat said.

"Thanks. Appreciate the help," Gonzales said. He sounded like he meant it.

"If you find McEvers or Hart…"

"We'll let you know."

She had no idea if he actually would.

They got the bill and threw down cash, then headed out to the rainy, dark day. As they hurried past the first alley, Cat spotted movement and tapped Tess. They shared a look and Cat pulled out her gun. Tess followed suit. On a different day, they wouldn't have.

They stepped into the darkness.

CHAPTER EIGHTEEN

Vincent emerged from the shadows into enough light for Cat to recognize him. He was wearing his pea coat and ball cap, and when he saw Tess and Catherine's drawn firearms, he said, "It's just me."

"*Vincent*." Catherine holstered her weapon and moved beneath the overhang of the building, out of the rain. Tess came, too. "What are you doing? It's broad daylight!"

"Well, no." He managed a small smile. "There's not a whole lot of sun out. Mostly snow." Then his smile faded. "J.T. told me about the Rikers security footage. The deliberate frame job."

"And you tracked me here."

He shrugged. *If you went to the end of the world I would find you.* He said, "I know you always say you don't want to be protected. But I figure we're working a case now. Together. And I have to watch my partner's back." He looked at her for confirmation, and saw, over her shoulder, that Tess was nodding at him.

"Completely agree," Tess said. "This case is getting complicated."

"And way too personal," Vincent said. "So what do you have?"

They explained about the call from Claudia McEvers. Cat went back over the fact that McEvers had worked for the Windsors.

Vincent said, "That could be weird or not too weird. Windsor was like DeMarco, in the stratosphere of money and power. They would have moved in the same circles. They probably hired each other's people now and then."

Cat's mouth pressed into a tight, firm line. "But doesn't all this feel like it's solidly linked? My father disappears during the power outage, IA tries to bust me with faked footage, someone who used to work security for Curt Windsor tells us not to trust two FBI agents we're supposed to be helping?" As usual, Cat got straight to the heart of the matter. He agreed with her.

"And key people are going missing," Catherine finished. "Lizzani. Hart."

"I think we're getting a good picture of how Angelo was kidnapped," Tess said. "Lizzani uses his biometrics to get them in, Hart reprograms the security system. No wonder he was so nervous. Click-click with that pen," Tess said.

"That's certainly a workable hypothesis," Vincent said, and then cleared his throat. It was time to move to his discovery. It was a game-changer, and he should have announced it as soon as they met up. "I have something to show you."

He saw that Cat heard how deadly serious he was; she checked her gun holster beneath her coat. Tess was on alert, too.

"What about Lizzani?" Tess asked. "We're trying to beat DeMarco's guys to his place."

"Take one extra minute for this," Vincent replied.

He turned and they followed him down the alley, hugging the wall to stay out of the snow. The Hudson River churned gray and stormy below the grade; and Vincent walked them to a Dumpster against the wall. He listened to Cat's increasing heartbeat. Maybe she only suspected what he was about to show her, but she was certain it was something bad.

He pulled a paper towel from his coat pocket, wrapped it around his hand, and opened the lid. The two detectives peered in.

There, sprawled among bags of garbage and flattened cardboard boxes, lay a redheaded woman. The very woman, he supposed, they had come to meet at the diner.

Her eyes were closed and she was curled up almost as if she were sleeping. But Vincent knew that she was dead. She had no pulse. To him, the smell of the blood that had streamed from the back of her head into the refuse was as strong as the rotting bags of food scraps surrounding her.

"Shut it," Catherine said.

Vincent closed the lid with the paper towel. The three stood beneath the overhang. He said, "The body is dry. That means that this happened before it started snowing."

"Are you saying that you think those two agents did this?" Catherine asked.

Tess frowned. "I wouldn't put it past them."

"Tell me about the FBI agents," Vincent said.

Catherine gave him the download. About Gonzales and Robertson, and the security footage from Turntable, and the phone call. Vincent listened intently. He could see why they were conflicted about how to proceed. He wasn't sure what they should do, especially now that Catherine was back on IA's radar. Once he found out who was causing her problems, that bastard had better run. Fresh anger seethed just below the surface and every protective bone in his body called out for vengeance. But he knew Catherine hated it when he stepped in to fight her battles.

He thought about the little girl he had saved in the burning building. And then he thought about Angelo DeMarco. If he could save Angelo's life, then this was just as much his battle as Catherine's. And that was not about protecting her. That was about doing the right thing.

He said, "Based on the scents on the body, I'll try to track down who did this."

Catherine nodded. "We can look into Lizzani while you hunt down the murderer. If it's Angelo's kidnapper, even better."

"No listen, let's split up, Cat. Stay with this. I'll go check on the address," Tess said. "That way we're square with Gonzales and Robertson and we can cover more ground."

"Let's withhold disclosure about the body," Catherine said, "until we see where it takes us. We can always 'discover' her body when it's convenient for our timetable." She looked over her shoulder. "I hope no one's watching us. Or taking pictures."

Vincent got quiet and went into predator mode. He said, "I don't think we're being watched. I see the murderer as very tall, male, has a beard. And he walked down this alley from the river toward the Javits."

"That counts Lizzani out," Tess muttered. "Unless he's an accomplice or has one who looks like that. I'll take the squad car to Queens. Did you drive over here?" Tess asked Vincent, who nodded. "Okay. I'll take our car and call you, Cat, as soon as something shakes loose."

"Good plan," Cat said.

Tess dashed through the rain toward their car. Catherine turned to Vincent and said, "The Dumpster's in plain sight. We may have already been spotted looking inside. Can you do one more check to see if anyone is loitering around?"

Vincent got still again. In his mind's eye, he saw Claudia McEvers walking toward the front of the diner. Then he envisioned the tall man following behind her. The man spoke; McEvers turned and followed him into the alley. He described the rest of the scene to Cat.

"She knew him. She wasn't afraid of him but she was surprised to see him. They walked down this alley to the midway point. Then she got scared and tried to leave. He grabbed her arm. He hit her over the head with the butt of a gun. She fell to her knees and he dragged her behind the Dumpster and beat her to death."

He walked behind the Dumpster to washes of blood swirling in the rain. Cat squatted down, observing but not touching anything. When she straightened she shuffled her boots to destroy any footprints of theirs.

Vincent stopped and inhaled a new layer of odors, scents that had seeped into the walls of the building. "Cigarettes. Cooking oil and food. Sweat. A man who was in the diner... could've been a lookout." Wood. Splinters. The memory-echo of scraping metal and antiseptic floor cleaner. "At one point he moved a stepladder that was possibly kept in a commercial kitchen." He kept focusing. "The ladder was in the alley, but I'm not sure when."

"The diner kitchen?" Catherine asked. "I think I saw that guy. I went out back and there was a young man sitting on the stoop smoking a cigarette." She frowned. "I wonder if he made us as cops. He had a strange reaction to me. When we were in the diner, we talked to the FBI agents on the phone but we kept it off speaker. But if someone had a parabolic listening device, they could have heard the whole thing."

Vincent grunted. "McEvers told you to meet her here, right? To tell you something, or to lure you into a trap? I wonder if the person who killed her prevented her from telling you something or saved you?"

"There was a girl texting the whole time we were there. She wasn't a very good waitress. I wonder if she was texting McEvers or Lizzani. Or even Robertson and Gonzales and telling them we'd arrived. Or someone else altogether. The killer."

"Maybe if we went back into the diner, I could get more information," he said, but Catherine shook her head.

"I probably shouldn't go back in."

"I'll go alone," Vincent said.

He turned and Catherine grabbed his arm. He scented her worry. Her body was practically singing with fear. For him.

"What if this is some kind of ruse to call *you* out?" she whispered fiercely. "People know we were together. And you're being hunted everywhere." Her shoulders were hunched; she was shrinking down, the very opposite of his brave Catherine. She was more like him than she realized: when she was unable to fight beside him or protect him, she felt lost. That was when she dropped her focus, her "tiger-cop" ferocity. Until he had been able to control his beast side as well as he could now, that would be the most likely scenario for him to begin to lose it. His powerlessness would enrage him most of all. He never felt more threatened than when Catherine was in danger.

"Catherine, we have to find this boy. His death is going to be unspeakable. Agonizing. I was a doctor. I know every single thing that's going to happen to his body if he doesn't get some insulin." "They have to know that. They won't kill him until they get their money," Catherine insisted. "They haven't even set a time for the money to be paid."

"That you know of. You said yourself you're not sure that all the messages from the kidnappers are coming through."

"Then we need to hurry." She tilted her head back to lock gazes with him. "Ever since you had to go back on the run…" She cleared her throat. "If it feels wrong, promise you'll pull back."

"I will."

They walked together back through the alley. Catherine couldn't know that his predator senses were replaying Claudia McEvers' last moments as if he were physically present. Ghostly white images projected how hard she had fought for her life. Martial arts moves, kicks, all to no avail. She had been very surprised. The pain and terror as the gun butt came down again and again.

And then, as he was about to step out of the alley onto the sidewalk, he smelled the weirdest scent. It took him a couple of seconds to figure out what it was, but even then he didn't know what it was called.

"Those bright red cherries that they put in drinks," he said. "What do you call them?"

"Maraschino cherries?"

"I can smell them. And... coconut. Popcorn. It's a mixture. Do they have something like that on the menu in the diner? A dessert?"

"I don't know. We didn't look at desserts." She sniffed. "I can't smell it."

"You're lucky. It's so sweet my eyes are practically watering." He began to walk out of the alley, and then he stopped. "It's strongest here. Right here. Whoever smelled like that waited here." He cocked his head. "The man who beat McEvers came up beside popcorn guy. A car pulled up and they both got into it."

"What about stepladder guy?" she asked him.

"I don't scent him down here. He must have gone the other way, around the Dumpster and back into the diner through the door you described."

"So he wasn't afraid to be seen. Making it more likely that he wasn't a stranger around here. So he might be in the diner right now, working. Or maybe he's lit out by now."

"One way to know."

Her lips parted in protest, and then she ducked her head in assent. He was going to do what he was going to do, and she knew there was no talking him out of it. It was game on, and Vincent was at bat.

CHAPTER NINETEEN

Ball cap low, Vincent strolled down the street with his hands in his pockets. There was a menu in the window of Mars, and he ran his gaze down the offerings until he got to desserts. Nothing with maraschino cherries, popcorn, and coconut.

He went in. He saw at once the texting waitress, who barely looked at him. But her heartbeat picked up and she took a step away as he approached.

Does she know who I am? Is she telling someone to call the police, that she's spotted the murderer, Vincent Keller?

She didn't seem agitated enough. She was on guard but she wasn't overly stressed. She was acting *guilty*, he realized. It wasn't that she recognized him. *She* was afraid of being recognized.

He sat at the counter. There were a few other people in a scattering of booths. Based on Catherine's description of the diner, it had gotten busier.

"Coffee, please," he said in a voice even lower and gruffer than his normal tone.

While she turned to a coffee warmer to pour him a cup, he slid off the bar stool and headed toward the back. It was convenient that the bathroom was located past the open kitchen. Vincent paused on the threshold of the steamy cooking area, pretending to search for the bathroom door, peered into the kitchen, and focused.

The man who had brought a ladder into the alley was in there. He was standing over a deep fryer. He had red hair, he was a little taller than average, and he wore a soul patch. The tattoo on his bare forearm read *Hendrix*.

Vincent looked around for a ladder and saw one in the corner of the kitchen, folded up rather incongruously beside a large stack of oversized cans of tomatoes. Vincent honed in on the ladder and went just a little beast, eyes averted. There was no blood on the ladder, as he might have expected. In fact, he didn't scent Claudia McEvers or her killer on it. No popcorn or maraschino cherries, either. But he did smell the other odors of the alley, the smells that had been there before Claudia McEvers' murder. That would place the man in the alley before she'd been killed. Maybe he was innocent of all of this.

Sometimes a ladder was just a ladder, and a cook was just a cook.

He must have felt Vincent's gaze on him. His heartbeat accelerated into overdrive and fear-sweat clogged Vincent's nostrils. The man was terrified. Feigning nonchalance, he walked over to a deep fryer and lifted up the basket, checking the fries dripping with hot oil. He was trembling.

Vincent continued his journey to the bathroom, opened the door so that it appeared that he had gone inside, and texted Catherine:

Yes. He's here. Wait. Conceal.

He waited for the guy to leave the kitchen.

Bingo.

Now in a black jacket, the cook furtively darted into the hall and hurried into the dining room. Vincent heard the front door open and close. He moved back into the dining area himself, dropped some bills beside his cup, and left.

Then Vincent made as if to wait at the curb for a break in the traffic to cross the street. In actuality, he was searching with his beast senses for the cook. Catherine was a few feet away on his right, waiting out of sight as he had requested. He counted her and heard her steady heartbeat. She was on the job, intent but not nervous.

There.

The guy was hurrying down the street to Vincent's left. Vincent began to follow him, maintaining a good distance with his ball cap down and the snow landing on his pea coat. He didn't turn to look back at Catherine, wasn't sure if she would stand still in the snowfall, which was getting worse, or re-enter the diner to examine the empty kitchen. Maybe she would start following him and his mark.

The cook looked over his shoulder, realized that Vincent was behind him, and his heartbeat picked up. He quickened his pace. A tiny flicker flared to life inside Vincent. Where it resided, Vincent wasn't sure—his brain? His body? It was the first flash of the interest of a predator in potential prey. But he was allowed to feel that, wasn't he? It was the same kind of charge a cop got when they tailed a suspect.

Wasn't it?

He didn't have to feel *less* than another human being so that he could actually claim that he *was* a human being.

So, okay, he permitted himself to enjoy the hunt.

The cook was getting increasingly scared. As he walked past a large window he glanced into it, searching for Vincent's reflection. Vincent slowed to make that impossible, and the flicker inside him grew.

Beasthood was ingrained in him, inside his very DNA. He had to work to control that side, and he couldn't relax his vigil, ever. He throttled himself back down and worked to see what the cook had done in the alley with the ladder, now that he had more sights and sounds to work with.

In beast-flashes, he saw the cook carrying the ladder into the alley. It had not yet begun to rain. The young man set the ladder down about five feet from the Dumpster. The body was already in the Dumpster by then, but it didn't appear that they guy was aware of it. Despite that, the man was afraid.

He climbed the ladder, looking constantly up and down the alley. Dripping with apprehension. Then he climbed to the top of the ladder, balancing precariously on the top, and extracted something from his jeans pocket, beneath his white work apron. Cotton fibers and tiny fragments of tobacco had cascaded out of his pocket onto the ground.

There was something in the man's hand, but Vincent couldn't see what it was. The roof of the diner was shingled, and there was a gap where part of a shingle had broken off. He slipped whatever was in his hand into the gap. Vincent concentrated harder. It was something metal...or *in* metal.

We have to go back and get that, Vincent thought. He thought about texting Catherine to check it out but he was too intently focused on his quarry to do it.

He let the vision-memory fade. The cook was coming up to a cluster of men and women in jeans, work boots, and jackets that read DICKINSON CONSTRUCTION, who were hurrying beneath the eaves of the buildings toward Vincent, possibly returning from lunch.

The young man broke into a run. He waved his hands and shouted, "Help! That man is after me! Help!"

The construction workers looked from him to Vincent. Their faces became ugly. Then one of them narrowed his eyes in suspicion and said, "Hey, man, what's up?" His eyes widened. "Hey, wait a minute!"

Recognized. Or nearly. He considered blurring past them but knew he couldn't. Even considered knocking them all out. But of course he couldn't do that either. He could only look on helplessly as the group spread themselves across the sidewalk, effectively barring his path.

He was afraid to even speak to them, for fear of being recognized, and hung a right toward the curb. He watched the cars as they trundled past and he darted into an opening. Once across the street, he disappeared into an alley.

Then, safe from scrutiny, he turned left and *blurred*, hoping to catch up with the cook. His mind was so fixed on triangulating his location that he missed the gaping hole in the ground before him—part of another construction site— and tumbled down hard onto his back. A crusty layer cracked beneath him and he fell into ice water. He lay stunned, the wind knocked out of him, and cursed Reynolds for taking away his ability to heal himself. Of course Reynolds had done it so that when it came time to kill Vincent, it would be easier.

His phone was still in his pocket. He rolled over onto his knees to protect it from the ice water. Finally able to take a breath, he crawled to the nearest side of the pit and searched for handholds—plant roots, rebar, anything. There was nothing but damp, packed earth; he pushed his fingers into the mud and made grabbing attempts with his hands. He pulled himself up, then extracted one hand, raised his arm, and drilled his fingers into a section of mud closer to the top. His ribs hurt and his head was pounding.

Still he forced his fingers in, and then in again, until finally he lifted himself out of the hole and lay on the ground for a moment, catching his breath. He held his hands straight out to let the rain wash them, then found the paper towel he had used to open the Dumpster and dried them. He wanted to tell Cat to search the diner's roof for something metal.

He texted her and hit send.

Message undelivered, his phone read. He saw that that he

had only one bar, and cursed under his breath.

He finally stood and then he *blurred*, seeing the cook's path down the block and attempting to follow it. But then he detected a car and put on the brakes. He ground his teeth in frustration as he watched a cab driving away. He knew the young man was in it, and soon it wove into the complex pattern of traffic. As he tried to decide if he should attempt to overtake it, he caught an elderly man beneath an umbrella staring at him.

Best not to chance it, he thought.

Daubed with mud and soaked to the skin, he trudged back to where he had left Catherine. She was standing beneath an eave, as wet as he was, colder, no doubt, and she heaved a sigh of relief when she saw him. He gestured for her to stay where she was—he would come to her—but as soon as he was within striking distance, she threw her arms around him as if she couldn't help herself.

He told her everything. Then together they walked back down the alley. Vincent did a long, slow scan of the area, checking for observers as she pulled on a pair of Latex gloves; then he laced his hands together to crate a foothold for Catherine and she did a leg-up. Balancing on his hands, she found the gap in the shingle he had described and felt inside.

"Found something," she reported. "I've got it." He lowered her to the ground and she held out a tin bandage box. He shielded her as she opened it, taking care to ensure the contents stayed dry.

It was a strip of notebook paper with an unconnected string of numbers beginning with a 2. Below that was the word *Rikers*. Vincent didn't immediately realize what it was, but Catherine did:

"This is a commitment number. An inmate ID."

"Your father's?" he asked and she shook her head with such certainty that he realized she had memorized Bob

Reynolds' prison number. She looked inside the can, then fished around with her gloved fingers. "That's the only thing in here."

"The cook wrote it and stashed it here," Vincent told her. "I can smell him on the paper and the can. That's why he brought the ladder into the alley."

Turning the paper over, she inspected the other side, then held it in one hand while she fished in her purse for a pencil flashlight. He watched the care she employed to glean all she could from the clue. He had beast senses, true, but she was good at her job and often she put together the data he gave her in clever ways he hadn't considered. He'd always admired competence—people who were good at what they did, and cared about the quality of their work—and Catherine never slacked or lost her edge no matter what was going on in her life.

She put the paper back in the can and looked toward the Dumpster, her brow furrowed.

"He was risking a lot to place it where someone could get to it. My money's on Claudia," she said.

"And she was killed before she could retrieve it."

Catherine looked fierce. "I want justice for her, but more than that I want to find Angelo DeMarco. But I have to call in her body now. It's just too much of a loose end if I don't. I'll say we were wondering why she hadn't shown up. Tess went to check out Lizzani and I searched the diner. I spotted the body in the Dumpster and climbed in to see if there were signs of life."

"Sounds good. Better if your DNA is in there."

"They're not going to sift through the trash. They'll check her body. After I search her, I have to call the homicide squad for this part of town. I have to follow procedure. So don't come into the Dumpster with me. I don't want there to be any chance of our CSU discovering your DNA."

"Got it."

She put the bandage can in her purse, muttering to herself about evidence bags; then she opened the lid and snow powdered the contents. He gave her another leg-up and she clambered inside, into the filth. Just part of the job. Most civilians had no idea what New York's Finest endured to solve cases. The good cops, that is.

She hesitated. "There could be surveillance. Go to your car and wait for my signal."

"Makes sense." He groaned inwardly, thinking of the mess he was going to leave in J.T.'s car. "How about I call Tess and debrief her about the cook and what you've found? She can officially request information about the diner's employees. Or have J.T. do it and keep it quiet."

"Yes. Good," she said. "I'm thinking J.T."

He hesitated. "I don't want to leave you here."

She narrowed her eyes in irritation, but it was in jest. A little. "Don't try to protect me. I'm just doing my job. You'll endanger us both if you're found with me."

She was right and he knew it. But it was still felt as if he were abandoning her. He had saved her life eleven years before, and he could still remember the sight of her flat on her back, a gash across her forehead, disoriented and pleading for her life. He had watched over her ever since. For years he had dreamed of simply meeting her. Ironically, once they had connected, she had ordered him to *stop* protecting her.

But Catherine could more than hold her own. She had become a cop. Because she was strong. And a great fighter. If those gunmen approached her and her mom today, his money was on both Chandler women walking away alive.

He loped on, drawing more stares because he was so filthy. He took a circuitous route to the car, then popped the trunk in hopes of finding something to cover the car seat with. He was in luck: he found not one but two thick blankets and a towel from J.T.'s gym. He draped both of the blankets over the car upholstery and cleaned himself up as best he could with the towel. Then he sat in the car, locked it, and pulled out his phone, already impatient for word from Catherine.

He started to dial Tess when a text from Catherine came in. *BFT. I have her phone.* "BFT" meant that blunt force trauma was the cause of death. That was how he had seen it go down. He was glad she was taking McEvers' phone. They might be able to identify McEvers' murderer from her messages and texts, and to deduce if the crime was linked to Angelo's abduction, and how Curt Windsor fit in.

Called it in, Catherine texted next. *Waiting. Did you call Tess yet? If not, I will.*

He texted back, *Go ahead.*

He knew that NYPD CSU and the medical examiner would come to the scene. And a detective supervisor and detectives from the homicide squad. Cat was Special Crimes. She'd hand off the case and leave. Homicide would canvass the area for possible suspects and witnesses. Surely the texting waitress in the diner would reveal the abrupt departure of the cook. Vincent could be placed at the counter and wandering back to the bathroom, but he had kept his head down. Security cameras wouldn't have been able to catch his face. Outside, witnesses had watched him, Vincent, go after the cook. One person had possibly recognized him.

He prayed that he and Catherine had been careful enough not to be linked.

She texted, *I can get a ride. Go look for cook.*

He texted back, *KK.*

Careful.

O&O. Over and out.

Vincent started the car and moved slowly into the traffic. Searching for the cook would be like looking for a needle in a haystack. There were over eight million people living in New York City. And yet, he and Catherine had found each other. They were destined, she had told him. She had insisted on that.

She had promised that.

If you were destined, that gave you an advantage over the cruel whims of fate. He knew that she believed it with her all her heart. He did too, although sometimes it frightened him to admit it. As if by owning it, he could lose it.

"So who are you?" Vincent mused aloud as he started the windshield wipers. He meant the cook. "What's your part in all of this? And, more importantly, just where the hell are you?"

Searching for answers, he drove through the falling snow.

CHAPTER TWENTY

Claudia had been a pro.

Cat thought of her as "Claudia" now that she had frisked her dead body and gone through her pockets. The phone Cat had lifted from the crime scene was a burner, but luckily for Cat, it contained the history of one other call besides the calls they had traded. It was a local New York number. Cat dialed it while she was waiting for NYPD homicide.

"Oh, my God, where the hell are you? Some guy was chasing me!" said a male voice. It had to be the cook.

"I can't talk right now," Cat whispered, trying to emulate Claudia's voice. It was easier to masquerade as someone if you whispered. "Where'd you put it?"

"Like we agreed. The broken shingle." The man's voice was shaking. "Why can't you talk? Where are you? You didn't come to the diner."

"*They're* here," Cat said, improvising.

"Bastards. God, I hope you can take them down. Joey's number's in the can. He's willing to testify."

Cat blinked. *Testify? About what?* She took a chance. "Heard anything about Angelo DeMarco?"

Tony DeMarco had managed to keep everything out of

the papers, but Cat didn't know how long that would last. Although the press might argue that the public had a right to know about such things, the better reason to go public was in case anyone could provide a viable lead. Hundreds of false leads would come in, maybe even thousands because the DeMarcos were so high-profile. But there could be gold buried among the dross. When a life was at stake, NYPD did everything they could. Cat had to assume DeMarco had told—not asked—the mayor to put pressure on the department. And on the Feds, too.

"Hello?" she said into the phone.

"The… TV's on," he murmured. "Hey… hey… what the *hell? Who are you?* Did you kill her?"

He disconnected. Cat heard a helicopter, then shouting and slamming doors at the end of the alley. The chopper was from a news outlet. Someone had alerted the press, or else a member of the press had successfully hacked a police call. Maybe they'd descrambled a scanner. At any rate, they were here before her homicide squad backup. Not good.

She grimaced, hoping the cook was too paranoid to tell anyone that someone had just called him using the dead woman's phone. She pocketed the burner and stayed beside the Dumpster as she called Tess.

Cat explained everything and gave Tess Joey's identification number. Then she said, "I really spooked the cook and I'm afraid he'll try to call this Joey and warn him not to speak to anybody. Can you get down to Rikers and talk to this guy stat?"

"Yes. And it actually makes better sense if I go, since someone's already tried to place you there once and you do not need to be asked why you went there again. If anyone asks me, I'll just say I have a C.I. and they might leave Joey alone. But they do log visits, and it might be a tip-off to whoever did this."

"It's a chance we'll have to take," Cat said. "Did you find anything at Lizzani's?"

"I'm still there. The guy's gone," Tess said. "He left in a big hurry but I didn't see signs of a struggle. Enough clothes were missing that I assume he packed a bag but he didn't take care of business like someone is going away permanently. For starters, he left a cat."

"Really?"

"Yeah. J.T. will take care of him."

"He will?"

"I'll convince him. Unless you want to take care of him, *Cat*. He's really cute. He's orange and he has little white socks, and his tail looks like it was dipped in white paint."

"I've thought about getting a pet before," Cat said, with a pang of temptation. "But with our schedules, I'm thinking it would be better for J.T. to take him."

"As I figured. Okay, checking that off my list. Mr. Boston White Sox is taken care of. I'm checking with the post office after I go to Rikers, see if they have a forwarding address."

"Any clues about where he went?"

"It doesn't look like he had a car. I told Gonzales and Robertson we should have someone canvass to see if anyone saw him leave. Of course they probably hired him a limo."

Cat heard a siren, a sure sign of the cavalry. They had probably realized the press was there and wanted to assert control as fast as they could so the crime scene wouldn't be compromised. Speaking of which… she traversed the area, running her shoes over the surface of the alley to make doubly sure that Vincent's footprints were erased. There should be no trace of him.

"Thanks for filling me in. It's show time for me," she told Tess.

"Break a leg," Tess replied. "Preferably a bad guy's."

Then Cat put her phone away and went to meet her fellow officers.

Rikers

An island of four hundred thirteen acres situated in the East River, between Queens and the Bronx. It was not a place you ever wanted to find yourself. Overcrowded, dangerous. Desperation and rage coated the walls like cooking grease, and Tess had to remind herself to stay on topic, because she knew that some of the inmates had been unjustly convicted, and that some of those innocents were barely sixteen years of age. You could be tried as an adult at sixteen.

And you could be sentenced to hell.

Rikers.

She had gotten recalcitrant suspects to break down and confess by threatening to send them to Rikers. Of course that wasn't up to her. She didn't pronounce sentences, she just made the arrest. But she could put in a good word for someone who cooperated.

Let this guy be cooperative, she thought, looking up at the gloomy sky. It was going to start snowing again any second. That would muddle the evidence at the Dumpster crime scene even more. That was convenient. It was also convenient that they had told Robertson and Gonzales that Claudia McEvers had wanted to meet with them. She and Cat hadn't taken it all the way by telling the two FBI agents that she'd gone as far as arranging a rendezvous, but the dots would connect.

But maybe it had been too convenient.

Tess had a very bad feeling that they'd already known that, taken steps to ensure that McEvers would not make that meeting.

They're dirty.

They were her prime suspects in Angelo's kidnapping. Did they participate in Reynolds' disappearance as well? That would give her and Cat more ways in to investigate them. And bust them.

Cops got fast-tracked to talk to prisoners, which was a good thing. She wanted to talk to Joey before he found out about McEvers' death. As it was, he might have gotten a call from the cook, or seen it on TV, the way the cook had.

She saw security cameras everywhere, recording, watching. J.T. had not yet located the footage of Reynolds' breakout. She wondered if it was being suppressed or if the cameras hadn't worked during the blackout. Special Agent Gayle Thurman was the Special Agent in Charge. Aside from Hendricks from IA, no one from Thurman's squad had questioned Cat about the case, which surprised Tess.

The badge was her golden ticket, and soon she found herself sitting at a Plexiglas barrier with a phone in her hand. On the other side of the barrier sat a very young, stressed-out guy with a thatch of red hair and matching eyebrows that made him look like Harry Potter's friend in the movies, only if Harry Potter had lived in the Bizarro World.

"Joey," she said quietly, "I'm Detective Vargas. Listen carefully and stay cool. A few things have changed." She figured she might as well be straight with him. If he already knew about Claudia's death, and she lied to him, there was no way he would talk to her.

"The person that your friend…" she began. And then it hit her: this guy had red hair, and so did Claudia. Maybe they were related.

Maybe this was her kid.

"Where is she?" he said querulously. He began compulsively pushing down the cuticle of his left thumbnail. It was bleeding. "Why are *you* here?"

Okay, he didn't know. She had limited time but she had to secure his cooperation. "I came in her place. What have you heard?" She kept her voice low.

"Man, they just dragged him out." He was excited. "Everyone was waiting for it. But I didn't think they'd be able to pull it off. Couple of other guys tried to go, too, while the lights were out, threatened to yell but the guards knew, too, so who cared? The guards knew the brothers were going to try to blow, and they put us all in lockdown. So he was the only one."

Oh, my God. He's talking about Reynolds. She stayed quiet in hopes that he'd keep talking.

"What was it like?" she asked him.

"It was *crazy,* man! Friend of mine said they had on ski masks and weapons. In a frickin' *prison.*"

It was hard to know if that was true. Prison gossip was like other gossip. She reminded herself that she was here to work on Angelo's case, but Reynolds was just as important. Just not as official.

"Do you know anyone who actually saw it happening? Maybe someone in the cell next to his?"

He flashed her a lopsided grin that startled her with its sweetness. She had checked his record: Joey Palmieri was in for possession of controlled substances with intent to sell. But it seemed like he was more the type to be hawking Girl Scout cookies or collecting donations for Unicef.

"Right now, everybody in here is claiming that they saw it. And that they knew the guy. Anyway…" He hunkered forward, eager to get back to business. "Are you guys are going to bust those a-holes?" His light-blue eyes were bright, expectant. "She's got everything she needs to make it stick? Because you say the word, I am testifying and they are going *down.*"

Her best guess was that Claudia had been collecting sufficient information to make some kind of case against

Robertson and McEvers, and that Joey was going to testify in that case. In exchange for a lighter sentence? Claudia McEvers was in no position to offer him anything like that... unless she was working undercover. Or it could be that once she amassed enough evidence, she could possibly aid in overturning a false conviction.

"Hey," he said slowly. "Something ain't right here." He sat back in his chair, putting more distance between himself and Tess. "Where is Mrs. McEvers?"

"Okay, listen," Tess said, leaning forward, attempting to establish her own connection with him, not simply as Claudia's proxy. "You and I have some things to talk about. But first I want to know a couple more things about the blackout." She just couldn't stop herself. "Did you hear anything about how it occurred? It wasn't an accident?"

He frowned at her. She remained silent. He said sarcastically, "Right. An *accident*."

She didn't react. She just waited.

"We heard it was some mucky-muck high up in the utility. He flipped a switch and the boroughs went out. He's long gone. And rich, I bet."

"Who paid him?"

"The guys who snatched the Feeb, I guess."

"The Feeb" had to mean Reynolds.

"So, Miss Cop, you better tell me what's going on." He gazed up at her through his false bravado like a little kid whistling in the dark. She felt bad for dashing his hopes.

"Okay, I'm going to be honest with you," she said. He took a little breath, afraid. Good. It was smart to be afraid at this point. "Claudia McEvers has been murdered."

"Oh, God." He could barely grind the words out. He fell backwards against his plastic chair, nearly tipping it over. "Oh, God, oh, God. I knew it. I knew they would never let me go."

She took a chance. "You mean Robertson."

So much depended on what he said next.

He keened, his voice high and crazed with fright. He rocked back and forth. Behind him, across the room, a burly guard took notice. Tess lifted a hand. *It's okay*, she signaled. But she didn't know if the guard knew she was a cop.

"He said he would bury me here. He said I would never get out. He was right." Joey started to cry. "I didn't do anything. I never did *anything*. That's why I'm here! Because I wouldn't!"

"Tell me everything. Quickly. Get it together," Tess ordered him as the concerned guard shifted his weight. Joey hadn't asked her how she had known to come to him—if Claudia had sent her, or given her Joey's name before she'd died—and she was glad he hadn't thought of it. It would keep her lies to a minimum, and she hadn't thought of a good lie to explain it anyway. If Robertson and Gonzales were involved, she had to stay well off their radar.

"*He* wanted me to be a mule. Carry drugs. And I said no. But I was so stupid. I said I was going to narc on him, tell the police all about him. So he planted some coke in my house and called it in."

Tess figured that he had already said all this at his trial, except maybe he'd been too afraid of Robertson to say anything. Copping a guilty plea might have been the only way he had to save his life.

"He *planted* it," he said again. His face was chalk-white. Prison was hell for just about anybody, but it had to be a special kind of hell for a tender baby-face like him.

"And Claudia had proof of that," Tess said. "That he did that to you."

"Yes! This morning she said she had everything she needed and she was going to go to the DA. She said if I would testify they'd find me innocent and let me out." He gripped the phone with both hands. "Listen, please, listen to me. I was in *college*. The first person in my family. I wasn't into drugs at all!"

She had been lied to many, many times in the past, and so her first impulse was to assume Joey was also lying to her. But this guy was convincing, and her heart tugged. Robertson was evil, doing this to him. Guys like Robertson were why Internal Affairs was necessary, as loathsome as she and the majority of her fellow cops found them to be. Law enforcement wielded a lot of power, and the checks and balances didn't always work.

Look at her and Cat—and yes, Gabe, before he had turned into Darth Vader—how they had broken not only protocols and procedures but actual laws to protect Vincent and destroy Muirfield. They had logged so much time off the books that they had almost lost their jobs. And they were "the good guys."

What was the saying? Everyone is the hero of their own story. She had no idea how Robertson could believe that. Maybe he didn't need to. Scumbag like him wouldn't rationalize his actions. He'd just act.

"Listen," she said, "we're in the middle of something really intense. It involves Claudia's death. But as soon as it plays out, I'm going to look into this. If you're not lying to me, I swear I am going to help you."

He kept crying. He wrapped his hands around his head and sobbed. Tess chewed her lower lip, willing him to calm down. If he kept it up, the guard was going to end this, cop or no cop. And that would close her window of opportunity.

He wiped his eyes and sniffled. He was in serious need of a tissue. He was just a kid. What the hell was he doing in Rikers? Why not minimum security?

So Robertson could keep an eye on him.

While keeping an eye on Reynolds at the same time?

"Listen," she began. "I am the real deal. Just don't tell anyone in gen pop that I was here, and—"

"You're all alike," he muttered losing hope. "When I saw the ADA here, I thought it was over. I figured she'd given him all the information and he had come to talk to me about my testimony. But he didn't ask me a single question."

Tess went cold. Ice cold. "The ADA," she said carefully.

"That guy who's on TV all the time. We call him 'the movie star.'"

Gabe? Was here?

"But he didn't talk to you," she said, and he shook his head. "Who did he talk to?"

"I don't know, I don't know." He started crying again. "*He* killed her. He *knows*. He's going to come for me!"

She knew he was referring to Robertson but the creepy thing was that she could substitute "ADA Lowan" for "He" and it almost worked for her. She had really liked Gabe. He had tried to kill Vincent to save himself from life as a beast. But then the beast in Gabe had been killed. After he flatlined, Cat restarted his heart with a defibrillator, and his beast side stayed dead. After that, he had remained in the city to make amends, risked his life for Vincent and stuck by Cat... yeah, and loved her so much he had gone all immoral on their butts.

She tapped the barrier to get Joey's attention. "Stay calm, okay? Do you know that for a fact? That Robertson knows Claudia contacted you? Or are you just scared?"

He stared at her as if she were crazy. "'Just' scared? *Just* scared? Oh, yeah, why would I ever be just scared in *here*?"

"Bad choice of words," she murmured. "Please answer the question. We don't have much time."

In fact, they didn't have any time. The guard *was* on his way. She assessed the man. He could be in Robertson's employ, keeping tabs on Joey for him. In which case, she was endangering Joey further.

"Play along with me," she said quietly. Then she raised her voice. She said, "Just think over what I said. It's not too late to keep your little brother from going down the same road as you."

"Palmieri, time's up," the guard announced.

Joey stared at her with a haunted look. "You stupid idiot," he hissed under his breath. "I don't *have* a brother."

The guard approached. Joey crumbled. "I'm sorry," he whispered to Tess. Tears streamed down his face. "I didn't mean to be rude."

"I know. Remember what I said." *I am going to get you out of here.*

And remember that you are not Wonder Woman, she told herself. But for this kid, she would be.

CHAPTER TWENTY-ONE

Rest in peace, Claudia. In the morgue.

Cat handed off Claudia's case to the Midtown homicide squad, and a uni drove her back to the 125th so she could write her report and get her car. No police office in the history of law enforcement stayed current on paperwork but again, there was that noose that IA had dangled in front of her. So Catherine took the time to file it.

On the subject of IA, she requested a meeting with Hendricks, wondering if proof of her altered footage might crack her father's disappearance. She nosed around the NYPD system as best she could and noted the APB that had been put out on him. Her father. Murderer, conspirator, fugitive. The fact that she was genetically related to him repulsed her. She understood Vincent's discomfort with the nature of his DNA all too well.

She had showered at the precinct, but she'd not replaced her usual spare set of clothes in her locker the last time she'd had to change at work, and she put her Dumpster-diving ensemble back on. She was looking forward to going home so she could change.

From texting, she knew Vincent was there and she had a

strange feeling of déjà vu as she entered the apartment to find him clean and in his bathrobe. He had made a pot of coffee in anticipation of her arrival and poured her a cup as she crossed the threshold. He moved forward to kiss her as he handed it to her but she gave her head a quick shake.

"I am absolutely disgusting."

"Never," he said. Then he dimpled. "Okay, maybe this once."

She savored the coffee as she went into the bathroom and took off her smelly, stained clothes. Maybe this outfit should be put out of its misery.

She washed her hair again and styled it into a loose bun rather than take the time to dry it. Then she put on her white bathrobe, the twin to Vincent's, and belted it as she padded barefoot back down the hall.

The house smelled great. He was making her a grilled cheese sandwich for dinner. Standing over the stove as he flipped the sandwich onto a plate, he had a mischievous little boy grin that seemed entirely inappropriate for a murder investigation, but it was infectious. She offered him half of the sandwich but he shook his head, and his smile broadened.

"I already ate," he said.

There clearly was a punch line to that statement. She waited for it.

"Someone *cooked* me a Mars burger."

"Oh, my God, Vincent, you found the cook!" she cried. "And I'm guessing from your smile that he wants to cooperate."

"On the nose."

She began to set down her sandwich to give him a hug but he gestured to her sandwich. "You haven't eaten for hours."

"I haven't hugged you for hours, either." She tore off a corner of the grilled cheese and popped it into her mouth. "Where is he? What's his connection?"

"He's Joey Palmieri's cousin. Joey, the guy in prison Tess

went to see." He picked up the plate with her sandwich on it and her coffee cup and carried them into the bedroom. She crawled onto the mattress, weary, hungry, and delighted.

"He's scared to death of Robertson and Gonzales," he said, joining her on the bed.

"Gonzales too?" She was disappointed, but not overly surprised. On the surface, Gonzales was the more likable of the two. But she had pretty much pegged him correctly: insincere to the core.

"Gonzales and Robertson are partners at the Bureau and in crime," Vincent confirmed. "The cook is named Nicolo Palmieri but he goes by Nico, and the whole family has been terrorized by those thugs. Seems Nico's father ran drugs for the two agents and he died. Suspiciously. Robertson and Gonzales wanted the family to stay in their operation but everybody else said no. So they made an example out of Joey."

"Why not make an example out of Nico? Their dealer's son?"

Vincent's mouth stretched into a tight line. "Joey's in college. Tess said he's the family's pride and joy. He had more to lose than Nico."

"A life is a life," she said fiercely. "One's not 'better' than the other. And they actually did more damage that way, destroying one branch of the family by killing the father and another by burying their son alive. No wonder Tess was a mess after she called me from Rikers." She paused, still unsure about discussing her father's escape. She let a couple seconds drag by. Sometimes the best way to get over something was to go through it. It was foolish to think that it wouldn't be on Vincent's mind. Constantly.

"She also told me what Joey said about my father's escape. The guards knew, Vincent. They let it happen." His mood went darker still and she saw the anger smoldering in his eyes. He could tame it now, most of the time. But how could she expect him to not to react when she could feel her own blood boiling?

"So did guards let him out? Or did people come in?" Vincent asked.

She said, "They wore ski masks and they carried weapons."

"So, covert ops all the way. I wonder how they made it happen, Rikers is huge."

She shared every drop of his bitterness. "You only have to buy off a couple of people if you know which ones to go to. But even Joey knew about it."

"Unless Joey's lying. Maybe he's trying to come up with the right information to make himself valuable to you."

"Tess wants to get him released as soon as we can." She drank some of her coffee. She hadn't realized until that moment that she'd used up all her reserves. She'd been running on empty for so long it had begun to feel normal.

"We'll help him," Vincent said.

"It's just… we can't help him right now. And I hate it that I can't go after my father *now*. And this kidnapping investigation is moving too slowly."

He rolled over on his side and gently brushed a tendril of hair away from her eyes. He kissed her temple.

"It's not. It just seems that way because you're not in the mix. They're sidelining you and you like to call the shots."

"No," she said, and then she thought it over. He was right. "I've worked on a team before. But there's no team here."

"Agreed. And we've taken matters into our own hands."

"But not with my father." She placed her hand on his broad chest, unaware that she was calibrating his heartbeat until its calm, steady beat soothed her. "At least, not while they're watching me," she amended.

"They're not watching *me*," he countered.

She cupped his cheek. "Everyone is watching you. Every time you do anything, you're putting yourself at risk. Does Nico know who you are?"

"Not so far, but I was pretty surprised that he didn't. All he knows is that we want to help. He thinks that's why I went after him in the first place. To scoop him up and keep him safe from Robertson and Gonzales." Before she could ask the question, he answered. "I took him to J.T."

Cat's stomach twisted in a knot. "But Nico will put two and two together. If he figures out that J.T. is your friend, he might make a deal with Robertson and Gonzales—his cousin for Vincent Keller."

"It's done. Tess and J.T. took him to a house Claudia had planned to take him to. He had the address, but he's never been there before."

She relaxed, but only a little. At least Nico wasn't compromising J.T.'s home with his presence. "So who does he think all of us are? He talks to me on Claudia's phone, and you scoop him directly off the street? And does he know Tess is a cop?"

"He thinks we're part of McEvers' undercover sting operation after Robertson and Gonzales," he said. He smiled grimly. "Which is closer to the truth than it's not."

She took another bite of her sandwich. She knew she was hungry but she didn't feel it. She needed to get back in the game, get things done. Claudia's crime scene was secured, evidence bagged and tagged, and her part was over. There would be an autopsy. Her discovering Claudia had probably red-flagged her, and the more she found out about Robertson and Gonzales, the more she realized that she needed to lay very, very low.

"Hey, busy brain," he said.

"I was wondering if we could link the blackout to Angelo's abduction. The blackout has been classified as an act of terrorism," she told him. They both knew what that meant: FBI jurisdiction. But a different task force would investigate it. Robertson and Gonzales would not be there to obstruct justice.

Thank God.

"I don't think it was intended to be a terrorist act," Cat said.

Vincent looked over at her. "Sure it was. Just for a different kind of war."

She took a drink of coffee. "I want to talk to Nico-face-to face. I'll need the address of the house."

"You've been working too long. You need a break."

"Now with all this going on." She set the coffee and plate on her nightstand. "You shouldn't come with me. You've been out on the streets too much in the last two days. You're playing Russian roulette."

He opened his mouth to argue, and she gave him The Look. Instead of acquiescing, as she expected, he wrapped his arms around both her shoulders and eased her onto her back. His eyes flared and his hand trailed to the belt of her robe. He loosened it, all the while his gaze locked on hers. He pushed the fabric away. His hand splayed across her bare stomach, and he stirred.

"We can't do this now," she whispered.

"We have to do this now," he replied.

Then his lips were on hers, and his arms came around her, and he was right. There was no decision to make; choice was an illusion. The imperative to make love with Vincent could not be refused. They were a nimbus of life in a black sky of death. They moved through that shadowy sky together as they had so many times before. Stars gathered in Vincent's eyes, in his hair, his smile. In the proof of his link with her.

Destined.

"Catherine," he murmured. "I love you."

"I love you, too, Vincent," she whispered back.

Weakened by weariness, they gave each other strength;

distressed by injustice, they soothed each other with hope. Unclothed and vulnerable, they dressed each other in the armor of warriors.

When it was over, they lay for precious seconds in each other's arms. Then she called Tess and told her she was on their way. She also told Vincent that he was *not* coming.

He went to the window and pulled back the curtain so that she could see the darkened sky. The city glow was there. For the majority of New Yorkers, all was right with the world once more.

They both began to dress. Cat wondered if Vincent realized that he was just as sexy getting dressed as he was when he was taking it all off. Then she wondered exactly what he was getting dressed *for*.

"You're not coming with me."

She prepared herself for an argument but all he said was, "I know."

"Oh." She was pleased.

"I'll check Turntable. See what I can glean from there." When she parted her lips to argue, he kissed them. "I won't talk to anyone. I won't let anyone see me."

She groaned. "You know, just… I guess it was yesterday… I was thinking how much I was enjoying being on a case with you again. It's like when we first met."

"I remember. We found out that we made a great team."

"Yes. Except I think there's even more danger now, rather than less." She felt pensive. "I thought once we brought Muirfield down, things would be different. That you would finally be safe."

He grunted. "At least I never had that illusion." She felt such a sense of loss for him until he added, "I've already accepted that *you'll* never be safe. You're a police officer."

"And…" She gazed at him in wonderment. "…you'd never ask me to give that up?"

"It's what you are," he said simply. "Unless you gave it up because you wanted to, you wouldn't be Catherine Chandler anymore."

"And I accept you as you are," she murmured.

"Beast and all?"

"All." She dimpled. "Well, except for the snoring."

He blinked, affronted. "I do not snore!"

They finished dressing and left Cat's apartment separately, she directly to her car and he off into the night. Troubled, she watched him go, replaying their conversation in her mind. She did love Vincent, did accept him as he was, but she didn't know in her heart if she thought of his beast side as a part of him, or *apart* from him. She had chosen to be a cop. He had not chosen to be a beast.

But I didn't chose to be Bob Reynolds' daughter, either, and Vincent has moved on past that.

She left the Village, and then the city, passing boarded-over windows, grim reminders that less than forty-eight hours ago, New York had been caught in a blackout. She called Tess.

"On my way."

CHAPTER TWENTY-TWO

CLAUDIA'S SAFE HOUSE

Tess and J.T. had driven Nico way out into the sticks in Yonkers. J.T. had left Mr. Boston White Sox at his place with his new litter box, food, and toys, and Tess was charmed by how worried her man was about his new, possibly temporary, pet.

The house was plain and old with solid bars on the windows. Nico didn't have a key, and neither did anyone else. Finally Tess went around to the back, scoured around under a million rocks and a cracked garden gnome, and found the key. Nico was very impressed when she came out of the front door and ushered J.T. and him inside. They found some canned food and coffee in the cupboard and Nico sat down to a bowl of fruit cocktail and coffee that she, Tess, made, so that her witness would live another day.

"Stay away from the windows. And *what* are you doing with your phone?" Tess said. J.T. looked up from his laptop— he was checking for news coverage on Nico's disappearance and Claudia's murder—as Tess held out her hand.

"Give it. I *told* you not to call anybody and you have not been that stupid, right?"

When he hesitated, she cleared her throat and said, "Unless you *want* Robertson and Gonzales to show up and kill you."

"Everybody is worried about me," he said. "My family. If I can just tell them I'm okay. My ma. She already lost my dad."

Tess was incensed. "You called her. You told her where you are."

"No."

This kid could not lie to save his life. Literally. She gave him a stern look and he flushed to his ginger roots.

"Okay, I tried to call my ma but I don't know, I guess something went wrong but the call didn't go through. I only tried the one time and—"

"*What?*" Tess looked at J.T. "Did it not go through because of some kind of jamming? I'm flushing it."

"In the *toilet?*" Nico cried. "Do you know how long I had to work to pay for that?"

"You can get another one. Unless they've got some kind of trace on it. Then you'll never *need* another one."

"It was the bars! I didn't have enough bars!" he pleaded. He held it out to her.

"Turn it off!" she yelled at him.

He cradled it against his chest. J.T. rose from his laptop and said in a pretty scary voice, "*Give her your phone now.*"

"Okay, okay," Nico said.

Tess was impressed by J.T.'s manly attitude. *That's my man. Supernerd,* she thought.

Nico pointed to J.T.'s phone, which sat beside his laptop on the dining room table. "See how many bars *you* have."

Tess grabbed the phone at the same time that J.T. looked at his own phone. "One bar," he reported.

"See? I'm telling you the truth!" Nico cried. "Please don't flush it down the toilet."

I'm never having children, Tess thought. She opened it up

215

and pulled out the SIM card. She put the card in one pocket and the phone in another.

"I'm going to take a look around outside. J.T., you have the con."

"Oh, my God, you made a *Star Trek* reference," J.T. breathed, with the same joy that some men said, "The Mets beat the Yankees."

"I can feel my DNA mutating," Tess muttered. "I'm going outside." To Nico, she added, "Stay away from the windows or I *will* flush it."

He nodded like a bobble head, then got quiet as Tess pulled out and examined her weapon. Given what a quivering mess he had been when she'd gone over to J.T.'s to drive him up here, she couldn't believe how stupid he'd been to use his phone when she had expressly forbidden it.

The Palmieri gene pool, Tess thought. *Not very deep.*

Porch light off, door open, out she went. Cat should be on her way, so she'd keep a lookout for her. The neighborhood was fairly secluded but there was still a bit of traffic from people at the end of their work days. She wasn't sure how to quantify when this workday had actually started. Or even what case she was on.

Hang on, Angelo, she thought.

A streetlight cast a glow on the house's cement walkway, which connected to the sidewalk. There were bushes and trees everywhere, and fences and the echo of a couple of barking dogs. She kept her gun drawn but down at her side. Listened carefully for anomalies between the surges of traffic. Looked back at the house. If someone was watching, she didn't want to get too far away. She retraced her steps and went the other way.

There was a glint of metal in one of the bushes fronting the next house over. Could be a tricycle or a sprinkler head or a .357 Magnum.

Soundlessly, she melted into the foliage and threaded her way in that direction. And just as soon as she had gone maybe ten feet, she *knew* she was in trouble. At that precise instant, someone jumped down from the tree above her, clipping her, sending her to the ground. *Keep the gun*, she told herself as she saw stars, then burst into action. The jumper would be disoriented, too, for one or two seconds. She grabbed that advantage and rolled as she fought to regain her equilibrium.

She flopped over onto her front, then pushed herself up to a standing position with knees flexed. Her assailant bounced back up and darted into the trees. Tess extended her arms and spread her legs, making a tripod to support her weapon.

"Stop. Come out. Or I'll shoot," she declared.

Her attacker's answer was a bullet. It missed Tess and she didn't pay any attention to where it hit. She stayed small but mobile, hauled ass behind a tree trunk, and worked very hard not to return fire in a residential neighborhood.

She held her breath so he—or she—couldn't hear her panting. Then she let her air out very slowly despite the protest of her lungs. One person had attacked but there could be others. There could be one behind her right now, in fact. As swiftly as a competitive swimmer drew breath, she looked over her shoulder. Darkness. There were no lights on in the other house. In fact, it looked to be abandoned. Good news; that would give her more leeway to discharge her weapon without the fear of harming civilians.

Her primary goal had to be protecting Nico. Secondary was capturing her attacker. She had to know if someone was after the kid—someone who would try again even if she fended them off this time. But if this was some weird random street crap and some unfortunate gangbanger had just attacked an armed police office, she had to know that, too.

Since Nico was number one, she checked over her shoulder again and ran backwards between the two houses, with the intention of moving to the back door of the safe house and securing her witness. J.T. wasn't armed, which appeared to be a good thing. It wouldn't be good for their relationship if he shot her when she came in barreling back in.

She held her breath again, listening as her feet made very soft swishing noises through the grass. She'd played cops and robbers with her five brothers during her entire childhood. That early training had come in handy, since all of them had joined the police force. And it was handy now, as she stealthily approached a wooden fence and dropped down into a crouch as the gate opened.

She waited a beat. Then, as a crouching guy in a ski mask slunk out, she leaped to her feet and put the barrel of her gun to his temple.

"Who sent you?" she whispered.

He swore, also in a whisper. She preferred not to shoot him so she got ready to knee him... just as a bullet zinged past her ear and slammed into the fence.

The first bullet was followed by a second and then things got a little confusing until she heard Cat shouting, "Tess! Tess!"

Then Cat was bending over her with something dark on her fingers. Probably blood; Tess said, "Whose is that?" as she scrambled to her feet... and nearly fell over.

"Whoa." Cat grabbed hold of her. "Yours. Were there two?"

"That I know of."

"I fired at two guys. They got into a black truck without plates. They're gone," Cat said, clasping her by the wrist. "Nico and J.T. are safe."

"Did I get shot?" Tess asked in disbelief. Her shoulder stung. "Who were they? Did you get anything?"

"Nothing," Cat said. "I should have come sooner." Her voice was strained. "I'm sorry."

"For what? Saving my life?" Tess touched her jacket. Her

fingers came away wet. She said something her mother would not have approved of and huffed. "Oh, man. I *did* get shot."

"Well, you're up and walking, so you must have been grazed."

"Where are all the concerned neighbors?" Tess asked rhetorically.

They went in the back way, as Tess had originally intended. When J.T. saw her, he went chalk-white.

"You're hurt." He began to sway.

"Are you going to faint?" she asked him. "Sit down and put your head between your legs."

"I'm not going to faint," he insisted. Then he fell down heavily into his chair at the dining room table.

"I'm sorry. I'm so sorry," Nico said. "I only called the once."

"Let that be a lesson to you." J.T. glared at him.

"We have to get out of here *now*." Cat said. "They might come back." She said to Tess, "Are you okay?"

Okay *enough* was what she meant, and Tess nodded. "Let's go."

"I'll take Nico this time, to mix it up," Cat said. "This just got more complicated because we have to find a new safe house. I guess a motel."

"You can go ahead and flush my phone down the toilet," Nico said. "Please."

Cat looked baffled. Tess understood the headshake J.T. gave her and said, "I'll explain later. Let's just go."

J.T. opened the passenger door and helped Tess sit down. Her shoulder was burning but her arm was completely functional. She fumbled around for the first-aid kit in her glove compartment and opened a package containing a gauze pad with her teeth while J.T. slid behind the wheel and started the car. The poor guy was completely unnerved.

"I don't like you getting hurt," he said flatly.

"Do you think it *was* his phone call?" Tess asked.

"Because we still have the phone."

"I don't know anything anymore," he grumped. "I'd say that would be too much like a spy movie, except that we're already living in a spy movie."

"I'm not hurt," she said. "I'm only grazed."

"Grazed is a subset of hurt. It intersects with you could have died."

"Not from being grazed." She regarded him fondly, then felt a rush of that J.T. mind-control-hotness and began to lean toward him to give him a kiss. Except that it made her shoulder hurt and she didn't want him any more freaked out than he was.

Besides, she had a job to do.

"Hold on," she said.

He looked at her quizzically as she opened the car door, got out, and placed the phone under his right front tire. She stood on the curb and gestured him forward. When he smashed the phone under his tire she exhaled a breath she hadn't realized she had been holding. The phone was history. But she also wished they could have taken it apart like some superspy couple, found the secret tracing chip, and followed it back to the hideout. Then they'd bust in and rescue Angelo DeMarco. She'd have to put on her cape first.

And maybe she was getting a little woozy from bleeding a lot.

"I'm sorry about the phone." Nico was weepy. And tired, scared, out of his element. Cat understood. "Miss Smith *told* me not to use it."

"You need to listen to us. We're trying to protect you," said "Miss Jones." "There are people after you."

Cat just didn't know who they were. It was getting to the point where the bad guys were going to have to take a number.

She and Tess drove back into the city using standard maneuvers to throw off a tail and avoid being boxed in on the road. As far as they could tell, no one was following them. She also knew Tess needed medical attention. Not immediately, but sooner would be better than later.

He sniffled. "I wish I'd never agreed to any of this. I mean, I'm a *musician*. I'm not some cop or anything like that."

"Wait." She was so intent on what he'd just said that she almost took her foot off the gas. "You're a musician. Is that how you met Ms. McEvers?"

"Yeah. She used to come around to the clubs with this dorky guy. He couldn't play for shit."

"What was his name?"

"I don't even remember. I tried to stay away from him because I was afraid she'd try to get me to play with him in return for helping Joey. She and I talked a lot about music but he would be all weird. He was very anti-social."

So he didn't connect Claudia with Angelo DeMarco. Despite her death, the kidnapping itself was still out of the media. That in itself spoke of the power of Tony DeMarco.

"Do you... record?" she asked.

"I've had some studio time. But it's really expensive. Do you play?"

"I played flute until my music teacher paid me to quit." A little white lie that made him smile and like her, which was the point. "What's the name of the studio?"

"Well, there was one called Deodato, and one called Maple."

Maple. A crackle of excitement charged through her like lightning. She remembered that name from their investigation into Angelo's financials. So, she had two hits so far: he, Claudia, and Angelo had seen each other at clubs and he had a recording studio in common with Angelo.

"Do you think you could make a list of the names of the

clubs for me? We want to figure out exactly how Claudia died."

He punched his thigh a couple of times. "But you already know. Those scumbags murdered her!"

"You watch TV, right? We need proof."

"Okay. There's Black, Soundlandia and Mania, Freak, Karmarama…"

"Can you write them down? I'll get you a pen and some paper at the motel."

"Yeah. Oh, Turntable."

When she had pulled up to the safe house, heard the shots, and saved Tess, her adrenaline spike had been off the charts. Now it spiked again. They were getting closer to making some connections, and she was becoming convinced that Robertson and Gonzales had a hand in Angelo's kidnapping. If she could get solid proof that would stick to them like glue, she could get them held on suspicion. If they were the brains, then the kidnapping scheme would fall apart. Their underlings wouldn't know what to do. However, at that point, whoever had Angelo might panic and kill him. Or they might have orders to kill him if things went south.

There were no guarantees that they would spare him even if Robertson and Gonzales continued to operate and his father paid the ransom. Kidnappers were brutal people.

A call came in. Her usual M.O. was to put it on car speaker but Nico would hear it. She glanced at caller ID: It was Tony DeMarco. Never in a million years had she anticipated that he would call her directly.

Composing herself, she put her phone to her ear. "Yeah," she said tersely.

"Detective Chandler, do you know who this is?"

"Yes."

"Can you speak freely?"

"No."

Nico looked over at her. She told herself there was no way

he could have seen her caller ID screen but a wary expression crept across his face.

"Make it so you can."

"Hold on," she said.

Nico was looking scared. She gave him a headshake to let him know the call had nothing to do with him.

She swung into the parking lot of a seedy motel. Tess and J.T. were directly behind her.

"Give me one second," she said to DeMarco.

"I want you to hunker down in your seat so no one can see you," she told Nico as she grabbed her purse, opened her door and climbed out. He did as she asked and she gave him a nod. J.T. was out like a shot. Cat held up a hand.

"I have a call I have to take," she said to J.T., who looked surprised and backed off as she put some space between herself and the rest of their convoy.

"Good girl," DeMarco said.

"I am not your girl," she said. "What can I do for you?"

"Okay, here's the deal. I did something stupid. This morning at dawn. I know it was stupid and I don't want to waste time with you telling me that."

Cat was listening hard. She said, "You made the drop without telling Robertson and Gonzales." *Much less NYPD.*

"Bingo. And no results."

"And you still haven't told Robertson and Gonzales."

"I knew you were a smart girl. Lady."

"Detective," she filled in. "You haven't told them because you no longer trust them."

"I never trusted them. I never trust anybody."

"Yet you called me." She didn't give him a chance to speak. "You can't bribe me. You can't control me. If you want my help you have to let me do my job. And I have to talk to my partner."

"Okay. We'll see where that takes us. So, yeah, I did a

drop. I have a way out of my building that no one else knows about. They thought I was in my bedroom sleeping. So I left and I did it. And… nothing."

"What has changed with Robertson and Gonzales?"

I think they're in on it. When the amount got bumped without warning, I wondered if they were engineering a better payday for themselves, know what I mean?"

"The same thing occurred to us," Cat said. "I'll talk to my partner. I'll get back to you in five minutes."

"I'll give you my private number."

"You could just call me from it so I can capture it," she suggested.

"I need to get to it. Just write it down."

"Okay." She fished in her purse and pulled out a pen and a notepad. She clicked the pen, registering that it wasn't one of hers. She must have picked it up somewhere. "Go ahead."

He rattled off a number. She read it back to him. Then he cut off the call without warning. Cat put the notepad back and clicked the pen to retract the tip, glancing idly at it to see whose pen she'd taken. It had been personalized.

30 YEARS DAVID WHITESIDE!
HAPPY ANNIVERSARY!

It bore the Con Edison logo. Cat wondered where she'd picked it up. Something tugged at her brain.

As she walked back toward the cars, J.T. gave her a wave. He had a phone in his hand.

"Burner phone," he said meaningfully.

Vincent.

J.T. crossed over to her and together they walked a short distance away from her car. Very short. She was getting worried about leaving Nico out in the lot so long; she pulled out her gun and kept it down as she connected. Her ear was immediately flooded with headbanger music that was so loud she felt as if it blasted through her brain and exited through her other ear.

"Cat," Vincent yelled. "Can you hear me?"

"Barely," she said. "I was expecting surf music. Aren't you at Turntable?"

"I was. Guess what was at Turntable."

She crossed her fingers. "Angelo DeMarco."

"The most disgustingly sweet sundaes you have ever had. They're made out of popcorn balls, maraschino cherries, and coconut. And other things."

"Yes!" Cat cried.

"What?" J.T. said. "What's happening?"

She held up her hand to ask for quiet. "And?"

"One of the waiters finished his shift at Turntable and came here to play a couple sets. He's actually a pretty fair bass guitarist. Then he placed a call to a music studio to complain about an overcharge."

She crossed her fingers. "Called Maple?"

"Good sleuthing," he said. "Why do you know that name?"

"Angelo booked studio time there. And so did Nico Palmieri. So maybe that's how the kidnappers put their plan together—they were originally going after the cook to get him to courier drugs for them. Then they decided to move on to Angelo."

"Makes sense." He paused. "Something's wrong. What is it?"

She licked her lips. "We're fine here."

"Catherine, I can tell when you're lying."

J.T. cleared his throat. She'd been so concentrated on what Vincent had been saying that she'd actually forgotten J.T. was there. Not a smooth move for a cop. He was gesturing for the phone and she told Vincent to hold on.

As she handed the phone to J.T., she said, "Remember to speak in code."

"Got it." J.T. took the phone. "Vincent, get over here. Tess has been shot and she needs urgent medical care."

"*J.T.*," Cat said.

"Here." J.T. handed the phone back to Cat.

"There's been *shooting*?" Vincent said. "Were you not going to mention that to me?"

"I was going to get to it." She flashed J.T. an exasperated look. He folded his arms over his chest and raised his chin defiantly. "There was shooting. Tess got grazed. Accent on flesh wound. She's functional and alert. They got away."

"How did they find you?"

"We think it was because Nico used his cell phone, but we aren't sure."

"Tess flattened it," J.T. said to Cat. "The phone."

"Where are you? I'll come check on Tess."

Cat gave Vincent the address, asked him to be careful getting there, and disconnected. J.T. headed back to his car. Cat jogged alongside him.

He scowled at her. "Were you even going to mention to my friend the doctor that my girlfriend was wounded in a firefight?"

"Of course I was."

"*Next week?*"

Catherine let him vent as they returned to the cars. She put her coat over her weapon and she went inside the motel to the desk, requesting an upstairs room "away from the street"—in other words, out of sight—trying not to wince when the desk clerk informed her that she would have to pay for a full hour whether or not she "needed" that much time. She told him he wanted it for the entire night and he scowled.

"This isn't a sting, is it? Are you a cop? Are you going to arrest all my customers just for having a good time?"

"What? No," she said. He hesitated, and she pulled out three twenties, even though the room rate was significantly less. "I just need a place to land."

He took the twenties as if they were dipped in acid, put a twenty in the register and slipped the other two into his pocket. Then he gave her a key and said, "I'm trusting you."

You're trusting my money, she thought.

She and J.T. moved the cars around to the back of the building. She pulled her car right up to the stairway; Tess herded Nico and J.T. up to the first floor and hustled everyone inside.

She told Tess about the call and Tess's reaction mirrored hers—relief that they might be out from under Robertson and Gonzales's thumbs, anxiety that if they went that route, they had to go off the books again. As for getting cozy with DeMarco, that didn't bother her much, either, so at least they were agreed on that. They had their principles, and DeMarco wasn't going to be able to buy them.

Then she showed Tess the pen and Tess's mouth dropped open. She took it from Cat and clicked it on and off, on and off, until Cat's mouth dropped open too.

"Do you think this is one of Bailey Hart's pens?" Cat said.

"When he fell backwards, and all his pens and stuff fell on the floor, I might have scooped this one into your purse," Tess said. "So what's *he* doing with a pen from an anniversary party for this David Whiteside at ConEd?"

"That name is really familiar," Cat mused.

Tess's eyes widened. "Wait. I saw him on TV at J.T.'s. David Whiteside is high up in the Electric Operations divisions of ConEd. He was being interviewed about the blackout and he kept saying that his team would figure out what had gone wrong."

Cat took up the thread. "Bailey Hart's alarm system went to hell during the blackout and there was all this programming to make it go off later. Which might mean that he knew the blackout was coming because he was in contact with David Whiteside."

Cat clicked the pen. "I'll bet you anything that David Whiteside is gone. And that we'll never see Bailey Hart again."

"Alpha niner correcto," Tess said, grinning, and they both went into the motel room.

CHAPTER TWENTY-THREE

2 A.M.

After Vincent tended to Tess's wound, they left the fleabag motel. At his suggestion they took Tess and Nico to his houseboat; then he went to J.T.'s to meet up with him and Cat just as Tony DeMarco showed up. Vincent still wasn't convinced they should be doing this and there was cold comfort in the fact that no one else was certain it was a good idea, including Tony DeMarco. They were all just one big happy circle of uneasiness. But Vincent had danced with the devil before, and he was sure he would again.

"This is nice," Tony DeMarco said as his two bodyguards inspected J.T.'s home. He was bending over petting Mr. Boston White Sox, who was a pretty cute cat, Vincent had to admit. "What happened to the wall?"

Catherine also looked at the large, jagged hole that Vincent had made when he had lost his temper. Of course, she didn't know that he had done it, and he couldn't cop to it while the crime lord was there.

"I hit it with my baseball bat during the blackout. There used to be a wall sconce over there." J.T. pointed to the other chunk that had been taken out near the front door—the one that he had actually done. It was good of J.T. to cover for Vincent, but he knew he should tell Catherine the truth at some point, and he would.

"If you ever want a job as a bodyguard, you just let me know," DeMarco said. Vincent could tell by DeMarco's heartbeat that he wasn't kidding.

Robertson and Gonzales had been very unhappy that DeMarco had informed them he was going "out" for a while and refused to tell them where. He agreed to remain in contact via cell phone. Then he and his bodyguards drove all over the city to shake any tail they might have put on him. Without his knowledge, Cat had asked Vincent to trail after DeMarco as well to make sure that he wasn't being followed by the Feebs.

"Tell me again how they were able to contact you directly," Cat said.

He shook his head, not to refuse, but in apparent disbelief. "Email. Sent straight to me from Angelo's laptop, which is in his room."

"It could have been programmed to send at a specific time," J.T. said. "If I had access to it…"

"Let's focus on this," DeMarco said.

"Okay," J.T. said, "let's see what we can do."

DeMarco took a seat beside J.T. at computer command central. Cat was bent over his shoulder, and Vincent stood beside her. One of the bodyguards was holding Mr. Boston White Sox, who was purring.

The crime lord handed J.T. a flash drive and J.T. plugged it into his computer.

Against the orders he had received from the kidnappers, DeMarco had dared to place a camera in a tree in order to record the drop. As the recording began to play, they were looking at a jogging figure from the back—sweats beneath a heavy jacket, gloves, hat. The figure slowed and walked toward an empty park bench that seemed to float on a snowdrift. Then he turned his face toward the camera, and it was obvious to Vincent that it was DeMarco.

The bench was already clear of snow and he sat down as if to rest. With his shoe, he dug a hole in the snow. Then he stopped, took a deep breath, pulled a small brown paper bag from his pocket, and buried it.

"You can't fit a million and a half dollars into a bag that small," Cat said.

"It's jewelry," DeMarco bit off. "Worth a million and a half."

Vincent watched Catherine think that over. She said, "You need to describe it. If they try to fence it, we could get a bust."

"Family heirlooms," DeMarco said. "A cameo from Sicily, which is the least valuable monetarily, but it means the world to me. Then they told me to put loose diamonds I had in a locket. Also very sentimental."

"The diamonds or the locket?" Catherine asked.

"It's cloisonné, enamel, you know? Of the Madonna and Child. Very religious. My great-great grandmother's. I gave them to Hallie, but only to wear. They'll go to Angelo's wife someday. If he..." Tears rolled down his cheeks. "If he gets married."

The man's sorrow was genuine. He was terrified for his son.

Then he added, "That's why I think Robertson and Gonzales may be in on it. They saw Hallie wearing both those pieces. And a guy like me always has loose diamonds around, you know what I mean?" He wiped his eyes. "She's not my most successful marriage. She's kind of a lush, actually. A drinker."

"She's scared," Catherine told him frankly. "She knows she's in over her head and she doesn't know what to do."

There was a beat. Then he said, "Did she tell you that?"

"Not in words," Catherine replied. "You may want to have a talk with her."

"Maybe I could buy her out." Then he raised a hand. "Okay. Here it comes."

They kept watching. For a moment the frame showed nothing. Then a shadow in the left-hand corner announced the approach of another individual. A man came into view. He was wearing a jacket with "Mets" across the back and a ball cap. As he sat on the bench, he kept his head down. Catherine groaned in frustration.

He was holding a box of popcorn. He tossed out a few kernels and a tree squirrel approached in that stop-motion way that forest animals moved. A second squirrel joined it, and then a third. The man kept tossing popcorn kernels. Then he "dropped" the box, and as the squirrels dive-bombed toward it, he leaned down and rapidly dug the brown sack out of the snow.

He began to rise. His head was still down.

"No," Catherine said.

"Wait for it." DeMarco leaned forward toward the screen.

Suddenly a little girl ran over to the cluster of squirrels. She clearly startled the man and he looked at her, displaying a three-quarter profile to the camera. He was very young with dark hair, and he had a piercing on his upper lip and eyebrow. He caught himself, raising his hand toward his ball cap and tugging on it, effectively concealing his face again. On the back of his hand was a tattoo of what could be an octopus.

J.T. selected the image and pasted it into the square so that the Homeland Security imaging system had a reference to search against.

"Wait." Catherine looked hard at DeMarco. "Let's go over this one more time. If we get a name and address, you're going to let us go in. Us, not you."

"One chance," he said, "and then I take over."

Vincent was amazed that Catherine was doing this. Surely she didn't believe DeMarco? He wanted to tell her that the man was lying. His heart was thundering.

"Once chance is better than no chance," she said. "Okay, J.T."

He gave the software the "go" command and it imprinted its grid over the face, triangulating thousands of variables in its search for a match. The system took over while everyone watched. Vincent noted that Catherine's heartbeat was steady, given the circumstances. He would have expected her to be far more excited.

She doesn't believe we're going to find a match, he thought.

Sure enough, about a minute later, NO MATCH came up on the screen. J.T. exhaled and DeMarco let out a few choice curse words. He reached for the flash drive and J.T. ejected it.

"Thanks for nothing," DeMarco said.

"We have leads," Catherine said. "We'll see if this takes us anywhere." When he nodded as if he didn't believe a word she was saying, she added, "Don't do any more drops without telling us, and don't let Robertson and Gonzales know you talked to me."

"Got it," he said. He put the jump drive in his pocket. He was about to go when Catherine gestured to him.

"Mr. DeMarco, can we speak privately for a moment?"

He looked around the room, gaze landing on his bodyguards, who were both playing with Mr. Boston White Sox, and shrugged. Then he followed Catherine into the bathroom and she shut the door. Vincent sharpened his auditory system, and he could hear them perfectly:

"Claudia McEvers worked for Curt Windsor some time ago. We have found some connections between your son and that family. Do you have any idea why?"

DeMarco's pulse quickened. "My son? What do you mean?"

"He had a picture of Curt's daughter Tori Windsor hidden away. And he's about to inherit a lot of money from Tori's mother's estate."

DeMarco's heart beast faster. "This is private family business. It doesn't have anything to do with his kidnapping."

"How can you be so sure?" Catherine asked. Her heart was beating faster too, and Vincent smiled faintly. She was enjoying tracking her prey, just as he would. Her quarry was answers and, ultimately, Angelo DeMarco.

"I just am." There was silence, and then a long, heavy sigh. "I can't tell you what you want to know. It would just open Angelo up to more danger. Don't ask me about this again."

The crime lord came out of the bathroom and headed out with his bodyguards, who handed off Mr. Boston White Sox to J.T. As Catherine walked back into the room, Vincent said, "I heard. So we're stuck?"

Catherine smiled. "Only half stuck." She turned to J.T. "Okay, let's do it for real. Hopefully we'll get a match."

Vincent laughed. They hadn't let him in on the scheme to fool DeMarco. J.T. saw his surprise and said, "Wait. It gets better. Did you see that thing on the back of mystery man's hand?"

"The tattoo?" Catherine said.

"It's not a tattoo. It's a rubber stamp. They use it at Turntable on people who aren't old enough to drink."

"All right, J.T.," Catherine crowed. "So this guy's been to Turntable. And we have his picture. If the system comes up empty, we can show it around at the club."

"Exactly. However, we'll get a match if this guy is in the database," J.T. reminded her.

They waited.

There was no match.

"This is for real," J.T. said. "Not the faked result for DeMarco."

"Not a problem," Catherine said determinedly. "Can you print out some copies of his face? We'll take them to Turntable and I'll also see if I can develop our lead on whoever was in the alley when Claudia was killed. The popcorn-smell guy." She turned to Vincent. "Can you watch Nico for us, so Tess can come to the club with me?"

"Sure." He grew somber. It was time to come clean about what he had done to J.T. "Catherine, listen," he began.

But she didn't hear him. She was collecting printouts of the guy's picture from J.T. while at the same time phoning Tess, planning to meet up at Turntable. J.T. glanced over at him and must have read the look on his face.

J.T. gave him a headshake and said, "Dude. It's all good."

It wasn't, but Vincent understood that there was a time and a place for confessions, and this was neither. Then Cat was kissing him and sailing out the door, asking him to hurry back to the boat basin to relieve Tess of Nico-duty so Tess could join her.

After she left, J.T. said, "It's forgotten, Vincent."

"It's not, J.T.," he said.

Then there was a ding from the computer speaker. J.T.'s eyes flicked to the screen.

"Oh, man," he muttered. "Vincent." Vincent came over and looked where J.T. was pointing. Bob Reynolds had been spotted in a gas station about halfway to the Canadian border.

"You have to protect Nico," J.T. said nervously. "You can't leave."

Vincent was quiet for a moment. "You could watch him for me. As a favor."

J.T. cleared his throat. "The biggest favor I can do for you is tell you no. So… no."

Vincent pursed his lips. "Then you give me no choice."

Without another word, he went out the door.

* * *

3 A.M.

Cat and Tess had no luck at Turntable with the photograph of the guy with the octopus stamp, despite several kids verifying that they'd seen him around. Just as they were considering giving up, a heavily pierced girl bounced up to them breathlessly and said, "I think I saw him with this guy. Older guy. Creepy."

"Can you describe him?" Cat asked.

The girl thought a moment. "He looked pissed off. He had a weird mark on his cheek. The older guy."

It had to be Robertson. Cat suppressed her exuberance. "Where on his cheek?"

The girl shifted her weight. "Um, like here." She touched her cheekbone. "Or... underneath it." She made a pout of apology. "I don't remember."

"Thanks. That's very helpful. Do you happen to know either of their names?" Tess asked.

She shook her head. "Oh, wait. I also saw the guy in the picture with Angel."

"Angel. The guitarist." Cat looked at Tess. She could feel dots connecting and it was a good feeling. She couldn't see the big picture yet, but it was almost there.

The girl rolled her eyes. "Wannabe guitarist. He's terrible."

"Seen him lately?" Tess asked her.

"Angel?"

"No. But I haven't been looking." She smiled like a little puppy. "Do you guys think you could buy me a hamburger or something? I kind of don't have any money."

They got her a burger and left. As they climbed into Cat's car, Cat handed Tess her phone and said, "I keyed in

DeMarco's private number. Why don't you call him and ask if Robertson is there? If he and piercing guy have been seen together… we're overdue to look at his house anyway."

"Got it."

Tess called. Robertson was at the penthouse, and DeMarco wanted to know why Tess was asking. Tess said, "Mr. DeMarco, is Robertson married? Is he living with anybody?"

"No. *Why?*"

"Anyone likely to be home?"

"I don't know. *Why?*"

"I just want to know. And please don't get your hopes up."

DeMarco told her that Robertson was divorced, but got the house in the settlement. He made sure they had the correct address and gave her the burglar alarm code. He promised to keep an eye on Robertson while they searched.

"You need muscle, honey? I can help out."

"No, Mr. DeMarco. No, no, no. And I am not a honey, sir." Tess smiled and shook her head as she ended the call.

"Do you think this is too much of a long shot?" Cat asked her.

"It's either check this out this or, I dunno, *sleep*," Tess said. She looked down at her shoulder. "And bleed."

"Maybe you should have stayed at the houseboat."

Tess made a *pfft* noise at her. "If this is the real deal, and they have Angelo at Robertson's house, we *do* call for backup. If we save him, Captain Ward will love us and we can fill in all the blanks about incorrect procedure when we need to."

"Agreed."

About forty-five minutes later, they had arrived in a beautiful wooded section of Westchester that had very few houses, all of them big.

"So this is *casa* bad guy," Tess said, and she let out a low whistle.

Before them stood a hefty two-story house with a mansard

roof shingled with slate, white wood exterior, and an attached solarium. By mutual unspoken agreement, Cat and Tess followed a slippery brick walkway around the side of the house. A redwood gate was partially open, and they peeked through.

"No, there *is* not a putting green," Tess murmured as she stared at a little flag sticking out of the snow.

"Or a swimming pool," Cat added, gesturing to a kidney-shaped pool adorned with a natural-rock formation waterfall. It was covered for the winter.

"We got jobs with the wrong agency," Tess muttered.

"There's no way he bought all this on an FBI agent's salary."

"Rich wife? DeMarco?"

"Or both," Cat said. "But I think what bothers me most is that he's not even trying to hide it. He's *flaunting* it. He must have a solid alibi to explain all this. And protection that will back him up if he's ever called on the carpet to defend it."

She looked around for the burglar alarm box and found it on the other side of the fence, half-concealed by bushes dusted with powder. A deep breath, and she punched it in, half-expecting that DeMarco had sent them on a fool's errand, although she didn't know why he would do it. Then she typed in the key code for the door. If DeMarco had all this information, why hadn't *he* checked Robertson out?

Then Tess said, "Someone's coming."

Cat cracked open the door and slipped inside, sliding against the wall so that Tess could follow. Cat heard footsteps. And then a man's voice.

"Yeah, some kid at the club. Had piercings. I don't know why they were looking for him. This stupid kidnapping couldn't come at a worse time for us. Yeah, that *was* close. I still say we should have taken the body with us. We'd have figured out where to dump her. Okay."

Cat slowly let out her breath. Either he'd hung up or walked out of earshot. Whichever was the case, they had to get out of there. She tapped Tess's hand and Tess tapped back. Very slowly and cautiously the door cracked open, and Tess stepped out. Cat followed.

They fled back to the car, got in, and glided away. Not until they had put a sizable distance between themselves and Robertson's house did either of them speak.

"Whoa," Tess said. "So this is what I heard: first of all, that was not Robertson in the house."

"I concur," Cat said.

"The guy had either been at the club when we were, or someone tipped him off that we were there. He and his accomplice don't know who that kid is, either. So they didn't participate in the drop. So they aren't in on the kidnapping. And they killed Claudia." She grunted. "The Claudia part is the part I'm the least sure of."

"I think you're right," Cat said. "Tess, what if Robertson and Gonzales are only involved in drug dealing? They may be genuinely trying to solve Angelo's abduction."

"When crimes collide," Tess said. "So Claudia was trying to help Joey and got murdered for that? And the fact that she was working for Windsor... I don't know, Cat, what do you think?"

"Angelo definitely has connections with the Windsors. But what if he didn't *know* that Claudia had worked for them? What if that was just a weird coincidence, like Vincent suggested?"

Tess considered. "But that girl described an older, creepy guy our young piercings guy was with. With a cheek thing."

"We just assumed it was Robertson."

Tess's phone rang. She pulled it out and said, "Hey, J.T. Oh, God." She looked over at Cat. "There's been a sighting of your father. He's at the border. J.T. thinks Vincent may have gone after him."

Cat gripped the wheel. She was about to say something

when two headlights on bright roared right up behind her, momentarily blinding her. The car was gaining, inches from her bumper; she put her foot to the floor and blew out of there. Tess held on tight and shouted "incoming!" as the car moved to the left going at least a hundred miles an hour.

Tess looked into the side mirror. "I think I see a gun!"

If their attacker was going a hundred, Cat pushed it to a hundred and five. Tess drew her weapon and turned around in her seat.

"Roll down the window," she said, aiming.

As they crested a rise, Cat saw a semi in the oncoming lane. She honked her horn to warn it and zoomed past it. Tess shouted, "Whoa!" and Cat braced herself for a horrible explosion of metal when the truck hit their pursuer.

The explosion did not come.

"Bad guys barreled off the road," Tess said. "Truck is fine. Go, go, go!"

Cat flew.

I made it.

Gabe swapped out Shannon's sedan for his car, worried that the sedan had been made and that she would be targeted. He wrote a quick note that he'd heard a strange scraping sound when he shifted gears, advised her to take it in to be checked, and offered to pay for it.

He checked for more messages from Celeste. Nothing.

Since he was at his office, he went inside and booted up his desktop to see if there were any responses to Reynolds' APB.

Yes.

Gabe's heart skipped a beat. Two beats. He felt dizzy.

Reynolds had been spotted about halfway toward the Canadian border, on a trajectory parallel to the one he just taken.

Gabe was caught completely off guard, exhausted and

shaken. Nevertheless, he made himself the strongest pot of coffee in the history of the DA's office and appropriated a prototype signal booster for his phone, a pet project of the DA. It looked like an extra large thumb drive, and could be plugged into a variety of phone models via a bouquet of connectors. He wasn't exactly sure how it worked, but he knew the DA said it would aid in the capture of targeted cell phone transmissions. Weak cellular coverage was not going to stand between him and Reynolds. It ended here. Now.

In his office, he had some warmer clothes he'd just purchased for an upcoming ski trip—a coat, silk underclothes, some snow boots he'd actually been planning to return because they were too big—and he slipped into as many layers as he could, gathered up anything useful, grabbed water bottles and snacks from the break room, got back in his car, and headed back almost exactly the way he had just come.

I am coming to get you, Gabe thought. He could feel it. *You're done.*

CHAPTER TWENTY-FOUR

I t was gone four a.m. when Cat knocked on Vincent's door. It opened at once, and he stood before in his belted robe. Relief flooded through her and he gave her a pained smile.

"I almost did it," he said. "I almost took off after him."

"But you didn't. Where is he?"

"J.T.'s best guess is that they're on the way to the border."

"I want to go after him too," she said, "but Angelo first."

"Angelo first."

She put her arms around him and kissed him. He lifted her into his arms. Nico was sacked out on his couch and they moved past him toward Vincent's bedroom.

"Nico's dead to the world," Vincent said. "I don't think he's had a decent night's sleep in forever."

"I know the feeling," she said.

Then they were in his bed, and she was in his arms, and after they shared a long, deep kiss, she told him about the night and what they might have discovered. And the car that came after them.

"It could have been the driver on the phone. Or someone

else in the house. Or it might have been some random crazy people. Tess isn't sure she saw a gun. The road was deserted and they didn't hit us. They overtook us and then they began to pull up beside us."

"You shouldn't have taken such a risk," he began, but then he laughed mirthlessly. "And why am I ever bothering to say that?"

"On the phone it sounded like Robertson and Gonzales aren't in on the kidnapping," she said. "The drugs, yes. Definitely."

He looked like he wanted to say something. Instead he put his arms around her for a long time. Finally he said, "You're quivering."

She smoothed back her hair. "I'm just loaded with adrenaline. And not sure of my next step."

"Remember that girl at the diner? Something was up with her. She was nervous."

"Yes. She was." She started to pull out of his embrace. "I wonder if she's got the breakfast shift today."

"The diner won't be open yet. You need to sleep, Catherine. I can track her..."

"I'll grab a few hours, and then I'll go."

He lay her on her stomach and began a slow massage as he took her clothes off one by one, gentling her like a distressed animal. She sighed and moved her shoulders. "I wonder what time Mars opens."

"Earth to Catherine. Ssh," he urged.

She kept seeing the headlights in her rearview mirror. Hearing Tess say, "I think I see a gun."

"At least lie still," Vincent insisted.

Next she saw her father in his cell, telling her that he had set Vincent up to keep him from killing her. "Because he will. Beasts only get worse. I *know*. I helped create them. Don't be fooled, Catherine. *He will kill you*."

"Catherine," Vincent said gently. "Try to relax."

His fingertips trailed along her arms like pieces of silk.

He is gentle.

Every day, he's getting better.

"Ssh," Vincent said again.

Tess knocked very softly on J.T.'s door, bargaining with herself that if he didn't hear her first attempt, she would go home. She didn't want to wake him up. But the door opened at once, and a fully clothed J.T. practically sagged against the doorjamb with relief.

"You've been worrying about me," she said.

At first he shook his head, but then he looked abashed. "I know you're a cop. I've accepted that. But... yes, I do worry. All the time."

Her smile was gentle and appreciative. "It's nice to be worried about."

"Worried *sick*," he said. "DeMarco coming here, and you two zooming off like—like Thelma and Louise—"

"They died." She decided not to tell him about what had just happened on the way back from Westchester. She was still trying to decide what actually did happen.

Mr. Boston White Sox approached, mewing, and Tess picked him up and cuddled him against her chest. "Are you going to stay up programming? If you don't mind my staying here, I am about to fall over."

"Mind," he echoed. He took her hand and led her toward the bedroom.

"Do you want to know about the case?" she asked him. *Except for the scary part?*

"Later," he said.

And opened the bedroom door.

* * *

Breakfast at Mars.

A large part of the cop game was waiting. There was a joke that the surest way to promotion was clocking the most hours in fruitless stakeouts, no-show meetings with confidential informants, and being put on hold. When Cat arrived with the breakfast crowd at the diner, she wasn't surprised to hear that the texting waitress, whose name was Staci, wasn't due for another hour. At this rate, someday Catherine Chandler would be the Chief of Police.

She took the time to go on walkabout outside in the cold, showing the pierced kid's picture to passersby and construction workers. None of them recognized him. Also par for the course in the cop game.

She stopped by the Dumpster, the same one Claudia had been left in. Sometimes Dumpsters were taken in as evidence. Not this time.

"I will get justice for you," Cat whispered. The dead had to depend on the living for justice. Mercy came from another quarter, or so it was said.

After her toes were completely frozen, she went back into the diner, to find Staci behind the counter, pouring coffee. She glanced up at Cat as if she'd been expecting her, and droplets of the fragrant steaming liquid splashed against the rim of the cup she was filling with a jittery hand.

Cat sat down at the counter. Staci walked over to her. "Hello, Staci," Cat said. "I'm Detective Chandler."

"This is about that dead lady in the Dumpster, huh," Staci said.

"I was wondering if you've seen this guy around." She showed Staci the picture of piercings guy. Staci went pale, and Cat added, "He's not a suspect. He's not in any trouble."

Which was a lie, but cops lied to people to solve cases. Even good cops.

"Yeah," Staci said. "I remember his name because I like poetry. There's a poet named Emily Dickinson and he's Paul Dickinson."

A name. Hallelujah. Cat battled the urge to whoop with joy.

"Has he been in lately? Maybe with someone else?"

Staci nodded. "A guy."

"Can you describe that guy?" *Weird thing on cheek? Creepy, older?*

"Yeah. He looked a lot like him. Young, dark hair."

That caught Cat off guard. She fished in her purse for the eight-by-ten glossy of Angelo. Staci nodded.

"That's him. They were in a band or something. They were having a fight. Paul told the other guy that he had to pay the studio what he owed or Paul was going to get fired."

Cat could feel all her nerve endings firing with excitement. She was on the trail. "So Paul worked at the studio." When she nodded, Cat said, "Did he say the name of the studio?"

She smiled a little, no longer nervous. Cat was being friendly and appreciative of her help.

"It was funny because they were eating pancakes and I thought he was asking me for more maple syrup. I knew they had a container on the table so I thought maybe it was empty or dirty or something. So I brought them more and they were *so* confused."

"Maple," Cat said. "That was the name of the recording studio."

"Yeah."

That shifty kid, she thought. *Befriending Angelo to get in on a kidnapping, really?*

"Do you know either one of them very well? Maybe you've texted them or you've seen them on your social media, something like that?" "No." Staci cheeks turned pink. "I kinda hoped but nada." *You are very lucky,* Cat thought. She put down a couple of dollars for the coffee she had yet to order and left.

As she walked to her car, her phone rang. It was Captain Ward.

"Yes, sir," she said.

"Just got a call from Agent Hendricks. He said you wanted to have a meeting with him and as it happens, he has some more things he wants to talk to you about."

Her body buzzed. *What things? Is this about the APB on my father?*

"I'm on my way in right now. I'll be there in fifteen minutes but I'm not sure when my union rep can make it," she said pointedly. But there was no way in hell she was going to wait for him.

"I'll sit in with you," he said. "If he's out of line, we'll stop."

Bingo. That was what she wanted. Although she was glad he was finally acting like her captain, she wasn't reassured. That couldn't matter right now.

"Okay," she said.

She called Tess and told her what she'd found out about the diner. And about IA.

Tess said, "If Ward doesn't back you up you need to do something, Cat. Okay? Seriously."

"Got it."

"And Paul Dickinson's got an employee locker at Maple. I'm thinking we don't get a warrant because we can't explain how we know to look at him."

"Right." Cat unlocked her car. "Charm the receptionist at the studio like you do. If it's my friend the career counselor compliment her on her hair."

"I will. So this is how I see it," Tess said. "R and G are involved in a crime we haven't even mentioned, and might not be involved in the one we've stopped sharing information with them about. But they still might have tried to kill us last night. Go figure. Let me know what happens at the precinct. Cyanide, while painful, is quick."

"Happy hunting."

Ding.

There was a second hit on the APB and Gabe was certain that any second, an announcement would go out that Reynolds had been apprehended. Gabe was desperate to get to him, but equally anxious about his own safety. Once Reynolds was in custody, he would have to ask him about the attack on the lake house. He wanted to know if he was a target now of the secret society.

If Celeste was.

Gabe drove too fast on the icy roads, slowing only when the car began to fishtail. He had rarely been so weary but the caffeine and the adrenaline were like a beast serum, fueling his body, keeping him alert.

He drove on.

"Detective Chandler," Agent Hendricks said. "We have reviewed your footage and we agree that what was sent to us was tampered with."

Cat and Captain Ward sat across from Hendricks in the same interview room where her previous interrogation had taken place. The camera was rolling. Beside Hendricks was a box of gloves and a large paper bag with something in it. She was edgy and skittish, wanting to be done with this, sensing that she might have a long session ahead of her. She noted the lack of an apology.

"We believe that the people who took your father

doctored the recording in order to confuse us," he continued.

"Gee, really?" Cat snapped. Captain Ward shifted uncomfortably beside her and she told herself to take it down a notch.

"However, we intercepted a message we believe your father meant to send to you in secret."

She blinked. "Intercepted? How? Was it a letter..." Her lips parted. "Did you hack my personal email?"

She was not as alarmed as, say, a civilian might be. She and Vincent were extremely careful not to use email, and anything important that she had to share with Tess, she told her face-to-face. Still, it was an outrage.

"That's illegal," she said.

"You know that as you are a member of the NYPD, the definition of protected speech is more... elastic in cases like this," he retorted.

"What did he say? If it was meant for me..."

"We would prefer to hold it for now. However, we would like you to explain this."

With great ceremony, he put on a pair of gloves. Then he reached into the bag.

There was a bundle of brown paper. He carefully unwrapped it, revealing a white T-shirt splattered with blood. Prisoners wore white T-shirts and boxers underneath their orange jumpsuits, so it likely could have belonged to her father. She swallowed hard, waiting to be told if it meant that her father had been injured, possibly killed.

"DNA test results indicate this is your father's blood." He looked at her expectantly. "Have you received other private messages, perhaps demanding money or services in exchange for your father's safe return? Are you under duress, and is that duress compromising your ability to perform your job?"

"No," she said. She grabbed the box of gloves and began

to pull out a pair, but he shook his head.

"I'll retain possession of this. Otherwise there's a break in the chain of custody."

"Are you *kidding*?" she said.

"Chandler," Captain Ward warned.

"Look," Catherine said, "I *arrested* my father."

"Maybe you've had a change of heart. Maybe you've come to regret your actions."

"I haven't," She bit off. "It's not my fault that my father is a criminal. It has nothing to do with me."

"Except… it does. The agents in charge of the DeMarco kidnapping have expressed some concern over these developments."

How do they even know about these developments?

She saw where this was headed: Robertson and Gonzales wanted to get rid of her and Tess. She shut her eyes to keep from exploding.

And then she realized that the best thing that could happen to the DeMarco case would be if they *were* released from it. She and Tess were already operating in secret, and the events of last night—and in this interview room—confirmed that they would have to continue to do so. It would be much easier if a clear boundary was established so that they no longer had to decide what information to share and when.

It's much easier for now. *For this case. But what about the rest of my life? My career?*

She licked her lips and lifted her chin. "Then my partner and I would like to formally withdraw from this case."

Captain Ward lifted a brow. "Don't you think you should talk to Vargas about this?"

"No. I'm speaking for both of us."

Hendricks said, "I think that's best. Detective Chandler, we would appreciate being notified if your father contacts you again."

Cat couldn't trust herself to speak. She rose and walked stolidly from the room. Captain Ward followed after her.

"We'll figured this out, Chandler," he said. "And for the record, I don't like the DeMarco case and I'm glad we're free of it."

"Thank you, sir." She kept her voice flat and neutral. There was no way in hell she would say anything else, especially on the record. But now she was certain of one thing: whoever had taken her father, they knew about beasts. They hadn't sent that T-shirt as some kind of threat or warning.

They had sent it so Vincent could try to track Reynolds down.

With as much dignity as she could muster, she walked to her desk and sat down. She opened the bottom drawer of her desk to put in her purse and froze.

Inside the drawer lay a dead rat.

CHAPTER TWENTY-FIVE

MAPLE RECORDING STUDIOS

Over the entry door hung a vintage sign of a pin-up girl holding a maple leaf, and it reminded Tess of the jeweled fig leaf on the David statue in the DeMarco penthouse. She shot a picture of the sign and took a moment to calm down. Cat had just called her to tell her what had happened with IA, and Tess was infuriated. She figured Cat had grounds for a lawsuit over the theft of her private email and, meanwhile, she had asked J.T. if he could find a way to retrieve it. He was actually pretty hopeful about it, but that did little to lessen her ire.

We are getting screwed over so many ways it's not funny.

Cat had tossed the dead rat, which was too bad, because Tess could think of so many people who deserved to get it next.

Tess took deep breaths. She had found an address for Paul Dickinson via a reverse-listing for his driver's license. Since his domicile was on the way to the studio she'd dropped by. Turned out it was one of those cold-water walkups shared by stoners, students, and low-wage earners. She hadn't wanted to tip her hand that she was a cop with a professional interest in Dickinson, so she hadn't asked for him specifically. She'd seized on the FOR RENT sign in the apartment next door as her reason for being there and asked them where the landlord was, fell to chatting and listening hard for information about her subject. Turned out Paul had moved out without giving notice and one of the guys had shyly asked her if she'd like to move in. They were pissed off at him because he had split, left half his stuff for them to deal with, and never heard from him again.

After some more chatter they'd urged her to check out the room for rent. She picked up an open notebook from the filthy bedroom floor, in which Paul had sketched himself as a rock star, and among the doodles was a set of numbers and the word *work*.

Locker combination?

She'd memorized the sequence and, as soon as she had left, telling them that she couldn't wait for the landlord to show but she'd be back, she had written the numbers on her hand.

Now she was at the studio, and she *needed* to get into that locker. If she couldn't make it happen with subterfuge, she and Cat had agreed they would fill Ward in, let the chips fall where they may.

Tess walked in to a foyer decorated in black and white with accents of bright blue, yellow, and red. Music was thumping loudly through the wall. There was a very bored young woman at the desk. Tess had expected Cat's phone buddy and career counselor, and she hoped this girl would be even easier to manipulate.

"Hi," Tess said above the noise. "I hope you can help me. My cousin Paul used to work here but, God, he's so crazy, he just enlisted in the army and he didn't get all his stuff before he quit."

"He didn't even," the woman yelled back, and Tess blinked. Was the receptionist calling her on her story? Had she just been busted?

"Didn't even quit," the woman elaborated. "Just stopped coming in. The jerk."

"That *guy*." Tess shook her head. "Well, he gave me his combination and if I could just get his stuff…"

"Whatever. Mrs. Myers was going to cut the lock off anyways."

The receptionist waved a hand toward a door. Tess opened it and went down a hall and into a room with a refrigerator, a microwave, and a row of lockers. One was marked PAUL. Making sure she was alone, she slipped on some gloves and tried the combination.

Open sesame.

Tess let out a whistle. Inside were a T-shirt, a pair of thick winter mittens and some socks, cans of baked beans and tuna, and quite a few plastic bottles containing different combinations of vitamin supplements as well as a prescription anti-anxiety medication. The patient listed on the label was Paul Dickinson.

And there was a picture of Paul with Angelo and a certain scruffy old man. It was the homeless penny-whistle player Tess and Cat had encountered during the blackout. Tess picked up one of the bottles, wondering if this was the medicine the old man had been talking about. Maybe Angelo had paid for all these things for the old guy and Claudia had supplied them. So then Paul stockpiled them and they took them to the old man every once and a while.

Only now, since Paul had turned into a kidnapper, the old man was going without.

In the break room she found a box of gallon-sized plastic freezer bags, put on fresh gloves, and took everything out of the locker. Then she took the lock and peeled off the Paul sticker from the front of the locker. She kept that too.

She thanked the girl and went outside. Her phone rang just as her feet hit the sidewalk. It was J.T.

"Okay, they didn't bother to delete-delete Reynolds' message when they captured it," J.T. said. "What that means is—"

"I know what that means," Tess said. "Go on. What did it say?"

"'It only gets worse.'"

Tess made a face. "Two guesses as to what "it" is."

"Vincent," said J.T.

"Yeah, I'm thinking." Her phone beeped. "Hold on. I have another call."

"Vargas, where the hell are you?" It was Captain Ward. "Did Chandler tell you that you're off DeMarco?"

"Yes."

"So you can resume the investigation into Easy Pickin's. I want you both to go over there now."

Tess bit back the first word that occurred to her because she was raised better than that and said, "You got it, Cap. On my way."

Then she called Vincent.

Gabe was lost.

Correction: Gabe *had* lost.

It was snowing, and he just couldn't go any farther. He hadn't had any real sleep in days; he had nearly been killed, then left in the snow for half the night. He thought he might have a concussion. He was completely done.

He was in the middle of a forest on a tiny road that barely registered on any mapping system. The car kept weaving as he nodded off and he was afraid he was going to hit a tree. He had to surrender and get some rest.

It was bitterly cold out but he couldn't risk running the engine. He piled all his extra clothes over himself, wishing for a blanket, and closed his eyes. The explosion replayed in his mind, and the tear gas, and Celeste. The images shifted in prisms like a kaleidoscope and he felt ill from exhaustion.

I'm probably going to die if I do this.

Just ten minutes.

He set his watch.

No way, Cat thought, as she glanced through the window of Easy Pickin's. Tess was emerging from her car just as Captain Ward pushed through the front door. He saw Cat and gave her a nod.

"Captain Ward," Cat whispered, "what are you doing here?"

The captain gave a wave to the cashier, a bearded man who looked like a gangbanger, and gestured for Cat to wait with him while Tess entered the store. Tess drew up short when she saw their boss and Cat shrugged and gave her head a little shake.

Captain Ward gestured for both of them to follow him past a row of "private viewing booths"—*blech*—and they trooped into a storage room stacked with cardboard boxes and a mannequin dressed in leather bondage gear.

"You'll thank me later," Captain Ward said. "I'm a witness. You are not in contact with your father. You are here with me. By the way, the store owners have agreed to cooperate and you two are going to interview Ralph out there and probably do a search of this storage room. And I'll be here the entire time."

Cat tensed. "Is something happening? Have they found my father?"

"We're here together. Your phone's put away," he said flatly. Tess nodded at him; after years of working together, Cat knew how to read Tess's subtlest gestures: Tess was freaking out. She had yet to tell Cat what she'd found in the locker and now here they were with a babysitter.

Cat's phone rang, and Ward shook his head.

"Don't answer it."

"But, sir," she began.

"*No*," he said. Then he looked at her full on. "Chandler, I'm protecting your career. I may not have appeared to support you in the interview room, but I do have your back." Cat slid a glance at Tess. The wheels were turning, and Tess cleared her throat. She said to Cat, "Drug case."

"You're sure?" Cat said, and Tess nodded.

"We're getting it from all sides," she said. "And if we could get our witness some fulltime protection…"

Cat followed. Tess wanted to free up J.T. and Vincent so they could deal with whatever she had found in the locker. Cat just hoped Captain Ward would still have their backs after they laid out the case for him.

"Okay," Cat said.

Tess faced Captain Ward, and Cat positioned herself next to Tess, to show solidarity. "Sir, we have reason to believe that Special Agent Robertson is running a drug ring. We have a victim we believe was falsely imprisoned at Rikers, and we have a family member who is willing to testify. We did not bring this to you sooner because of the precinct's connection to the DeMarco case, and we were afraid that if we exposed what we knew while were working with Robertson and Gonzales, we would endanger not only ourselves but our witness and the victim."

His shock was impressive. His anger, even more so. He narrowed his eyes and clamped his jaw and said, "Run it down for me. *Fast*."

Half an hour.

Gabe wiped the muzziness from his face as he processed that he had slept through his beeping alarm for twenty minutes. The interior of the car was frigid. He saw his breath in the glow of his phone.

As dangerous as it had been, he was grateful for the extra rest. He wasn't refreshed, but he was functional, which was the best he could hope for at this point. He unwrapped a granola bar and made himself eat it. As he chewed, he examined the APB site for more Reynolds sightings, preparing to note them on his phone's mapping function.

Both of the previous responses had notes appended to them. One said *False sighting*. The other, *Inconclusive*. So was he on a wild goose chase in the middle of an ice forest?

Or are they feeding us false data?

At the same time, his phone signaled that he had an incoming message. He punched open his message window. There was nothing there. Then the signal booster made a strange sound, like electrical pulses on a competing channel. Perplexed, he flipped to his message screen again.

A string of gibberish had appeared in the text box, numbers and letters and emoticons... but mixed within the garbage were what appeared to be mapping coordinates: latitude and longitude.

Am I intercepting something?

He checked the map. If he applied the numbers as coordinates, then whoever was transmitting was at an inn thirty miles due west of his position. Had the signal booster made this data capture possible? Keeping it connected to his phone, he gave the object a cursory examination. He mentally replayed the few seconds Celeste had had his phone. Had she done something to it?

He had just survived one trap. Was he so eager to rush into another?

* * *

Tess's goody bag.

Vincent found it just where Tess said she would leave it—in a trashcan close to his houseboat at the 79th Street Boat Basin. He inhaled a world of scents, including Angelo's, and nodded to himself as he closed it back up and called J.T.

J.T. recognized Cat's ringtone and picked up.

He said, "I was wondering when someone would ca—"

"Hi, J.T," Cat cut in. "Okay, here's the deal. I've filled in my captain and he's willing to place our witness in protective custody. We can meet you both at that abandoned subway station on Worth. He understands why we have kept this off the grid and he guarantees he will not pursue any legal action against you."

"Against *me?*" J.T. said. His other line beeped. "Hold on." He took the call.

"J.T., it's Vincent. I want to park Nico with you. Tess left me some evidence and—"

"This is so perfect it's scary," J.T. said. "Cat's on my other line telling me to bring 'our witness' to an abandoned subway station. Worth. She and Tess have told Captain Ward about the drug thing and he's taking Nico into protective custody."

"You're right. It is kind of scary and kind of perfect," Vincent said. "I'm in. I'll bring Nico to you and then I follow you in, protect you. Worth is a good choice. It's dark."

"But what if Nico says something to Ward about *you?*" J.T. asked. "What if he, like, IDs you? He knows where you live. He knows we know each other."

Vincent hesitated. "We can ask him not to. Cat and Tess can say he's wrong if he tries to blow my cover. And if worse comes to worst... I run."

J.T grimaced. "I'm all for saving lives, but this is a huge risk, Vincent."

"And some things are worth the risk. You've risked your life for me for over a decade."

"And I thought it would have gotten easier by now, not harder," J.T. riposted. But he knew they really had no other choice, now that the status quo had changed. "All right. I'll be here."

The abandoned subway station reminded Vincent of the Canal Street station, where he had saved Catherine from a speeding subway train after Special Agent McCleary and his goons had ambushed her. He hoped this wouldn't be a replay of that day.

He kept to the shadows, certain that Catherine knew he was watching over Nico as Captain Ward took custody of him. He saw the way her gaze lasered into the darkness, searching for him. He tried to send her a text message but they were underground. After he was sure the handoff was complete, and Cat, Tess, and J.T were safe, he went above ground and resent it.

Then he headed for the old man's shed, which Tess had described to him. He found it, but the old man wasn't there, and it appeared that his little hovel had been ransacked. The food and sleeping bag Tess had mentioned were gone. His pennywhistle was cracked in half and lying on the frozen ground.

Vincent smelled Angelo and Paul Dickinson everywhere. The Angelo-smell that lingered here was of an Angelo on insulin. He isolated the Dickinson scent from the items Tess had collected from his locker. They mingled on a set of three photographs tacked to the wall.

He caught his breath.

The first photograph featured a slightly younger version of Angelo DeMarco, and of a pretty, red-haired girl:

Tori.

He swallowed hard. Angelo and Tori were sprawled in a grungy room that looked like it was in an old warehouse or factory, and there were stacks of paperback books behind them. Angelo was holding a guitar and Tori appeared to be singing. Her head was thrown back and she was laughing. She had not laughed very often when they had been together. On the back, someone had written *torimacto*. According to Cat, that was Angelo's nickname for Tori.

In the second picture, Tori was posing at the head of a stone corridor with sharp hooks and chains dangling overhead. She was holding her nose and pointing to the hooks. She was pantomiming that something smelly was dangling from the barbs. Meat? Was this a slaughterhouse, maybe a packing plant?

He turned the picture over. There was a scribbled set of numbers. *1293.*

The third picture showed Angelo standing by himself, standing outside a large factory with a falling down sign that read SANT MEAT PACKING. On this one, *Lantus* was written on the back. Lantus was the name brand of a synthetic insulin for type-one diabetics.

Like Angelo.

Vincent looked inside Tess's sack again and found a couple of empty plastic freezer bags. Attempting not to add any more of his own fingerprints to the photographs, he slipped the three pictures into a plastic bag.

He did some Internet searching on his smart phone. Then he texted Catherine again:

Tracking. Santangelo meat packing plant. 1293 Egret.

It wasn't dark out yet. He would have to be carful. Head down, Vincent headed out.

* * *

Fisherman's Inn wasn't an inn at all. It was a cheap motel that had never seen better days and never would see them. A white panel van was parked not in the lot but about twenty feet down a snow-encrusted path. Aside from the dead desk clerk and the sentry stationed at the front door of room 103, Gabe was the only person within fifty feet of the motel.

Except for Bob Reynolds, who was tied to a chair inside room 103.

Gotcha, Gabe thought, as he moved around a pine tree and drew his Beretta.

A branch cracked behind him.

CHAPTER TWENTY-SIX

After Captain Ward, Tess, and Cat returned from Worth Street, Pamy approached the group with a sticky note and held it out toward Cat. Captain Ward intercepted the little square of yellow and said, "Who is Shannon Richardson? Oh." He read the note. "*Detective Chandler, ADA Lowan borrowed my car. Left a msg that something's wrong w/it? I tried to call him but his phone makes this weird clicking noise. Can you ask him to call me?*"

"Thanks, Pamy," Cat said. Obviously the woman didn't know that Cat and Gabe weren't on speaking terms. Cat did think it very strange that Gabe had borrowed her car, and hadn't even had the good graces to—

Reynolds. Gabe's gone after him.

One look at Tess, and Cat knew that she was thinking the same thing. Cat said, "Well, Captain, we're closing in on end of shift and I'm wondering if you plan to maintain surveillance on me?"

"We are bringing you a beautiful drug case," Tess reminded him. "You have our witness in protective custody. How is he, by the way?"

"You are bringing me the possibility of a drug case. So far all

I have is hearsay evidence," he countered. "And… he's scared."

"Tess, please call our union rep for me right now," Cat said.

"You got it, partner." Tess pulled out her phone.

"I'm doing this to protect you," Captain Ward said.

Oh, my God, he sounds just like Gabe. And my father. Maybe they're working together.

Her lips parted. Maybe they *were*.

"Cat? Are you okay?" Tess said.

Stress and exhaustion and suspicion tugged at her. But shooting straight through it all were her priorities: *Keep Vincent safe, find Angelo DeMarco alive.*

"Place the call," Cat said, and Captain Ward raised his hands in the air as if she were holding him at gunpoint.

"Okay. Backing off," he said. "If you get any emails that incriminate you—"

"That *appear* to incriminate her," Tess said.

"File your paperwork," he snapped, and walked away.

Once he was out of earshot, Tess said, "Oh, my God, is Gabe MIA? What's going on?"

"I don't know." Cat pulled out her burner phone. "Tess, Vincent sent me a message. I think he's found where Angelo's being held." She texted him back *on our way* but the message was undelivered.

Then Tess's phone rang. "It's J.T.," she said. She put the phone to her ear. "Yeah, hi, babe, *what?* Oh, my God, are you all right? I'll be right there."

She was a blur of movement as she grabbed her purse, hat, and gloves. "Someone roughed him up," Tess said. "He's at his place."

"What? Who?"

"Two guesses," Tess said. "Agents Ass and Hat."

"Go," Cat urged her. "I'll catch up with Vincent."

Tess was halfway to the door. "Call me."

"Same. Let me know how he is."

Tess had just made it out the door when Captain Ward planted himself in front of Cat. "Where did Detective Vargas go just now?"

"A C.I. she's been developing just called in," Cat improvised. "He's afraid he's been made and he wants an assist."

He pursed his lips and raised his brows, the perfect picture of skepticism. "And you stayed behind to do the paperwork."

She took a breath. "Yes."

"Good. Because I'm staying late tonight. So I'll be here when you finish it."

He's here, Vincent thought. *I can smell him.*

Most illnesses brought with them odors that a beast could detect—part of a predator's arsenal was its ability to cull a sick animal from the herd—but doctors also learned that some diseases carried with them a detectable smell. Diabetes was one of these. And Vincent caught that scent now, in the air.

But it was the scent of a diabetic on insulin, which was different.

The compassionate doctor inside Vincent rejoiced. Whatever else was going on, Angelo DeMarco probably wasn't puking his guts out, or in a diabetic coma. Someone had shown him mercy by increasing the shelf life of their captive.

So Paul and any co-conspirators—Vincent could tell there were other people in the vicinity—had not followed through on their threat to murder Angelo. He would be dead by now if they hadn't dosed him.

But that was just one of many things that didn't add up. The inertia of ransom demands, the awkward drop and retrieval... a scarcity of leads and then a set of "clues" so obvious that they might as well as written the address of the

Santangelo Meat Packing Plant, abandoned since the 1930s, in neon. Not to put too fine a point on it but this whole situation smelled. He had begun to think it was a smoke screen for Robertson and Gonzales' drug activities, but he couldn't figure out exactly how.

That was why he had ditched the car on the outskirts of the gutted factory district of Washington Heights—block after block of derelict buildings that reminded him of the training grounds where he and his buddies in Special Forces had run a hundred simulated ops until they could complete their missions without "dying."

The warehouses on the next block were in even worse shape, featuring rows of broken windowpanes and blasted-out loading doors. Beer bottles, cans, paper napkins and trash were mixed into the snow like buried treasures.

He felt his burner phone vibrate. It could only be Tess, J.T., or Cat. He pulled it out and read a text from Catherine: *there soon.*

He texted back, *No. Stay away.*

He jogged in the shadows. The sun was just going down, slanting on crumbled toward and silos. He heard the sibilant whoosh of tires on asphalt. Four blocks behind him, a car moved very slowly down the street. Its lights were off. Vincent ducked behind a rusted-out mailbox and held his breath. A sentry on patrol? Had he been spotted?

A thick whirl of snow splotched the top of his head, startling him. It was followed by another. And another. Wind blew snow like ocean waves and then fresh snow drifted down from the sky, weaving itself into the tapestry of odors that told him stories about the ramshackle, forlorn wasteland.

And then the car smell became a diesel smell became a diabetic smell, and he dodged behind a concrete wall beside the mailbox lined with broken glass, walking in a crouch as fast as he could go as the car rolled past him.

The car turned left onto another street. Vincent had to cross the street to keep up, and he wondered if it was a ploy to flush him out of the darkness. They might have infrared trackers on. If so, they probably already knew where he was. He selected the darkest section of the street, the angle of the weak sunlight obscured by the jagged roof of what appeared to be some kind of storage elevator, and blurred across the street. Hopefully anyone who was manning surveillance would assume they had a glitch and lose interest. Maybe they would continue to point at where they had last seen a dark orange human shape, focusing on where he had been, not on where he was.

He blurred until he was pacing the car. It was going very slowly. They had to be looking for cops or maybe DeMarco security. Or maybe even renegade FBI agents out for a private payday.

The car turned right. Alarm bells clanged. Every time he had to cross the street, he was taking another risk of exposure. There could be sentries posted on rooftops. If only they had some idea of the size of the operation that had snatched Angelo. His soldier's reflexes and training served him well as he wove through the deep shadows, and a part of his subconscious traveled back in time to wartime Afghanistan, when he had been turned into a beast. The wilding had come over him and the men and women he served with; they had lost all sense of strategy and coordinated tactical maneuvers and became ravening monsters, like superhuman versions of horror movie zombies.

Only much, much worse.

He zigzagged, a boot crunching down on a can, crushing it. The *pop* of escaping air sounded like a gunshot and his adrenaline spiked. He morphed and the world was doused in a white glow. He heard dripping water and a low-level electrical hum. It was possible they were jamming cell phone transmissions. He couldn't check his phone now; his eyes were on the car.

The vehicle glided like a shark toward an enormous brick building topped with a four crenelated towers like castle turrets. Angling down, it slid aloud into what had to be a garage, and Vincent raced toward it. Then something tripped him—a thin wire stretched parallel the length of the building down the last one-fifth of the street.

I can't believe I didn't see it! he thought angrily as he went flying. As he hurtled through the air he fully beasted out. With a roar he stuck a landing. His ankles screamed but he did not crumble.

Suddenly the car picked up speed and a gate began to zoom down behind it. Still beasted, Vincent roared again and ran full-tilt to make it beneath the plummeting metal.

He was a second too late.

Thousands of volts of electricity rocketed through him. Brain, skull, eyes, groin, toes… heart. Everything was seized and shaken by savage, man-made lightning. Vincent broke into a seizure, completely helpless as continued contact with the gate jetted fresh pulses of electricity through his agonized, fully stressed body.

Then something fell over him—a wire mesh net sizzled and burned him. His body no longer responded to the stimulus. He lay inert, quivering. His mind was gone. The world became one tiny pinprick of platinum light.

And then light was gone too.

Slicing.

Through his shoulders.

Muscle tearing. Searing pain.

The coppery tang of blood. The acrid odor of sweat.

Ice water hit Vincent in the face and he didn't so much

come to as become slightly less unconscious. The very first word that formed in his mind was *Catherine*.

He kept his eyes closed and tried to take a breath.

He couldn't.

His arms were stretched outward and slightly behind his torso, so that his chest was already over-expanded. He was unable to inhale. As he began to suffocate, he opened his eyes.

He saw nothing. Something was covering his eyes. Blindfold. Fabric grazed the deep wounds in shoulders. Hood.

A protesting sound struggled from the upper quadrant of his chest cavity. Then something crashed into him like a bolt of lightning and his body contracted, hard. His spine folded back on itself and bones cracked.

With a mighty animal shriek he became the weapon Reynolds had fashioned him to be. His right arm was suddenly free; then he landed with bare feet onto white-hot coals. Pain seared through him and juiced him with adrenaline. He sprang forward, but the restraint around his left arm swung back onto the coals. The stench of his own burning flesh dosed him with more adrenaline.

"Run! Run!" someone yelled. "He's loose!"

His left arm pulled free and he hurled himself forward, blind. Somewhere in his brain his human intelligence walked Beast-Vincent through the required motions to rip the hood off from his head.

Dungeon, came the word.

He had been locked in a dungeon before. Imprisoned.

His mind conjured the sight of an unconscious, alabaster-white woman with brilliant-red hair. A dead woman, in a dungeon cell with him.

Tori, came her name.

Then Beast-Vincent lost purchase on language and the language of his existence was *Kill*. Mayhem, chaos, destruction: he had zero human awareness as three figures cowered together, then forced open a thick door and disappeared through it. The door closed with a ringing clang.

His blistered feet oozed as he stumbled after them, fists slamming down the on the metal. The muscles in his shoulders clutched. Blood poured down his chest and back. The door held fast. He pounded on it again. Again.

He whirled in a circle, raging, roaring, seeking other prey. He was in a large room illuminated by electric camping lanterns. The bed of coals had been spread beneath a configuration of dangling meat hooks and heavy chains, each of the links an inch in diameter. Supported by the chains, he had been hung from the hooks.

A cattle prod lay on the blood-smeared concrete floor. As Beast-Vincent attempt to pick it up, overwhelming pain and weakness conquered him and he fell to his knees. He began to lose his edge and he became just Vincent again, battered, burned, beaten.

He grabbed the cattle prod as he panted. Despite all the pain, the sensation of breathing freely was what he focused on, rejoiced in.

They'll come back, he told himself. *Move, soldier.*

But he was so hurt, debilitated. He didn't know if he could stand, much less take on any adversaries. He tried to beast out, but instead he only fell forward, landing on the cattle prod as his face hit the concrete.

Get up, get up. If you don't get up you will die.

But Vincent couldn't get up. He could only lie utterly still. And pass out again.

Gabe couldn't believe his luck.

The snapping sound behind him had only been the sound of ice cracking on a tree limb, but faced with an instinctual fight-or-flight reaction, Gabe had chosen to flee—toward the motel, just as chatter from a radiophone covered the noise. He flattened himself against the wall, trying to catch his breath. All his life, until less than two years ago, he had been strong, and agile, and never short of breath.

I chose the wrong path.

I can fix that.

The sentry said something into his radiophone and walked away from the door. He kept talking, turning back around once, then moving on.

Gabe put his hand around the door. Locked. He could shoot the lock but he didn't dare. He didn't know how many people were traveling with Reynolds. He didn't know what their agenda was—why they were restraining the ex-agent, why they had captured him in the first place.

He ran around the other side of the building, to discover that there was a window minus storm shutters. The drapes were pulled back and he could see Reynolds.

And as he turned his head, Reynolds could see him. His eyes widened, and then he smiled very oddly. He mouthed, *Raise the window.*

Gabe was confused. Reynolds moved his head toward the bottom of the sill and Gabe felt along it. He understood: the window was not quite shut. Possibly it had been opened to allow in a little fresh air.

Gabe slid his fingers into the space and pulled upward. He was able to raise the window maybe six inches, and then it stopped, stuck. Gabe applied more pressure; he was so tired.

Another inch.

He heard the squawk of the radiophone. The sentry was returning. He had two choices: retreat and wait for another opportunity, or risk it all.

He risked it.

The window slid up. There was a screen, no doubt left

over from last summer. He pushed it in. It clattered and he winced. So did Reynolds.

Then he climbed in, grabbed the screen, thrust it under the bed, and closed the window.

The door began to open and as Reynolds watched, Gabe rolled under the bed, on top of the screen, and sucked in his breath.

"Here's our Easy Pickin's report," Cat said. She handed him a hard copy. She felt like a student who had been given detention. Captain Ward paged through it at an infuriatingly slow pace, then gave her a nod.

"Tell Vargas I want her to give me a rundown on this C.I. tomorrow," he said. "I need to make sure some of my detectives keep me a little more in the loop."

That would be all your detectives, she thought, but did not say.

"Yes, sir." She remembered the days when they called Captain Bishop "Joe" and "boss" and missed him. She didn't miss his devotion to the cause of bringing in the Vigilante but, pre-Vincent, he had been a good captain. Except for the part about messing around with Tess.

She called Tess now, to ask after J.T. He'd been jumped on his way to teach a class, shortly after the handoff of Nico to Captain Ward. In New York City it was difficult to know if you had been mugged for a reason or mugged just because. While he was shaken and he had some bumps and bruises, he was basically all right. But she could tell that Tess didn't want to leave him. And, given that it was possible that J.T.'s attackers might try again, this time invading his home, Catherine told her to stay put.

"You can be the backup to my backup," Cat said.

Then she got in her car and followed her phone's driving

directions to the street address of the Santangelo Meat Packing Plant, texting Vincent all the way, receiving no response.

"C'mon, c'mon," she murmured, becoming more and more worried. The sun was down and it was dark. The buildings all around her were like a set for a disaster movie. A total war zone of blasted-out brick buildings, decay, abandonment.

She called Tess. "Have you heard from Vincent?"

"Cat, you're breaking up," Tess said. "Where are you?"

Then she saw the ruins of the packing plant. It was a big hulking wreck against a blackening sky. A handful of windows revealed light like yellowed teeth. Wary of rolling right into a trap, she pulled onto a side street and got out of her car. She put on her coat, hat, and gloves, shut the door quietly, and drew her service weapon.

"Tess, I'm going into the meat packing plant," she said into her phone.

Her answer was static.

"Tess."

Call failed.

She placed her phone into her coat pocket. Then as quietly as possible, she shuffled through the snow. This situation had turned on a dime. Suddenly this didn't feel like it was about rescuing Angelo DeMarco.

Vincent's in trouble, she thought. She didn't know how she knew it, or even if she did know it. Maybe she only feared it. But she could feel her cop brain making connections of which she was as yet consciously unaware. Her mind had been trained to piece together sensations, discoveries, suspicions, revelations until the puzzle was complete. Awareness was building, and soon would become answers.

Then the roar of a beast echoed over the destroyed landscape, raging, crazed, inhuman. It rattled her bones and took away her breath.

Vincent.

He had beasted. Why? What was happening?

There was another roar, and another. They were coming from the factory. Cat broke into a run, skirting snowdrifts and piles of rusted chains and machinery. She sucked in icy air and kept going. The snow muffled her footfalls and the darkness cloaked her.

Another roar.

She stopped across the street and took in the large building. There was an open, illuminated loading bay with a gate stretched across it. The light spilled onto a door and beside it, a broken window.

She checked her weapon. Locked and loaded.

Then, as she began to cross the street, someone came up from behind her. She turned, preparing to fire.

But Officer Lizzani of the 123rd precinct brought his gun butt down hard on the crown of her head, and Cat collapsed to the ground.

CHAPTER TWENTY-SEVEN

FISHERMAN'S INN

The sentry came in with a cup of coffee and a bowl of soup. The group had commandeered the living quarters of the motel's manager—the man they had shot—and three more men and one woman entered Reynolds' room. He was untied and moved to the bed, where he dangled his right foot over the edge, possibly so Gabe would have a reference point... or maybe because he could almost be seen. Reynolds was hiding him, protecting him, and Gabe wasn't sure why.

"We're going to move across the border tomorrow morning," said the woman. "We need to know if you're with us, Reynolds."

Reynolds laughed hollowly. "The way I see it, I don't really have a choice."

"You do," she said. "We'll leave you here with food, water, and a phone. We'll be across the border by the time anyone comes."

Gabe listened hard.

"No need," Reynolds said. "I'm with you. You're right. I *am* eminently suited for the position you're offering me."

"We don't want another Andrew Martin incident. We want to make absolutely positive that there are no more beasts anywhere. They need to be wiped from the face of the earth."

"That's obvious," Reynolds said.

"Unbelievably, there are some among us who disagree," said the woman. "They want to make *more* beasts. Of course, their leader's dead. And we're pretty sure we got Celeste Ellison, too."

They must have been watching her. Maybe Bruce Fox is a plant. She doesn't trust him. Gabe spared a thought for her, which was the closest he could come to a prayer. He was with Sam Landon: he couldn't believe in a god who would permit the injustices he had seen. When beastly men died, would such a god allow them into heaven? He doubted it.

"Well, I'm in. The Muirfield Project was an unmitigated disaster and I'm sorry I was ever involved," Reynolds said. "As you know, I programmed Vincent Keller to exterminate his own kind, but he thwarted me."

"Do you think he'll come?" asked the woman. "We have to go. We've taken too much time as it is."

"Oh, he'll come. I threw down the gauntlet with that bloody T-shirt. He wants to kill me. He'll risk everything to make that happen."

But Gabe detected the uncertainty in Reynolds' voice. He wasn't so sure of his beasts any more.

And I'm not about to enlighten him.

Cat woke up lying on her back on an old mattress that had been covered with a sheet. There was an icepack on her forehead and as she squinted, a figure loomed over her holding a flare of light.

It was Angelo DeMarco with a lantern in his hand, scowling down at her.

"...been looking for you everywhere," she slurred. She looked around. There were stacks of moldy paperback books in a half-circle around the mattress. This was the setting for the photograph of Angelo and Tori.

"Yeah, and you weren't too good at it. We had to plant the most obvious evidence on the freakin' *planet* for you guys to figure it out."

A shape came up beside Angelo. Piercings, dark hair.

"Paul. Dickinson," she managed.

Angelo blinked and frowned at Paul. "You moron."

"Whatever." Paul huffed and turned away.

"He wasn't supposed to go to the drop," Angelo said to Cat. "Minute I heard he actually *went*, and took my family's stuff..." He shook his head. "What an idiot."

"It actually worked out," Cat said slowly. "We weren't getting anywhere. It was Lizzani and Bailey Hart, right? Inside?"

He preened. "Pretty impressive for twenty years old, don't you think?"

"You're almost twenty-one. You're going to be really rich. So why did you do this?" she asked.

"Help her up," Angelo said.

Officer Lizzani came forward. He bent over Cat and put his hands under her arms, raising her to a sitting position. She was so dizzy that her head fell back. Then he jerked her to her feet. She swayed.

I've seen their faces, she thought. *Would Angelo actually kill me?*

Lizzani clamped his beefy hands around one arm and Paul took the other. She shuffled forward. Her clothes were wet and she was shivering. Angelo carried the lantern.

Then Angelo turned to her and for a moment, she saw

the same frightened look she had seen on Hallie DeMarco's face—frightened, drowning. Then it was gone, replaced by his sneer.

He opened the door.

What she saw made her knees buckle.

They were in a black pit, its filthy floor grooved with channels. Coals glowed in a rectangle. There were hooks overhead. Lanterns blazed light on an unholy image:

Vincent was chained to the floor, wrists shackled and pulled through loops, a beast collar around his neck. His face was bruised and cut. He was shirtless and there were horrible, deep wounds in the tops of his shoulders and bruises all along his arms and across his chest. The soles of his feet looked burned. She sucked in her breath and the room spun. She didn't know how he could withstand such terrible damage. It was mutilation, pure and simple.

Then her gaze moved from his feet to his amber-colored eyes. He was staring at her as if she was the only thing he saw. Half-dead, beaten... and focused on her.

We make each other stronger, she thought. Her panic didn't disappear, but she was able to control it.

"He killed her," Angelo said. "He killed Tori."

What was she to you? Why are you connected to the Windsors?

"No," Cat said. "Why would you think that?"

"I don't *think* it. I *know* it!" he shouted. He nodded at Lizzani. The dirty cop picked up a cattle pod and pressed it into the wound in Vincent's shoulder. A bellow tore out of Vincent's throat, echoing through plant. *Someone hear him,* Cat pleaded. *Hear him like I did.*

Then there was a gun at her temple, pushing so hard into her skin that she imagined it drilling a hold through her skull.

Angelo was holding the gun.

"Vincent didn't cause her death," she said again. Even if

her captor pulled the trigger, Cat would not be silent.

"Yes! Yes, he did!" Angelo shouted. "He turned her into the monster that he is and killed her!"

"No," Vincent said. He sounded utterly human... and in terrible agony.

"Liar." Angelo nodded at Lizzani. The horrible electric zap of the device was lost beneath Vincent's screams of pain. He slumped forward, his head bowing.

"Wait!" Cat said. "Just wait! I can tell you what happened."

"I *know* what happened!" Angelo said.

"How?" Cat asked.

Angelo pointed to Lizzani, who sneered at Cat. Then Lizzani grabbed Vincent by his hair and yanked back his head. He was enjoying the torture, the power to cause pain. Try though it might, the New York Police Academy couldn't screen out all the bad elements—the misfits and miscreants who were drawn to the job not to protect and serve, but to bully and torment. Men and women with rage issues, wounds from childhood that had never healed, only festered through the years. People like Sam Landon who would never stop hating and hurting no matter what vengeance they wreaked. They had holes in their souls that would never be filled.

Angelo, for the love of God, do not be a person like that, she begged. If he was, he would not only kill Vincent, but take pleasure in giving him a slow, agonizing death. Vincent was drooping forward, prevented from falling onto his face by the chains around his wrists and neck.

"My father the big shot. He thinks he's the only one in our family who owns people. I'm not even old enough to drink and I got people all over this town. Police department, fire, mayor's office... You know who caused that blackout? *My* guy." He snickered, and he seemed younger than his years. He was like a spoiled kid who was bragging about what he had gotten away with. Like a petty little shoplifter or a minor buying beer with a fake ID.

Pieces of the puzzle were still missing. Cat had to put them together so that she could find a way to talk to Angelo, get through to him. Had Angelo and Tori been boyfriend and girlfriend, the Romeo and Juliet of two warring mob families? Had Vincent unknowingly taken Tori away from Angelo? But no, Vincent had told Cat that Tori had been locked away in her family penthouse, like a princess in a castle made of spun sugar. Angelo obviously knew a few things—that Vincent was a beast, and that Tori's death had some connection to him—but Cat didn't know how much she should say.

"I know that Windsor was a bastard, and Tori was terrified of him. I know that he—" Angelo indicated Vincent with a wave of his hand "—was sent in by rivals of Windsor's to assassinate him. But he failed and he kidnapped Tori to use as bait. And he—he..." He seemed to go blank, as if he had just suffered a horrible shock. "...she was *so* lonely, and there he was, rescuing her like some prince charming. But he had a secret. He was a monster."

Cat opened her mouth to speak, but forced herself to stay silent. She gazed at him steadily, willing him to keep talking. They would find out what he believed Tori's story to be. And, hopefully, correct the parts he had misinterpreted.

"So to protect this monster, she told me she couldn't see me any more. She chose him over me." A heavy sob made his body convulse. "She loved him more than me!"

Wordless, she waited for his grief to submerge again, to be overtaken by his fury. She didn't have long to wait. He strode over to Vincent and kicked him in the jaw. Vincent's head snapped back and blood poured from his nose.

Cat balled her fists and lost her breath. She fought wildly for composure.

Angelo loomed over Vincent, glaring down at him. "I wanted to know more about you. I saw pictures of you and her, together, all over town. She was in love with you. She looked so happy. I couldn't believe that I was that easy to forget.

"Then I found out that you're some... some mutant. *I saw you change.* And I *had* to get her away from you. I went to the houseboat but she wasn't there. Then Lizzani saw her near a hundred and thirty-ninth. She disappeared, and he couldn't find her."

She was going to the dungeon, Cat thought, her stomach twisting. *That was the day she saved J.T.*

That was the day she died.

Vincent's head rose slowly. Blood was dripping from his chin. His eyes were glowing, his muscles bunching. He had fully beasted out and he was growling at Angelo.

Not now, Cat pleaded. It was as if even the mention of Tori's name called to his beast side. Through no fault of her own, Tori had been born a beast, and her nature brought out Vincent's beast side—with tragic consequences.

"Next thing we know, she was brought into the ER. Dead. The ambulance records indicated that someone had called nine-one-one and she was found carefully wrapped in a blanket in an alley close to where Lizzani had been looking for her. An old lady just happened to see the man who lay her in that alley. *Him.*" He pointed at Vincent.

"No," Cat said. "Let me talk to you, Angelo. Let me tell you what it was like." She glanced at Lizzani. "Alone."

"We've got no secrets," Angelo said. Lizzani's answering smile was calculating and cold. Angelo didn't see the greed of a man who could be bought... and who would easily resell himself to a higher bidder. He used men more powerful than he by allowing them to use him first.

"Please," Cat said. "This is about Tori. The truth about her and what happened. It's... for you only."

Speak to his heart. To his pain, she told herself. *He's lost someone he loves and he has no one else.*

"Paul, cuff her," Angelo said.

Paul approached gingerly with a pair of handcuffs. Cat assessed the situation. Angelo had tortured Vincent, was threatening to kill her. If she fought, Vincent might attack. They might get out of here alive. But she sensed there was a spark of humanity left in Angelo. If she could just reach him...

Go ahead, say it, a voice inside her whispered. *You're not certain that if Vincent beasts out, he'll spare you.*

Without looking at her, Paul closed the cuffs around her wrists.

"Go outside. I'm going to talk to her," Angelo said.

The pressure of the gun lessened, then vanished. Lizzani came over and yanked hard on the handcuffs. The edges dug into her wrists and she grunted. Then he and Paul walked toward the door, shoes ringing on the stones. Beast-Vincent tracked them the way a cat tracks a mouse.

They went through the door and shut it.

"Make sure they're not listening," Cat told Angelo. He complied. His commanding demeanor as ringleader was slipping a little. He looked tired, as if the energy he had expended executing his plan and collecting his pound of flesh from Vincent had exhausted him. He made a point of picking up the cattle prod and aiming it at Vincent as he skirted around him and walked toward Cat. When Angelo drew closer to her, she saw that he was sweating and his skin was pasty.

Beast-Vincent was sniffing the air.

Angelo needs to take his insulin, she thought with a shock.

"Talk fast or you'll be the one who will get this," Angelo threatened her.

"Tori's father was like Vincent," she began. "He chose to become that way. A beast. But Vincent didn't. He was a

282

soldier in the army and they injected him with chemicals that changed his DNA. He was a victim."

She took a deep breath.

"And so was Tori."

"A *murder* victim," Angelo said, his anger building again.

"A beast," Cat said. "Tori was born a beast, because of the choice her father had already made."

Angelo's went stark white. The cattle prod dipped as if it weighed too much for him to hold. Then he scowled at Cat and aimed the prod at her.

"Nice try."

"I'm telling you the truth," Cat insisted.

"She told me to stay away," Angelo said. "For my own good. She was trying to protect me. From *him*."

"She was trying to protect you from herself," Cat said gently. "Because she loved you. She cared about you. She didn't know how to control it."

Angelo swayed. The cattle prod dipped again. He wiped his forehead. "She—she was not like him. *She was not like him*. A—a..." He whirled around. "Look at him! Look!"

Vincent lunged at him but somehow managed not to roar. His chains brought him up short and he howled in fury.

"Listen to me, Angelo," Cat pleaded. "There was a man who knew about beasts. He was trying to create a beast that he could control, and send out to murder the people he blamed for the death of his son. To do that, he needed the blood from a beast. He held someone that Vincent cares about hostage, expecting him to save him. But Tori found out and got there first. So he took her blood.

"It was a terrible tragedy and it shouldn't have happened, but Vincent didn't cause it. She went to the dungeon on her own, to try to save someone's life. That was the Tori you knew and loved. Someone who would take risks for someone she loved. Like she did with you."

"Don't you try that on me!" he bellowed. "Don't you dare! We were fine. Tori and me. She was all I had. My life… all my life, people have been afraid to be my friends! Except for her."

"And… and she was your first love?" Cat said.

"She was my half-sister!" he screamed at her. "My only decent family. My father slept with her mother!"

Cat gaped at him. "But then how… did Windsor *know?*"

"They broke up for a while. Separated. Windsor was such a bastard. My dad moved her to Sicily and she had… me. And he made her give me up. To him." His lip curled. "You never keep anything my father wanted. In exchange, he never told Windsor. Tori's father would have killed my mother if he knew."

"Angelo," Cat said, "I—I…" She didn't know what to say.

"Our fathers were monsters. We were both so lonely until we finally met. She brought me a guitar. My first guitar."

"It's pink with blue flowers," Cat said. "You hid her picture inside it." He blinked. "You—you saw it? Did my father see it?"

What does it matter now? Cat thought, but she heard the fear in his voice, and she saw how impossible it had been for him to have a life of his own. Tori was out of harm's way, but he was not.

"Your father didn't see it," she assured him.

"And you took her away from me!" he shouted at Vincent. "I begged her." He let out a sob. "Then I saw her in the newspapers with *him*. Everywhere."

"She had discovered that she was a beast," Vincent said groggily. Each word was an effort. "Her father nearly killed her. I saved her. And together, our beast senses were heightened. She kept going out of control."

Vincent lifted his head and gazed up at Angelo. "It's like Catherine told you. She cut herself off from you to protect you. Because she loved you."

"Shut up!" Angelo screamed. He pressed the cattle prod against Vincent's forehead but did not turn it on. For Cat, the world stopped spinning. All she saw was the prod, and Vincent's eyes as he gazed unflinchingly up at Angelo.

Vincent said, "Tori died saving my friend's life."

Cat shut her eyes for a moment. When she opened them, she saw tears running down Vincent's cheeks.

"Fake tears," Angelo sneered, but his voice was shaky. "She wasn't even cold in her grave before you went back to *her.*"

"That's not true," Cat said. "He mourned her. He grieved for her. He was so afraid that anyone he loved—" her throat closed up and she tried to clear it."—that anyone he loved would die like she had."

"She said she had no friends," Vincent said. "But I knew there was something she wasn't telling me. I didn't speak up because things were happening so fast, and then it all fell apart. That day, it was awful." He shut his eyes. "Angelo, honor what she did. You know how lonely she was growing up. *You* were all *she* had, and she never had me. She knew that but she risked her life to save mine anyway."

"For *nothing.*"

"For love," Cat said. Now it was her turn for tears. "Let us go. I swear to you that we'll never tell anyone that you planned all this. We'll 'save' you and take you home."

"You're a cop. Cops lie. My father's got more dirty cops around him than just Robertson and Gonzales. He's got enough to populate a small country." He didn't sound proud. Despair leaked from every word.

"Then kill me," Cat said. "But let Vincent go. He didn't kill Tori. He loved her. Like you did. Tori wouldn't want you to go down this road. To become a monster. He went out night after night tracking you so he could save you. Risking his life, like you knew he would. *You knew he would.*"

Angelo looked down. She saw shame in his posture, and that gave her hope.

"Everyone in New York is after him, but he risked everything to find you."

Angelo's gaze darted from Vincent to her, and Cat's heart skipped a beat. If Vincent could snap out of it, blur, he could save them. But his heavy chains made his shoulders droop, and his head was bobbing.

"I thought *you* would come," Angelo murmured. "*You're* the cop. You'd come and then I'd get a message to him and then I would kill him."

"But *he* came here first," she emphasized. "Without me. To save you."

He slumped. Vincent smelled the air and looked hard at her. Angelo sobbed and said, "I hate my life. I hate my father. I hate everything. She was the only good part."

"Angelo, listen. You need to take your insulin."

He kept crying.

At the motel, the group left Reynolds' room and he turned off the light. Then he got down on his hands and knees and said, "Lowan. Come out."

Gabe complied.

"You're on our side, right? Will you help us, serve as our eyes and ears back in New York?"

Not in a million years, Gabe thought. He said, "Of course. This is what I want, too."

He stood there and lied. And because he was so convincing, Reynolds let him go.

In the hellish torture vault that he had built for Vincent, Angelo DeMarco collapsed.

Still chained to the floor, Vincent said, "He's starting to deteriorate. He has to have insulin."

There was banging on the door. Both of them looked over at it and Vincent smiled thinly.

"They must be locked out."

"Lizzani will never let us out of here alive," Cat said, and Vincent knew that she was right. Now that he was more lucid, he was fairly certain that Lizzani, not Angelo, had been the one who had tortured him. As long as that door held, they were safe. But the longer they remained in this room, the more likely it would be that he, Cat, and Angelo would die.

Vincent pulled at his chains, but he knew that fully human, he couldn't break free. He told Cat to look for a key anywhere, everywhere. As she searched he smelled the acetone-scent of untreated diabetes.

"No luck," she said, and he thought, *No luck. This kid growing up in a crime family. Not allowed to be with his mother. Losing Tori.*

He would have to make some luck for Angelo. And for Cat. And for himself.

"Cat," he said, "can you pick him up fireman style?"

She cocked her head at him, thinking it through and then she got to her knees, raised Angelo up so that he flopped over her shoulder, and grabbed onto Vincent's wounded shoulder as she struggled to her feet. Vincent clamped his mouth shut to keep from groaning. He didn't want her to stop.

She stood before him with Angelo draped over her body.

"Good thing you work out," he said.

"I know what you want me to do." She licked her lips. "You want me to use the cattle prod on you until you beast out."

The banging on the door was louder. Both Lizzani and Paul Dickinson were bellowing to be let in.

"First, I need to tell you something. I lost my temper with J.T.

287

during the blackout when he told me about your father's escape. I grabbed him around the throat, and I almost choked him."

She took that in. And then she said, "You won't hurt me, Vincent."

"I want to believe that." *I love you so much*, he thought. *I would rather die here and now than hurt you.*

She picked up the cattle prod. She touched it to his wound.

Rage and fury and power and strength and brutality and hatred and violence and

save her save her save her.

And Lizzani was running after them, shooting wildly, while Paul stumbled through the charnel house screaming, "Save me!"

Catherine said, "Then help me," and Paul took Angelo from her, carrying him through the corridors while Vincent tore away a door, and then another door. They were out in the fresh snow and as they staggered toward the car the beast quieted. Vincent was human again.

He opened the back door and lifted Angelo from Paul, yelling "Get in!" Then he carefully draped Angelo across the back seat and jumped into the passenger side while Catherine got behind the wheel. She drove forward. Lizzani was off to one side, shooting. One of the bullets hit the car. Startled, Catherine swerved. At the same time, Lizzani jumped into her path—whether on purpose or by accident, they never knew.

She hit him.

CHAPTER TWENTY-EIGHT

Angelo was home, safe and sound, insulin injected, and sleeping comfortably. Cat returned Tony DeMarco's family heirlooms and diamonds.

Vincent and Paul waited in the car. Paul was a mess, and Cat wasn't sure what to do with him.

Tony DeMarco wanted details. He wanted to shower Cat with gold and make her his "goddess."

"I'm still in the middle of something," she told him. "I'll get back to you, all right?"

He was weeping with joy when she left.

EN ROUTE TO GABE

"All I can figure out is that there's some kind of device attached to Gabe's phone, and when you dial his number, you patch into his location," J.T. said. "He just left a motel called the Fisherman's Inn."

"Is my father with him?" Cat asked.

"No idea," J.T. said.

Then Tess was on the line. "Are you sure you're up for

this? I can get on the road—"

"We're on it," Vincent said into the speakerphone. "We're not turning back now."

En route to New York

Gabe was on a hill, heading downward into a valley, when he saw a pair of headlights. He tensed, figuring his incredible string of good luck was about to run out. He was afraid that someone was coming for him. That they had figured out that he had been with Celeste Ellison at the lake house, had escaped, and would live to tell the tale unless they killed him. Perhaps that wasn't entirely rational—what tale could he tell that anyone would believe?—but he pulled off the road behind a copse of trees.

He got out of the car and crept through the snow to a better vantage point. He was so ragged by then that if someone came for him, he didn't know what he could do except call 911.

That was a bit of a joke, but it dawned on him that maybe he could do just that. So he pulled his phone out of his pocket, realizing that the signal booster was back in the car. As he walked back toward it, he ran his gloved hand over the faceplate, wishing he had been able to bring his touch-sensitive gloves, the ones he could make calls with. As it was, he'd have to take off his gloves to—

Wait. He pressed his fingertips over the front of the phone again. In the upper right corner was a tiny little bump that shouldn't be there. A piece of dirt?

Something Celeste put on it?

He hurried into the car and turned the key so that the instrument panel lit up, reaching up quickly to turn off the dome light. He took off his glove and scraped at the bump with his fingernail.

It detached, and he caught in his palm.

He got back out of the car and ran to the road. He pulled off his other glove with his teeth and rubbed his hands together briskly. He felt the bump, and he kept rubbing until he didn't feel it anymore.

Then he returned to his car, made sure that all the lights were off, and watched.

The car crested the hill.

His mouth dropped open in surprise.

Catherine's car zoomed right past him.

"J.T.," Cat said into the phone.

"I lost the signal," J.T. reported. "But you're close to the motel."

Catherine turned off her headlights and slowed to a crawl. Beside her, Vincent got quiet.

He said, "There are people there. And one of them is your father."

Cat pulled to the side of the road and they both climbed out. She pulled her weapon.

Vincent prepared to become a weapon.

As they approached, a cry went up. Someone had been keeping watch from the roof of the motel, and they spotted Catherine and him in the moonlight. People came at them, half a dozen, and before he beasted out, Vincent said, "Your father's in there." He pointed to one of the motel room doors.

Shots rang out. People began to yell.

"I should be out here with you," she said.

"Get your father," he replied.

She heard Vincent roar as she ran to the door and tried the knob. It was locked. She shot it and kicked the door open. Moonlight filtered in from a window, to reveal her father crouched on the floor.

She kicked him in the face and he tumbled backward. She stepped on his shoulder and aimed her weapon right between his eyes.

There was no gunfire outside.

There was no roaring.

"Hello, Dad," Cat said.

"Hello, Keller," he replied loudly.

"He's not coming in here. This is between you and me, just like before. You have the right to remain silent..."

Her father gazed at her with his intense, gray eyes.

She never wavered.

"Remember the last time we did this?" he said. "Vincent made you crash your car. Then he almost ripped out my throat. And he's been mutating since then. That's what his body is programmed to do. I know. I programmed it. And he's going to become more and more beastlike, Catherine. There's nothing you can do about it. It's like a fatal disease. Ultimately, it will kill the part of him that's still human. And then he will kill you. If he hasn't by then."

"Anything you say can and will be used against you in a court of law," she said.

"Look how you're shaking," he said. "You know I'm right. Push too hard on a bad day and what's to stop him from losing his temper in a very bad way? Will he tell you he's sorry after he breaks your neck?"

"You have the right to an attorney," she said, and then she heard a soft growl.

No, Vincent, she thought. *No, please. Don't give him the satisfaction.*

"You had to shoot him that first time, just like a rabid dog. It's not his fault, just like it wouldn't be the dog's fault. He's a time bomb."

She heard movement outside. Another growl.

"If you can't afford an attorney, one will be provided for you."

"Why is he growling?" Reynolds asked her. "You have the situation under control. You're not in danger. *He's just angry.*"

Then she heard the crunch of leaves and a slight breeze as Vincent walked through the doorway and stood behind her. Reynolds' eyes widened but Cat didn't take her attention from her father.

Vincent stood beside Cat.

"How many of them are dead?" Reynolds asked.

"None. They're resting comfortably," Vincent said. "Like you."

"There's more of them," Reynolds said. "They'll come after you."

"There's always more of them," Vincent said.

Cat gestured with her gun. "Come on, Dad. Let's go home.

ONE NIGHT LATER

In his penthouse, DeMarco poured three glasses of scotch. "Single malt like you've never tasted. Not on your salaries."

He held two of them out to Cat and Tess. "I don't know how you did it. Lizzani, who'd have guessed? And Bailey Hart. I've got my people out looking for him, that's for sure." He shook his head. "Never dreamed anybody else knew about my escape route out of the penthouse. Hey, they ever figure out who that kid was they sent to collect the drop?"

"No," Cat said. Paul Dickinson had received a plane ticket out of town.

And David Whiteside had been apprehended at the airport.

All in a good day's work.

"I told you I would spread the love around generously.

And I will. The ransom was for one point five, so I'm giving you a commish. Ten percent? That's just seventy-five thousand each. Not enough to corrupt you, just enough to help out with bills, maybe start a college fund your kid."

"No kids," Tess said.

"Yet." He smiled at her. "You can have it in cash, unmarked bills, no way to trace it. Free and clear. My gift to you." He bowed from the waist.

"We're on duty," Tess said. "We're not allowed to drink. Or accept… tips."

He looked at Cat. "It's chump change."

She didn't reply.

He shrugged. "Well, you're young yet. A few more years and those stars in your eyes will go out. Trust me. I've seen it a million times." He drank his scotch. "That's why I have so many friends on the force."

"You're depressing me," Tess said, and he guffawed.

"I don't know which one of you two I like more. You're both so…" He mock-growled.

"Honest," Tess filled in helpfully.

He laughed again, and then he drank the second of the three glasses of scotch. "I can't let you go without doing something for you," he said.

"So we can be indebted to you?" Cat asked, and he grinned. He was as jovial as Santa Clause.

"Okay, listen. Here's what I've got for you. I put the word out and you are going to be able to make the case on Robertson stick. That kid Nico? He'll be safe for the rest of his life. Guaranteed. And his cousin will be out of Rikers by summer. Bet on it."

"Sure hope you're right," Tess said.

"And I've got so much dirt on Gonzales you could grow potatoes on him. I'll make sure it gets to the right people. No one will ever connect it to you. I swear."

"Thank you," Cat said.

"Those mooks forgot who they were messing with." He lowered his chin and peered up at them both through his lashes. "*Capisce?*"

You did not just say that, Tess thought, her mouth twitching. She could almost hear the theme to *The Godfather* playing in the background.

"What about the old man who lived in that shed?"

"Got him into low-income housing." He preened. "I take care of mine."

"For the record? We are not yours," Cat said.

"*Yet.*"

"We'll be going now, Mr. DeMarco," Cat said.

They turned to go. Then he said, "Angelo would like to speak to you."

In the grubby room, Angelo sat in bed. He looked wan and thin. Ill. But his eyes were cold and hard.

"I was going to kill him," he said defiantly.

"I know," Cat replied.

"I had insulin there. Paul would have given me a shot. You didn't do anything special. As far as I'm concerned, *you* owe *me.*"

I'm sorry, Cat thought. *I'm sorry that you're lost. That you're hurt. That you're angry.*

"Tell him that. He owes me. Double. Once for him, and once for *her.*"

"I will," she said.

And then she walked away.

It was a slam dunk.

The grand jury brought back indictments for both Robertson and Gonzales.

A wiretap had revealed that Justus Zilpho had hired a

couple of shooters to go after Catherine and Tess. They'd shot at Vincent as he'd left Cat's apartment during the blackout, then come after Tess at Claudia's safe house, and tried to run them off the road when they'd gone to check out Robertson's house. They were in jail now, too.

Gabe knew the 125th was celebrating, even though this was technically a win for the DA's office, not for them. But there was no way he could show his face at Rosie's Bar.

So he was home, uncorking his own bottle of champagne, planning his plans, scheming his schemes. He poured two glasses and carried them into his bedroom.

In his bed, Celeste smiled at him and took the glass he offered her. She held hers.

"To the future," she said. "One that I predict will be very interesting. A future with beasts in it."

"To the future." *With me in it*.

They touched glasses and sipped. Then she stretched and purred.

Like a cat.

Seven-thirty on the dot. Cat said goodbye to Tess and J.T. and hurried home. She smiled as she unlocked her front door. She knew that this time, her apartment was not empty.

This time, it was filled with candles, and champagne, and chocolate.

And Vincent, in his white bathrobe.

She went to him and he put his arms around her. Their lips touched, and then she poured all the passion that she had for this man into her kiss. He answered in kind, and then he pulled a red rose from his bathrobe and handed it to her.

"For you, my beauty," he said. His face glowed with love. They walked together to the window and gazed at the bright lights of the city together. Then Vincent pulled the drapes.

And they went to that world, the world that was theirs alone.

We are better together than we are apart.
And we always will be.

ABOUT THE AUTHOR

Nancy Holder is a multiple award-winning, *New York Times* bestselling author (the Wicked Series). Her two new dark young adult dark fantasy series are Crusade and Wolf Springs Chronicles. She has won five Bram Stoker Awards from the Horror Writers Association, as well as a Scribe Award for Best Novel (*Saving Grace: Tough Love.*) Nancy has sold over eighty novels and one hundred short stories, many of them based on such shows as *Highlander*, *Buffy the Vampire Slayer*, *Angel*, and others. She lives in San Diego with her daughter, Belle, two corgis, and three cats. You can visit Nancy online at www.nancyholder.com.

BEAUTY & THE BEAST

SOME GAVE ALL

BY NANCY HOLDER

When Vincent Keller is approached by the family of one of his fellow supersoldiers, a woman who went missing in Afghanistan, he vows to help them to uncover the truth behind her disappearance. Meanwhile, Catherine is on the case of a young girl so traumatized by the brutal murder of her aunt that she is unable speak. Cat knows how it feels to grow up haunted by a terrifying past, and Vincent will do anything to ensure that justice is served. Together, they will risk everything to prove that even in the darkest place, there is hope.

For more fantastic fiction, author events, exclusive
excerpts, competitions, limited editions and more

VISIT OUR WEBSITE
titanbooks.com

LIKE US ON FACEBOOK
facebook.com/titanbooks

FOLLOW US ON TWITTER
@TitanBooks

EMAIL US
readerfeedback@titanemail.com